FALL FAR FROM THE TREE

Fall Far from the Tree Book One

AMY MCNULTY

Fall Far from the Tree by Amy McNulty

©2016 by Amy McNulty. All rights reserved.

First edition.

No part of this book may be reproduced or transmitted in any form, including written, electronic, recording, or photocopying, without written permission of the author. The exception would be in the case of brief quotations embodied in critical articles or reviews.

Published by Snowy Wings Publishing, PO Box 1035, Turner, OR 97392

Cover by RebecaCovers and cover images by Ipedan and AnoushkaToronto, courtesy of Shutterstock and Depositphotos

The characters and events appearing in this work are fictitious. Any resemblance to real persons, living or dead, is purely coincidental, and not intended by the author.

ISBN: 978-1-952667-43-5

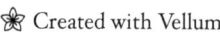 Created with Vellum

I

ROHESIA

I'd lived only five winters the first time I saw an infant drowned.

Father's hand lay lightly on my shoulder as the horse jostled us slightly, shaking her head and whipping the tips of her silky black mane across my eyes. Father noticed the instinct that took over, the mere moment my eyelids closed despite how hard I'd fought to keep them open. "Watch, Rohesia. Burn the moment into your mind."

The shrieking woman held aloft by two soldiers kicked her legs, sending her skirt upward. I noticed the mud that collected along the hem, the strands of straw-colored hair that escaped her kerchief and swung wildly across her mouth. The hair billowed with each shriek like curtains in the breeze, the skirt a gale that tore through a field of wheat, the woman the only source of movement beyond the scuffing hooves of the horses beside me.

"The child, Rohesia. Not the mother."

The soldier by the river tossed the tattered cloth that had wrapped the baby to the ground and held the crying infant as far out in front of him as his stocky arms would allow. One gauntlet supported the baby's head and neck, the other gripped the child's body loosely, and I saw one impossibly small leg kick upward vainly.

The horse tossed her mane again, whipping the black hair across my eyes, but I leaned sideways and turned my head away so I wouldn't close them. Father let go of the reins with one hand and ran his fingers through the horse's mane gently, his voice almost a whisper. "Settle down, Sunset." He placed the same fingers atop my head, patting my scalp as he tugged on Sunset's reins, leading her sideways so my gaze was forced again to fall upon the soldier and the infant at the side of the river. "Can you see? Can you see the child?"

I tried to speak, but my voice caught in my throat. I swallowed and forced the sound out, the word I knew he wanted to hear. "Yes." I did not say that Sunset's ears flickered across my view, sometimes blocking what the soldier held in his hands. I wasn't allowed to be comforted by such a thing.

"What do you see?"

I clenched my teeth. There could only be one answer. "Black hair. Golden skin." I took a deep breath. "The eyes..." I couldn't see them clearly from Sunset's back, but there could be no other reason Father would show me the scene.

"Black," Father finished for me. He pulled too hard on my hair, causing my scalp to twinge slightly. He didn't say the rest, what I knew he would only imply: *Like yours. Hair, skin and eyes that you and no one else on this island shares. You and no one else but that baby.*

"Please! Have mercy! She's just a child!" The woman still kicked, forcing the words out between shrieks.

From behind me, Father's composed voice answered the woman. "There is no mercy for traitors." He spoke louder. "Send the outsider back where it came from."

I couldn't blink, but part of me prayed that Sunset would whip her mane across my face to shield me, to comfort me. But I learned long ago there was no one who would ever comfort me. No one but Father. That's what he told me. That's what I knew.

The soldier bent to the river and placed the screaming bundle atop it. The current tore the bundle from his gauntlets, and I watched as the mess of black hair floated further and further away, as if the river were as eager to rid our isle of the child as Father was. For a moment, I thought perhaps it would make its way back home. The child was too far for me to hear its screaming. Perhaps it kept crying. Perhaps it would cry all the way home. But it was the kicking leg, the tiny kicking leg, that brought me back to the truth of what I'd witnessed. Just as the baby reached the horizon, just as I was sure it would drown far beyond where I could ever see it, the tiny leg stopped and faltered, descended and vanished from view.

"Apparently the outsiders don't want it, either." Father gripped Sunset's reins with both hands and pulled her back to face the shrieking woman. I blinked, giving my eyes relief at last from the sting.

The woman slumped at the side of the river, the soldiers stepping back to mount their own horses. "Demon!" she sobbed quietly. "Bastard!"

"This is what happens when you shelter an outsider," said Father. "When you let him into your home, shelter him in your heart." I looked up at Father and saw his gaze turned up to the sky, at the moon that appeared against the blue, the moon that had come out even before the sun had finished setting.

He pulled Sunset's reins, turning her back, back to the heart of the duchy, back to the castle. I slipped my fingers through her mane and gripped tightly, afraid that if I fell into the river then, the waters would sweep me up to join the child who was just like me.

Father nodded at the soldier who'd placed the baby in the river as the man stepped beside us. "If she has nothing more to say about the outsider who left that child within her, let her join it."

The soldier said nothing. I couldn't tell if there was any life at all in his eyes.

Father whipped the reins and Sunset was off. I exhaled as we put the river behind us.

"Demon!" I heard the woman scream behind us. "Your rule is hypocrisy!"

Hypocrisy. The other words I knew, but that was one I'd never heard before. I turned my head, trying to lean around Father to get one last look—

As if he'd heard my thoughts, Father answered the question I'd never dare ask. "She means she doesn't think it's right that I killed her baby and let you live."

I swallowed, faced forward, and stared at the castle. I focused on the rapid clopping of Sunset's hooves, straining to put the muffled screaming far, far behind me.

"Lady Rohesia. His lordship wouldn't approve of you taking this rather, uh, *scenic* route."

Leave it to the sniveling swine to refer to streets covered in fish guts and dog shit as 'scenic.' Sherrod ran his knobby fingers through his limp straw hair, somehow managing to stain his grease-covered fingertips with yet another layer of grime with the gesture. Father often warned me to stay a good few feet in front of the man unless I hoped to wake up with a coating of white flakes and scabs on my scalp the next morning. He had his uses, but companionship was not one of them. Nor was stealth.

I stuck my right hand out to stop Sherrod from overtaking me, my left wrapping around my sword hilt. "We're not here to pick posies, Sherrod." I nudged the tip of my steel-toed boot forward so I could lean around the corner for a better look. "Father won't care how I got here, so long as I get the job done."

I didn't have to turn around to imagine the pinched look on Sherrod's face, the way he ran his tongue across his protruding front tooth whenever something bothered him. "But may I ask why the stealth was so necessary?" he asked. "Why couldn't we take a band of soldiers and just march right up to the dock, swords extended—"

"Quiet," I hissed, leaning back and retreating to the safety of the alley. I drew my blade out slightly. A sailor pulling on one of the ropes that rolled the barrels down the plank had stopped to wipe his brow, and his gaze had wandered too close to our alley for my liking.

"My lady," Sherrod tried to speak softly, but the best he could manage was sounding like a man told to whisper while screaming, "you've seen only seventeen winters, and are perhaps not quite as familiar with the, uh, position of leadership as you may think, and the duke's guard is at your command—"

"As are you," I reminded him. "And your sole command now is to refrain from speaking."

Sherrod's tongue whipped out and smeared saliva all across his upper lip. Even with his mouth shut, his tooth bulged out, as if it couldn't be contained behind his lips, like most of the refuse the steward felt compelled to tell me. Satisfied he'd keep his tongue occupied with his lips for the time being, I leaned back around the corner for a better view of the newly-arrived ship.

The Duke's Favor was an old ship with golden sails, marking it as a trading vessel under the protection of the duchy's lordship. I'd read up on it before I left that morning, although I'd been familiar with its most recent captain, who'd often dined with Father. It was supposed to supply the duchy with rice, opium and spices, and had done so faithfully for decades, since the time of my father's father. But Father had received word by pigeon that Captain Tierny had died of fever after they made port, and the ship was late. Too late. Families had gone hungry, and divans had started demanding more gold for their opium, causing a bit of a problem with inflation. Father had put an end to it all by hanging a few divan owners in the market, a reminder to the people that greed would not be tolerated when others go hungry. He'd had to ration the rice, too, and supplement what was left with some of the grain from our fields, but there was never enough wheat to feed the people.

I counted the men pulling the barrels and watched the one who seemed to be shouting the orders. The new captain. Father said the man was softer than Tierny, and younger, too. That wouldn't bode well for what I was there to do. At least, it wouldn't bode well for the new captain.

There were forty-two men on and around the ship that I could see. The rest of the fifty—forty-nine, I suppose, disregarding Tierny—could be below decks or dead at sea. Or if they were too loyal to Tierny, to the duchy... Dead by mutiny.

"My lady," scream-whispered Sherrod from behind me. The simple command of keeping his mouth shut was never bound to last long. "What's the point of skulking in the shadows? Do you even know what to look for?"

"Yes, I do." I smiled, watching as a row of the barrels broke free of the ropes, rolling freely off the side of the plank and thudding to the ground. There was one that bounced and rolled further than the others, causing the captain and a few of the men pulling the barrels to panic and chase it down before it could fall into the harbor.

I straightened my back and slid my sword all the way back into its scabbard. I took a step forward, noticed a bit of dirt on my shoulder plate and stopped to flick it away. I felt Sherrod slam into the back of me, his nose crunching against my cape and jingling the mail beneath my chest plate. I turned, grabbing my cape and inspecting it for a Sherrod-shaped dirt imprint. Finding a dark spot, I glared down at the steward as he took a step back.

He ran his tongue over his tooth twice. "I'm so sorry, Lady Rohesia." He bent his head and averted his eyes to the shit beneath our feet, as if willing himself to sink into the muck. "I thought we were going—"

"Four feet."

Sherrod wrung his hands together, pausing to wipe the sweat that accumulated on them across the front of his tunic. "Pardon?" He dared to look up.

I let my cape fall, and it swished, blowing air back and rustling Sherrod's greasy hair. I leaned forward, sticking a gloved finger toward his chest, too repulsed to touch it. "You stay four feet behind me at all times. Or is that a problem?"

Sherrod took four exaggerated steps back, his eyes back on the grime below us. "No! Of course not. I mean, of course. I'm so sorry. I have no excuse—"

"Enough." I turned back, my cape swishing once more behind me. "I better not hear you speak. I don't even want to realize you're there."

To emphasize the point, I paused, daring Sherrod to speak in acquiescence. He didn't. A shame. I'd have liked to remind him that I'd outgrown him, in more ways than one.

I stepped forward toward the docking bay, my head held high, my feet slamming into the cobblestones and wood with more force than necessary. I turned a few heads as I weaved my way through the men still attending the remainder of the barrels, stepping over the taut rope a few of them held without acknowledging them or letting my back or shoulders slouch in the slightest. By the time I'd made my way across the crowd of sailors, only the crew and captain attending to the lighter barrel hadn't noticed me. They finished tilting it upward, a few stopping to wipe their brows. The captain crouched beside it, his lips moving.

"Does opium often talk back to you, Captain? That is, when you're not inhaling it?"

The captain's shoulders stiffened. Unfortunately, I didn't hold the advantage long. The captain rolled his shoulders, relaxing as he stood. His face—weather-worn and caked in lines, but not entirely displeasing—lit up with a grin that slithered its way across his features.

"I wouldn't know about opium," he said, placing his right hand on his waist, not-so-subtly close to his blade's hilt. "I never mix business with pleasure." He laid his left hand on the barrel casually. "And besides, this here's spices that's doing the talking."

I sniffed the air, searching for the telltale giveaway of cinnamon and nutmeg, but the air smelled like nothing but rotten fish and sea salt. A gust of wind that changed direction and a flicker of movement out of the corner of my eye demanded my attention. "Seems to me like your spices are bobbing in the sea, Captain."

Like sheep, the captain and the crew looked at once into the harbor. I watched, pleased as the grin dropped off the captain's face and he shouted orders to retrieve the barrel that they hadn't bothered to save from rolling into the waters. The captain was the only one left attending the barrel atop which he still rested his forearm. He smiled again, moving his other hand from his belt to wipe his brow of excess moisture. He laughed. "Two squalls on the return trip, and not a scratch on 'em. Two minutes with this lot, and we lose two barrels." He pointed at the men scrambling to throw a rope down to the floating barrel, but I refused to follow his gesture.

"I don't recall ever having this problem when Captain Tierny led 'the lot.'" I jutted my chin toward him. "I don't think we've had the pleasure."

"I was about to say the same myself. Captain Hann of the Duke's Favor, at your service." The captain bowed deeply, removing his hat and revealing the thinning dark hair clinging to his scalp. He fastened his hat back on his head, careful to leave his left arm on the barrel all the while. His eyes drifted over my head to somewhere behind me. "And you. I'd have thought to call the soldiers over immediately, but I know that fellow, and I can't imagine him trailing behind an outsider dressed to battle an army."

I clenched my jaw and waited for Sherrod to confirm the acquaintance. But of course, I'd warned him not to speak, and he had chosen this one inopportune moment to decide to follow my commands. Whatever it took for him to make my life more difficult.

I gave up and spoke his name. "Sherrod." Silence. This was getting ridiculous. The captain's grin twisted, resembling something closer to a genuine smirk. I turned and saw the useless man face first on the ground, one foot in the air dangling from the taut rope above him. The remaining sailors holding the rope were frozen in what was probably confusion, neither continuing to pull down the barrels or offering at all to help the steward. I couldn't say I blamed them.

"He's been that way a few minutes," said the captain coolly. "You might want to see if he conked his head in the fall."

The captain still leaned on the barrel, scuffing his boot on the dock and examining his boot toe. If he thought I was going to turn my back on him long enough to help someone who would be no use to me whatsoever, he was grossly underestimating me. "He doesn't have much there to injure."

The captain raised an eyebrow. "Is this how the duke rewards such ardent devotion?"

I smiled, doing my best to echo the sculptured grin Hann had. "There's no reason for the duke to reward what's expected of all men. And I'm not my father." I nodded toward the barrel as I let my left hand pull my sword a little out of its sheath, calling attention to gesture. "Open the barrel, Captain."

Hann laughed, letting his forearm fall from the top of the barrel at last as he threw his hands in the air and then crossed his arms, trying a bit too hard to seem casual. "The duke is so hard up for soldiers, he sends his own daughter to pick up the delivery? Is he that eager to get his first cut of opium and spices?"

"No, the duke, as you phrased it, never 'mixes business with pleasure.'" I pulled my sword out further, knowing the sun would gleam off the metal and draw the captain's eyes toward it. "You're late, Captain. Too late. And smuggling outsiders."

Before I could fully pull the sword from its scabbard, I flicked my right hand. The small dagger I kept there slipped out, and I wrapped my fingers around its hilt. The captain fumbled for a moment but drew his sword in time to cross with mine, but by then, my dagger had already slipped into his arm. He shouted and his sword faltered, drooping slightly. He gritted his teeth and raised the sword back upward to move more in tune with mine. "You missed."

I grabbed my sword with both hands and spun, tearing it free from his weakened resistance and bringing it down toward his shoulder. He dodged, rolling out of the way but grunting as the dagger hit the deck and slid further into his arm, and my sword reached its intended target: the barrel. The wood that chipped off was no bigger than the size of my hand, but I didn't need to see more to recognize the eye that stared back out at me. The dark brown, almost black iris.

The captain scrambled to his feet, sweat pouring down his brow, his hat crooked and in shambles on his head. His arms shook as he struggled to lift his sword out in front of him, his boots slipping on the wood dampened by blowing seawater. "How could you let your father do this?" The words were difficult for him to get past his purpling lips. "You're one of them."

I let myself look one more time at the eye that peeked out from the chip I'd made in the barrel. It darted from me to the captain and back again. I wondered, not for the first time, what an outsider found so appealing about the duchy, knowing what fate would likely have in store for them there. But Father could be generous to his people. Perhaps the risk was worth it to them.

"Captain, you're mistaken." I swapped my sword into my weaker hand, reaching into the pouch at my waist and sliding out the thin silver tool I kept hidden there. Hann flinched but dragged himself protectively in front of the barrel, draping that same elbow on the top, no longer from some futile effort to appear casual but because every step he took was enough to send a weaker man sprawling headfirst to the deck, where he would never get up again. I watched his struggle, thinking of how pathetically he'd tried to fool me with wide grins and teasing. "My feet have never touched soil outside of the duchy. You're more of an outsider than I am."

I brought the flute to my mouth and blew three notes. The notes hung in the air for a moment, reverberating into silence. And then the hooves began to echo on the stones leading to the docks, the clomp of foot soldiers stomping in time to an unsung melody.

"You... bitch..." Hann's legs gave way, and he struggled in vain to stand as his weight collapsed down on top of them. His sword fell numbly from his fingers, clattering to the ground.

I slid the flute back into my pouch and bent forward, ripping the dagger out of the captain's shoulder. "If Ytoile exists, perhaps you'll give Her my regards. Unless you're sent flying into the flame kingdom." I wiped what remained of the blood and poison from the dagger's blade against the top of the barrel.

Hann's eyes fluttered shut and his shoulders slumped forward. "Hypo... crisy..."

Yes, yes. It was sort of a death cry for these types. The whole line was left unsaid: "Your whole existence is hypocrisy."

I straightened my shoulders and turned, sparing one last look for the quaking eyeball seen through the hole in the barrel. The soldiers I'd summoned from the town square were engaged in battle with the remaining sailors, although their armor put them in little danger from the ragtag attack of whittling knives and daggers. I walked back in the direction I'd come, paying no attention to the cries of anger and pain that erupted all around me.

I gazed at the tip of my sword and the scratch in the metal the barrel had put there. The blade was lined with such scratches, the metal almost dangerously close to cracking into pieces. I slid the blade into its scabbard and reached down toward Sherrod, grabbing him roughly under the armpit and dragging him to his feet, feeling his weight tug at the tendons in my arm but determined not to let the strain show on my face. His foot twisted and freed itself from the rope just as his eyelids fluttered open.

"My lady?" His eyes had sort of a glossy look as they darted back and forth wildly, searching my face and what I presumed to be the men gathering behind me. Convenient that he knock himself out while I made my inspection. Too convenient.

"We're done here, Sherrod." I gave him another tug and lurched forward, ignoring the pain in my sword arm. When at last the steward heaved himself up entirely and made a great show of dusting off his tunic, I rolled my eyes and gladly let go of his armpit.

"Was his lordship right about the captain then, my lady?"

I wiped my moistened glove against my cape. "Father is always right, Sherrod."

"*Let them take you for a fool, Rohesia,*" Father had instructed. "*It lowers their guard, and it's more fun to see them act brash before they squirm.*"

"It's just a matter of toying with your prey before you slaughter it."

I stepped aside into a puddle to avoid the swinging sword of the nearest soldier, washing away the shit and dirt on my boot in the jumble of blood and sea water.

2

FASTELLO

I let the gem dance across my fingers, knowing Luana would be drawn to the gleaming green bauble as it weaved over my knuckles, under my pinky and back up by my thumb. Her wide brown eyes were hungry, practically drinking in the movement of the pendant the way I drunk in every inch of her body when she pressed it flat against mine.

She reached out a hand, hesitant, curious. "How do you do that?"

I smirked, dropping the emerald between my fingers and down my sleeve just as her soft fingertips were about to clasp her prize.

"Hey!" She did her best to scowl, but the corners of her mouth gave her away. "You said I could have that one."

"I didn't say I would give it to you for nothing." I grabbed her hand in mine, bringing her knuckles up to my mouth for a kiss on each little hilltop. She laughed, muttering something about how it tickled as I tugged her lower so I could lean forward and place my lips against hers. She hesitated for just a moment, so I let her pull back and lock her eyes with mine. Then that little shy smile of hers—so strange on one so brash—broke out and she flung her arms around my neck, settling onto my lap as I'd intended.

I ran my hand through her dark curly hair. I wondered not for the first time at the buoyancy of those curls, so lively compared to the straight brown hair that brushed against my own shoulders. "Look," I said, pulling my mouth away from hers for a chance to breathe some cool, dry air for a second, "I found it." I held up the gem I'd slipped back up my sleeve between my thumb and forefinger.

She snatched the emerald from my fingers, kissing me on the nose. "Thank you, Fastello." She pulled her tunic slightly away from her skin and dropped the jewel out of sight somewhere between the peaks that poked out from the top of her shirt. They glistened sweetly with the sweat she'd earned from all the dancing around the bonfire. The rest of the clan was still out there, with muffled laughter and muted music, but no Luana dancing. So I had no reason to join them.

I took a deep breath to keep my cool, lest she notice and make fun of what was going on in my pants. "Just don't let my dad know, all right?" I ran my now gem-less hand across the three-day-old stubble poking through the bronzed ruddiness of my cheeks. "You know how he feels about taking for ourselves."

Luana rolled her eyes and blew a loose curl away from her mouth. Her lips were so enticing when they were pouty. "If he was serious about all that, then he'd have to banish half the clan."

"Somehow I think you'd be safe regardless." I nuzzled her neck.

"Oh, please." Luana let me kiss her throat and collar bone a few more times, laughing and throwing her head back. Then her hand pressed against my chest, sliding slightly under the tunic, and she pushed me back. "The day I become a Mina or Gilia is the day I become an old maid with no other prospects." She grinned and kissed my forehead before swinging her legs off my lap and escaping from me, tossing her hair back over her shoulders. "Why would I go for an old man when I have the strapping young sixteen-year-olds sneaking me emeralds?"

"Just don't let my *old man* catch you calling him an old man." I reached forward to tap that temptingly plump bulge that was her ass, but she spun and dodged the playful slap, one hand lifting her skirt off the ground oh-so-slightly and the other hand angled above her head. The fast movement resembled not a mischievous dodge but an elegant dance.

"Oh, no," she said, smiling and twirling out of reach. "That will cost you another gem, I'm afraid."

I stood, mesmerized by her dance around the dying fire to the muffled music outside, her lithe shadow flickering across the canvas of the tent. "Oh yeah?" I lunged at her as she made a turn around the fire, but she jumped deftly out of my grasp. "What's the going price? Will it cost me a diamond?"

She stopped in a pose with one foot and one arm extended, just as the music came to a pause in the tempo. She smiled impishly. "*Could* you get me a diamond?"

I lunged and wrapped her in my arms, and this time she didn't squirm away. I bent to kiss the top of her soft curls. "I'd get you all the jewels across the sea if it meant you'd be mine forever."

Luana pulled back slightly to gaze up at me. "And what would Elisabetta and Abella have to say about that, I wonder?"

I laughed. To think she would bring *them* up, after all these weeks together. "They're children," I said, doing my best to make my voice sound even deeper. "You're a woman."

Luana shook her head, but she didn't drop the smile from her features. "*You're* a child, Fastello."

I pulled her tighter against my torso. "I'm only four years younger than you."

She tapped her forefinger against my nose. "And I remember you as a baby suckling at your mother's breast. A rather annoying, loud baby at that. Kept the whole clan up every night with all the moaning."

"Hmm." I grinned. "Things haven't changed much, have they? Only it's not my mother's breast I'm suckling." I loosened my grip so I could sneak a kiss on her collar bone, but she used the opportunity to slip entirely out of my fingers. She stiffened and rolled her shoulders, straightening the sleeve I'd pushed aside in my eagerness to expose the skin beneath.

I reached a hand out to stop her. "Don't be that way—"

"What is this about mother's breasts? Please don't remind me of your mother's breasts. I'm never going to get my hands on another pair so fine and ample."

The man had entered the tent without first announcing himself outside the flap. When you reigned as king of the clan, you got exempted from things like common courtesy—

"I couldn't even wrap one hand around one of 'em." He made a cupping gesture with both hands. "Had to use both, and even then, flesh was spilling every which way."

—and tact.

"Thanks, as always, for that image, Dad." I swallowed the bile that had formed at the back of my throat, which was probably corroded with years of the unpleasant stuff formed from Dad's reminisces of my mother. I supposed the most important thing Dad thought I should know about the woman who'd birthed me and died just a few years after was that she was buxom and had an ass that "no piece of gold, no decades-aged liquor would ever rival."

Dad clasped his hands and rubbed them together like he had just uncovered a stash of spices some aristocrat had hidden beneath the sole of his shoe. "Missed you at the celebration, son." He grinned as his eyes searched Luana from head to toe and back again, lingering far too long at the place where my gift to her had vanished from sight. "Missed you too, Luana."

I had a feeling it was mostly knowing that both his son *and* Luana were absent that made him bother to put down the ale, get off his ass and find out why we'd decided to sneak off for a rare moment of privacy.

"Oh, really?" Luana tossed her hair again, her eyes betraying just a little of her impatience even despite the smile she forced onto her lips. "Took you a while to notice I was missing."

Dad chuckled. Luana had a way with him that Mina and Gilia no longer had, perhaps more than any woman had—at least until he chose his next conquest. "I had other things on my mind, Luana." Dad pulled the tent flap back, and I could see the shadows of the revelry and dancing flickering off the other tents in the darkness. Dad gestured for Luana to go first. "But you're never far from my thoughts."

"That's little comfort, Davazanto." Luana spared me one last glance, raising an eyebrow before she turned to exit. "I have a feeling those thoughts aren't too far from the gutter."

"The gutter? For such a pretty lady? Perish the thought!" Dad ran his hand through his shoulder-length brown hair, a twinkle in his hazel eyes. When you managed to see past the lines and sunspots that had formed on his skin, I supposed Dad was like a somewhat less handsome version of myself, beaten down by a few more decades of living.

He let the flap fall behind Luana, stepping in front of me in my eagerness to follow her into the darkness.

"Fastello," he said, turning a palm up to halt me, "you ride again tonight."

I stopped as if he'd reached for the knife at his belt and stabbed me. I pointed to the flap behind him. "*Tonight?* Might I ask what we're celebrating?"

"A fine haul. One of the best in weeks." Dad tsked, crossing his arms and inviting himself further into the tent. *My* tent. "But what good are we to the people starving if we limit ourselves to one raid an evening?"

He exaggerated. Raids were rarely held more than twice a week, let alone twice per night. I think we'd done enough to scare the prosperous from ever venturing far from their hidey-holes.

As if on cue, the music outside the tent stopped, a roar of bellyaching laughter filling in the brief gap of silence between one melody and the next. I threw my hands wildly into the air. "Well, maybe you should have decided this before you passed out three pints and then some to every able-bodied rider we have."

Dad shrugged his shoulders, his arms still crossed. "So they're not able-bodied. They've earned their respite. You seem alert enough. Too busy drinking in the view to drink your share of ale?"

I ignored the question. Luana was intoxication enough for me. "And what have *I* earned exactly?"

Dad dropped all pretense, letting his lips slip into cold hard lines. "Nothing, to be honest."

I scoffed. "You've got to be kidding me. I don't think I need to remind you that I was the one risking my neck the most—"

"Oh, because rich little skins and bones put up such a fight, do they?" He waved a hand and let it slip back into the crook of his arm. "I was doing what you do at half your age, and I didn't skim from the takings, either." He stepped closer, poking a finger against my chest. "Green leaks through white shirts, son. And I noticed Luana was sporting quite a shiny green bauble from between those ripe peaks of hers. Hardworking families count on what we give them, Fastello. Our takings are the difference between life and death."

I clenched my jaw, doing my best to speak through a grim smile.

"And I suppose the jewels your whores wear couldn't buy enough rice to feed a dozen families?"

Dad laughed and stepped back, shaking his head. "It's good to be king of the nomads, son. Maybe someday you'll learn. Or your brother will grow up and show you." I snatched up my mug and unloaded the rest of the ale that I'd left untouched when I felt Luana's smooth fingers dance across my collar bone by the bonfire. Dad nodded at the belt filled with daggers, knives and other tools of the trade that I'd tossed to the ground when I'd entered with Luana. "Put that on, but wear your cloak. It's a genial job. You and Rento will be enough."

I almost choked. "Rento? What's he going to do, ask them to adopt him?"

The twinkle returned to Dad's eye, and he shook his forefinger at me. "Watch and learn, son. Some boys are born to be a nomad."

And some nomads are born to arrogant assholes.

RENTO HAD BEEN EXCITED TO BE INVITED ALONG TO HIS FIRST RAID. Too bad his eyelids could barely stay open.

"Quit rubbing your eyes," I hissed, leaning my head lower so I could get a better view of the dirt road between the leaves of the tree. "Each time you do, it'll take you another few seconds to re-focus. We're supposed to be watching the road."

Rento snorted and readjusted his back against the trunk. "I thought you were so good at this. Why do you need me to help you look?"

Yes, born to be a nomad indeed. Rento kicked out a foot lazily, almost brushing his boot against my cheek. I whipped out a hand and grabbed his ankle. Rento jumped in place, almost losing his balance and slipping off the bough that we'd both made our lookout.

"You jerk," choked Rento. "I nearly fell."

I pushed Rento's leg away from my head. "And you nearly kicked me in the face."

"Your face could benefit from a little improvement." Rento pulled his leg underneath him, putting his hands down on the bough where he'd been seated and slithering closer toward me on shaky arms. I let his comment go. He was wrong about my face needing improvement and he was shaping up to be no looker himself, but he had the wit of a man twice his twelve years. I wondered if he got that from emulating me. Besides, I wasn't eager for another face like Dad's to be out there. It was hard enough getting attention from his leftovers. And Luana.

Rento reached out to grab the second bough and slid his face beside mine. "What are we looking for exactly?"

"The Stargazers." I pointed toward the spike of the tower against the moonlit sky. I knew that there was a sea beyond that tower and the cliff behind it, but I couldn't help but feel like it was somehow the edge of the world, perfectly poised at the end of the dirt road. The moon and starlight seemed made to reflect the silver stones of the tower, casting its shadow on the fields around it almost as far as the eye could see. "Every full moon, they hold some ritual." I pointed to the glowing orb in the sky, as round as the sun, and almost as bright in the darkness. Its light offered a calmer, more delicate glow.

Rento hung off of my every word, his eyes drawn to the glowing orb like one of the devout. I smirked and nudged him with my shoulder, pointing back at the dirt road in front of us. "The wealthy don't often bother leaving the heart of the duchy." As if he needed to be reminded, I shifted a little to look in the opposite direction of the tower. Rento's eyes followed suit. The city was almost invisible in the night, but the candles and torchlights flickering from the castle and a few of the taller surrounding buildings gave the dark shapes the illusion of eyes watching us from the darkness. The moonlight danced off the calm waters of the sea beside the city, and I could just make out a ship docked in the harbor. I turned back to face the spiral tower. "But they will tonight."

"But you already went on a raid earlier this evening." I felt Rento shift as he looked forward and backward, rustling the leaves and shaking the branches. "When the people left the city." I reached out a hand and placed it on his back to steady him, putting a finger to my lips to quiet him.

I nodded toward the tower. "Apparently Dad got information that some people made it to the tower after the raid, and those people will be headed home tonight."

A bobbing movement, like a small herd, appeared at the gates of the tower. They moved awfully fast for a late night excursion, kicking up billows of dust as they drew closer. I checked back over my shoulder for signs of soldiers from the heart of the duchy, but as usual, the duke couldn't possibly have cared less about the safety of his citizens once outside the protection of the walls. I gripped the tree branch hard and shifted my legs off of the second branch, swinging back and forth a few times to build momentum for a leap the few yards down to the grass below. My knees bent to absorb the jump, and I dusted off some leaves that had accumulated on my tunic.

It took Rento a full minute and a half to slither back down the tree trunk, but I waited patiently, glad he wasn't fool enough to emulate my landing. We didn't have time to deal with a broken ankle on top of a raid. Rento hobbled over a bit, perhaps having wound up with a sore ankle even from the few inches he'd dropped at the landing. "Where's Dad?" he said, between deep breaths.

I shrugged. "Back at the tents, for all I know." That was Dad's way of 'participating' in most raids. Especially if there was no one but his sons around to praise him. I pulled my hood over my head, wrapping my cloak tighter across my chest. If Rento wondered why I was wearing a cloak that was clearly not my own, a velvety soft and lightweight thing more suited to a ballroom than a chilly night in the middle of nowhere, he said nothing. Perhaps the deep gashes and the dirt stains explained anything he needed to know.

"Did Dad tell you what to do?" I slipped the dagger hilt, the leather stained red and the blade completely missing, out of my belt and lined it up with the red-stained gash in the cloak. It slid into the leather thong I'd tied around my arm, making it appear as if I had a dagger blade protruding from my bicep.

Rento shuffled his feet. "Yeah." He watched me, his head tilted, his hands clutching his own shabby cloak. "He didn't say what *you* do, though, exactly."

I ruffled the dagger-less arm through my hair, pulling a few tendrils over my face. "Watch and learn, little brother." I pointed to the tree. "And stay out of sight until you're needed."

If things went well, as I expected them to, chances were he'd never be needed.

Rento shrugged and slipped away behind the tree, his hands

fumbling at the small dagger hilt he'd attached to his belt. I didn't feel it necessary to warn him there wasn't going to be much to worry about from where he'd be watching. Unless he was worried about squirrels gone rabid.

The pounding of the hooves grew louder, so I got into position, clutching my elbow and drawing deep breaths. I stood in the middle of the road at the bottom of the hill, leaving the group enough time to see me before they barreled down and ran me over. Of course, I wouldn't be letting them think they'd run me over. Lying down in a raid and feigning injury was a bit risky—more than one nomad had actually gotten hurt or worse in the attempt. Besides, if Dad called upon me for my expertise, there were easier ways for me to win them over.

"Help!" I shouted, forcing some rough hoarseness into my throat. I didn't bother shouting at the top of my lungs, as it'd be difficult for them to hear me at that distance. Still, it helped the facade to at least try. "Help me, please!"

They came over the hilltop. I studied the group. Only three horses, two ridden sidesaddle, with two luxurious golden skirt hems peeking out beneath thick and coarse woolen cloaks. The ladies had no doubt tried fruitlessly to cover their wealth. The fine dresses aside, women like Luana never bothered to ride sidesaddle.

"Stop, please!" I screamed, taking one intentionally labored step forward. I reached my hand without the blade hilt out. "Help me!"

Although I doubted they heard me over the pounding of the earth beneath them, I must have finally come into view. I stood my ground, challenging them to ride around me if they were determined to ignore a poor wealthy man in trouble. Or through me, if they could stomach it.

As expected, they could do neither. "Bernard! Watch out!" one of the cloaked women screamed, pulling back on her horse's reins and deftly steadying the beast beneath her, barely shifting at all from her saddle. The woman behind her followed suit. The man leading the trio turned his head to look behind him, coming dangerously close to running me down. But his horse did me the favor the man wouldn't, roaring and lifting its front legs upward, demanding the man focus on stopping and soothing the horse until it ceased moving.

An uncomfortable sensation of my heart pounding almost to bursting tore across my chest, but I took deep breaths and reminded myself the fear would play well with what I had to do. If Rento noticed and asked later, I'd tell him a skilled nomad could summon such convincing terror as needed. "Thank you," I sputtered.

Bernard didn't seem to share my terror, despite the fact that he'd almost run a man down without hesitation. He looked me over, scowled and turned to the lady behind him. "My lady, the Stargazers told us to stop for nothing."

"I'm sure they couldn't have expected us to come across a man in distress." The woman removed her hood, letting a tumble of golden-colored curls fall out, framing an oval-shaped face. She was pretty—not gorgeous, but nice to look at. She pursed her lips.

"My lady—" started Bernard.

"You have saved my life, my fine woman." I hobbled past Bernard and his horse, pointedly ignoring the man's glare, and laid my 'uninjured' arm's hand on the neck of the horse carrying the lady. Perhaps used to courtesans, she extended a pale hand, which I took and kissed liberally. "Thank you. Thank you."

"He's injured." The second woman let her hood fall back and revealed frizzy brown hair, hanging in two limp bunches around a rather wan, freckled face. She shifted to slide off her horse and turned to face me. "Let me see it—"

"Lady Cecily, please stay back." Bernard swung his leg across his saddle and jumped down, tripping over his feet in his attempt to stop the woman from approaching. He passed me like a worm on the side of the road and stood in front of the brunette, turning around and putting himself between us.

I glanced up at the blonde, whose hand I still gripped in my palm. Her blue eyes sparkled in the moonlight, and she looked amused. I did my best to reward her with a pained grimace. "No brave protector for my lady...?"

"Agnes," she said withdrawing her fingers. She smiled, although the turn of her lips did not quite soften up the rigidity of her features. She nodded at the manservant behind me and made a point of examining her horse's reins. "And I expect Bernard is doing his best. He's quite overwhelmed."

"My lady," began Bernard, stepping forward. I wondered if he was capable of saying much else.

I used the moment's distraction to groan loudly and grip my upper arm. It got Agnes' attention. Something like concern danced its way across her face. "Bernard," she said, sliding off her horse. "This man needs our help."

"This *man*, my lady, is suspiciously alone in the middle of the night—"

I slowly smiled, as if the mere effort caused me pain. "We were waylaid on the way to the Stargazers." Agnes reached out for my 'injured' arm and examined the knife and the stain of pig's blood. "I only just managed to get away."

"There you go." Agnes' eyes met mine. "The Stargazers said they were expecting another group from the duchy, but no one ever came."

"My lady," said Bernard, stamping his foot impatiently. "That's precisely why they told us not to stop for anything, or anyone. If you'd just allowed us to wait until morning—"

Agnes arched a golden eyebrow, her eyes searching my arm. Her face soured at the sight. "And have the night's ceremony count for naught? You know that only the unholy are allowed in the Stargazers tower when the sun rises."

"I just think that they could make an exception if there was a risk of danger—"

"And where were you headed?" The plainer woman, Celia or something, arrived at my other side. She didn't seem as concerned for me as I'd expected. "I didn't catch your name?"

"Gilbert." I grunted. "To the Stargazers, of course." Agnes reached up to grab the dagger's hilt. I darted my fist out and grabbed her hand. "No, don't!" I gazed adoringly at her. "You're too kind. But if we take it out without a doctor, it'll bleed out."

"I've worked with doctors before," spoke the brunette, stepping in front of Bernard to reach for my arm.

Agnes rolled her eyes and positioned herself between me and the plainer woman. "Cecily, now's not the time to pretend your occasional charitable work makes you a nurse. We'll take him back to the city and have Doctor Audemar look after him himself."

She let my arm go gently and turned to grab onto her horse's saddle. She paused. "Can you ride horseback with a dagger in your arm, do you think?" Her smile told me she didn't care if I was bleeding out a dozen holes in my body, she wanted my arms wrapped around her torso on the back of her steed.

"Agnes," I heard the quieter woman speak, my eyes locked on the flirtatious blonde. "I think it's safer to leave him here and send help." There was something in her voice that made me leery. I adjusted my hood. In the moonlight, it ought to have been hard for her to get a good look at my face, at the slightly darker shade of skin than the wealthy were accustomed to.

"Yes, yes, of course, Lady Agnes!" There was no mistaking Bernard's nervousness, but I did my best to ignore it as I offered Agnes a boost with my 'good' arm. "Even if what he says is true, we need to alert the guards."

I turned to face the dithering man. "*If* what I say is true?"

Cecily put a hand on Bernard's chest, pushing him back before he could open his mouth. Her cloak moved just enough to reveal a rather large blue jewel hanging from a silver chain across her neck. "Where's the rest of your group? Who attacked you? Why did they let you go, and why were you headed to the tower when the city is closer?"

Damn, this lady is good.

Agnes laughed at some joke that no one else heard. "Honestly, Cecily. Are you a judge as well as a nurse now? We haven't time to lose."

"I'm not going anywhere with him—"

Bernard crumpled beneath her touch, saliva gurgling at his lips. I had a sinking feeling. *I've seen that look on a man's face before.*

Cecily screamed. One of the hands she brought to her face was covered in red. My gaze followed the trail from her hand to Bernard's chest, which was stained red, a red still gushing, a color far deeper than the pig's blood smeared on my arm. Rento stepped back, his red hands empty.

"Rento, what are you doing?"

He bent down, and with an effort, rolled the dead man's body over to grab the dagger that was still stuck in his back. He had to stomp on the poor manservant's body in order to get leverage. "What Dad asked me to," said Rento, as casually as he might if Dad had just asked him to put down the tent stakes.

I turned to Agnes and saw for the first time an emotion that had dropped the stiffness out of her attractive features: pure terror. I slapped the horse's ass. "Run," I hissed. Before she could say anything—if she was even capable of speaking—the horse took off, down the dirt path toward the duchy.

"What have you done?!" screamed Cecily. "Agnes! Help!"

I grabbed the woman, who was clearly in hysterics. "Relax," I said, dropping all pretense that I was exhausted or injured. "We just... We just want your valuables."

"All right! Take it." She pointed to the jewel around her neck, her dark eyes searching mine, looking for something she couldn't find. A guarantee of safety maybe. She started beating her bloody hand against my chest. "It's all I've got. Let me go!"

"Settle down!" I had to get control of the situation. I gripped her arms tighter. "Just settle down and you can go..."

She gasped and fell, suddenly limp in my arms. I almost fell to the ground, the sudden weight was so unexpected.

Rento pulled his dagger out of Cecily's back with less effort than he'd used to get it out of the man and wiped the red off of the blade with her cloak. He whistled as he ran the cloth back and forth over the dagger, cleaning it even as the blood ran onto my arms and chest, staining the pig's blood with the blood of a woman. A woman who had yet to offer much resistance.

"What?" Rento asked, stopping his careless tune when he saw my face. He slid the dagger back into his belt and put his hands on his hips. "I wasn't going to wait all night for you to seduce them."

3

CATELINE

Almost as if it knew I was watching it, the firefly blinked, fading in and out of existence, swooping up and down and up again, and landed on my stump. I watched it breathlessly for a moment as it danced across two pale, scarred knuckles. It blinked its warm yellow glow over the ragged surface of the skin—light and dark, light and dark. Almost like it was telling me I was meant to have five fingers there, same as on my left hand, same as on all those around me. As if I could ever forget.

Durand stopped skipping through the meadow, his eyes drawn to the little gift from Ytoile that still tickled my skin. The firefly flew off, returning to its brethren who peppered the meadow, awash in the pale moon glow. When it vanished amongst its many sparkling siblings, and I lost track of it at last, I turned back to see Durand still staring at me. My smile began to falter, but I did as Mother Jehanne had told me, and I forced my lips to curl upward again.

"Did you know," I told the small boy, "that fireflies are Ytoile's children on earth?"

Of course, he'd had to have been asleep for the past five or six years not to understand that. He nodded, and sat down on the grass beside me. I felt that stirring of heat inside me, the feeling that made me dread what was sure to come, even if Mother Jehanne had told me time and again not to get so heated at the curiosity of others.

"Why is your hand broken?"

There it was. The question I'd been dreading since he first locked his eyes on the firefly and intruded into my private moment with the stars. The question they all asked once, when the mothers were out of earshot and they thought they could finally speak without reproach.

I shifted my arm to hide the hand under my left elbow. "It's not broken," I said, perhaps a little more bitingly than necessary. I forced the smile back onto my face. "I was born this way. Oh! Isn't the night sky so beautiful?"

Durand bit his lip and continued staring at my stump, as if he could somehow look through the silver cloth of my mother-in-guidance dress, through the skin and bone of my elbow, and see what I'd hidden beneath.

"That hand has led you here, Cateline. That hand that Ytoile blessed you with led you to become one of us." I don't know how old I was, young enough to crawl into Mother Jehanne's lap, old enough to wonder why I was different. It was my earliest memory of her, patting my back and whispering blessings into my ear as twilight ebbed and the sun was dangerously close to rising.

The thought reminded me of Durand's young age. His eyes flit closed and snapped open again. I reached across my lap to touch Durand's knee with my left hand, ignoring the look he gave it, like he were searching for some deformity in that one as well. "Is this your first full night up, Durand?"

The question seemed to do the trick. He grinned, meeting my eyes at last and showing off a gap in his front teeth. "Yeah. Mother Flore said I could try."

I stood and waited for Durand to follow my example. The moonlight reflected off of the silver of my long skirt as I took his hand in mine. "Only the most holy of Stargazers wake at night and sleep during the sunlight." I squeezed his hand. "You're very lucky to be chosen, Durand."

The compliment seemed to snap all thoughts of tiredness out of his drooping eyes. I led him toward the other children, and he let go of my hand, all thoughts of me forgotten as he joined in a game of tag that Ide and Aymon were engaged in.

I watched the children scream and laugh and play for a moment, marveling at the way Ytoile's children sparkled amongst them, Her blessings for the least of us, the cast aside, the unwanted, so evident here in the moonlight. I gazed at the waterfall pouring its sparkling white and blue water into the reservoir, and the two rivers that birthed out from it. One to the forest, the other through the fields. This truly was a blessed place, giving life and protecting life throughout the entire isle. I noticed the small white figure beside the water. I left the other children to their game, slipping beside the child in her white dress and crouching beside her.

"You're not playing, Oriabel?" I searched her face for some sign of tiredness, but if she felt at all lulled to sleep by the false promises of the sun demon, she didn't show it.

"I had a vision." Oriabel pointed to what had so drawn her attention, a pile of white pebbles beside the reservoir, pebbles covered in small black ants. They looked like stars being devoured by darkness. "Yesterday, when I was asleep."

"The sun demon sends visions while you sleep during the daylight," I told her. I thought of my own dreams, those achingly false promises. "He's angry you spend his hours fast asleep."

Oriabel shrugged. "It wasn't like that. It was just a moment with my family. My real family."

I shook my head, thinking of Mother Jehanne's arms wrapped around me, her gentle rocking as she sung me to sleep. "*We* are your real family, Oriabel."

Oriabel's lips puckered like she'd eaten something sour. "It's different for you, isn't it?" Her eyes flickered tellingly to my right arm, but at twelve years, she knew better than to let her gaze linger. "You came here as an infant."

I sighed. It wasn't as if I was the only infant abandoned at the gate of the tower. Oriabel had to know this. But she knew, also, how few survived past those first few months. After all, why else would a parent abandon her baby here if not for the child being sickly? My surviving to live sixteen winters was proof of Ytoile's plan for me. My sickness wasn't in my bones. It was just something that ordinary parents couldn't possibly understand.

"You've been here six years, Oriabel." I sat on the ground and crossed my legs. "I'm surprised you remember your old family at all."

Oriabel tucked a strand of yellow hair behind her ear. "Well, I do."

I reached out to touch her shoulder, doing my best to follow a mother's example. "Ytoile has plans for the least of us." I paused to let the gravity of the statement sink in. "Your parents may have had no use for you, but She wanted you here."

Oriabel snorted. "Every day you sound more and more like a mother, Cateline."

I could tell from her tone that she meant no compliment, but I couldn't stop the smile that spread across my face. I let go of her shoulder, twirling a strand of my wavy red hair in my best attempt to exude the humility expected of me. "Thank you."

Oriabel hugged her knees against her chest, the retort she was about to say quickly lost as her thoughts turned back to visions planted to test her. "I'm not so sure my parents had no use for me."

Most of the kids came to the tower a little later than I did, and they all had these memories of their birth families. Good memories. Hugs and kisses. Laughter and dancing. Stories told around the fireplace on cold winter nights. For some reason, they never spoke of the work they were forced to do from dawn until dusk, how they toiled only in the hours of the sun demon. They never spoke of receiving no education behind the safety of closed doors in the daytime, of having no time to play and frolic through the meadows at night, like they did at the tower.

They didn't speak of that day their parents died, or more likely, their parents decided they'd had enough of feeding them. The days their parents decided the endless hours their children put into harvesting crops and tilling fields would never equal what they could get from hiring an adult, an adult who would take a few gold coins to waste on import food or opium and not eat up precious wheat and vegetables.

I tossed my hair over my shoulder. If I told her the whole truth, she wouldn't believe me. *"Spare the sufferer the harshest truth, if you can."*

Mother Jehanne always told me. *"All the sufferer, all the sinner needs to know is that Ytoile has a plan for them."*

"I'm sure your parents wanted to keep you, Oriabel," I lied. "But they probably knew how much happier and healthier you would be under the mothers' instruction."

The look Oriabel gave me as she peeked over the top of her knees was like she was determined to prove that she was actually in abject misery—just to be contrary. "Do you think your parents wanted *you?*"

She hadn't said "wanted to *keep* you," as if it was simply a matter of me not being able to toil during all the hours of the sun demon for a plate of food on the table. Just "*wanted* you."

I stood up, keeping my nose held aloft and refusing to watch the histrionics any longer. "You'll never become a mother if you don't learn compassion," I said coldly.

"*Good.* I have no intention of becoming that kind of mother anyway."

Against my resolve, I spun to face her, a lecture on all the mothers had done for an ungrateful child on the tip of my tongue, when Mother Ermessenda's voice called out across the meadow. "Children, we have finished. You may return to the tower."

By the sound of the sigh Oriabel let forth, you'd have thought she was disappointed that she was a day sleeper, that she'd be free from the rays of the sun demon as she slept. It was clear to me that she would never become a mother, never have any special relationship with the goddess in the night sky.

"Go on, then," I said, pursing my lips. I gently pushed her shoulder. My eyes scanned the meadow for the other children chosen for the night's frolic.

"Cateline!" called Mother Ermessenda, beckoning me over to an area a few yards away. I made my way to her, smiling at the grinning Ide and Aymon as they ran past me into the tower.

"I caught five of Ytoile's children!" shouted Aymon.

"But I caught six!" sneered Ide.

"Liar!"

"How would you know? I let them go!"

I cupped my hand around my mouth to focus my voice in their

direction. "Hush, children! Be quiet in the tower! The others are sleeping."

They giggled and disappeared inside just as I reached Mother Ermessenda. She crouched over a sleeping Durand, who lay curled up amongst the stalks of grass like one of the kitchen kittens. Mother Ermessenda scooped him up in her arms. "You let this one fall asleep." It was a statement, but her tone was heavy with accusation and disappointment.

I bit into the inside of my lip, bowing my head. "I'm so sorry, Mother. Oriabel wasn't participating and I was worried—"

Mother Ermessenda grunted, leading the way back into the tower. "Not participating isn't as offensive to Her Holiness as falling asleep after committing to a night awake in Her honor."

I could feel the heat rise to my cheeks, knowing the pale, freckled surface would express my shame and glow deep red. "I'm sorry, Mother."

Mother Ermessenda shifted Durand in her arms, throwing him back over her shoulder. "Who recommended this child was ready for a festivity night?"

"Mother Flore, I believe." I was eager to shift the focus from my own failings.

Mother Ermessenda paused as we reached the entryway to the tower from the inner meadow, and then she clucked her tongue. "Some are always eager to think our children are ready before they truly are." She looked me up and down pointedly, drinking in the silver of my mother-in-guidance dress. I'd received it only two weeks earlier, on a night that ranked among the happiest of my life, in all my many happy, happy nights and even days as a Stargazer.

"Of course." I let my eyes fall, desperate to show remorse. I reached my arms out, offering to take Durand back to his quarters. "I will pray for him as he slumbers."

Mother Ermessenda exhaled sharply. "A mother-in-guidance to pray for a child's soul? I think not. The boy and Mother Flore will have to beg for forgiveness. I don't care if either of them were set to sleep during the hours of the demon. His eternal happiness is at risk."

I swallowed nervously, both for the reprimand to my audacity, and for the idea of poor Durand and Mother Flore spending the next few hours in contrition because I failed to notice the child drifting asleep. "I will beg for my own forgiveness, then," I said, taking a deep breath.

"As should we all, every night, and every day." Mother Ermessenda sniffed. "But you will have to pray with Mother Jehanne. She's asked me to summon you."

I couldn't help the smile that burst onto my face. My gaze locked with Mother Ermessenda's, and I could swear I saw the emeralds of my eyes reflecting off of Mother Ermessenda's dreary blue ones.

Mother Ermessenda's own mouth puckered. "Well, go on then. She's in her chambers. And there's less than an hour left until the end of the night. You wouldn't want to be responsible for Mother Jehanne offending Ytoile as well, would you?"

I made the smile vanish on my lips. "No, of course not." I curtsied and turned to go, not bothering to hide my grin once my back was facing the sour mother's direction. *Mother Jehanne. She summoned me!*

"Come in, child."

I had just raised my fist to knock on the large wooden door leading to Mother Jehanne's chambers, but she knew I was standing on the other side of the door. It was no surprise, really. As I entered, I marveled at her commune with the stillness of the night, how her relationship with Ytoile, her almost entire existence in the blessing of darkness, could allow her to discern even the quietest of movements.

"Good night, Mother Jehanne." I kept my hand over my stump in front of my abdomen, my eyes averted to the large black and silver rug covering the grey cobblestones.

"Good night, Cateline." I could hear Mother Jehanne rocking in the chair she kept at the sole window in her chambers. "The stars were bright tonight."

"Yes." I took a deep breath. Perhaps it was best to get it over with. "I'm so sorry, Mother. I failed one of the younger ones at the night's festivities. He fell asleep before the end."

I dared to look up just a bit and saw Mother Jehanne rocking in her chair, gazing up at the stars without pause. She waved a hand to beckon me nearer. "Come, child, and help me draw the curtain. Dawn is breaking."

I dutifully reached in front of Mother Jehanne and tugged at the dark black material, adorned with silver stars to match her rug. Only the slightest crack of waning moonlight slipped into the room from beneath the thick material, and it took my eyes a moment more to adjust to the near total darkness.

I felt Mother Jehanne grab my hand before I could properly make her out. She cupped it in both her hands, patting the back of it gently. "Do you think me totally devoid of sin, child? Devoid of suffering?"

I thought a moment, chewing on the softness of my cheek. The truth, or the answer she might be seeking? I couldn't tell. "No person is," I said at last, settling for a mixture of the two.

"That's right. And if the holy mother is unworthy of Ytoile's perfection, a mother-in-guidance is bound to make mistakes as well." She squeezed my hand and let it fall. "Fret not over a sleepy child, Cateline. It takes time for a chosen child to adjust to the night. And sometimes a child simply isn't meant to be chosen."

"But I..." It'd been the first time I was asked to watch the younger children alone, without a mother. I'd tried to emulate the mothers who'd watched over us in the past, quietly drinking in the moonlight on the sidelines, only coming to speak with those off by themselves in danger of sleeping. "I wanted so badly to please you."

Mother Jehanne sighed, but it was more of a weary sigh, as if she were burdened by all of the tasks she had to do, and less of a disappointed sound than Mother Ermessenda might have offered me. "It would be impossible for you to displease me, Cateline. Why else do you think I chose you for the mother-in-guidance position? You, and you alone?"

I thought of the other two girls who'd turned sixteen this year, Ava and Malle, who'd left the tower at the same time I'd officially started my training. Sent off to the heart of the duchy, along with the boys our age, sentenced to a life of servitude and day-time existence. For I knew, from what the mothers had told us, what sort of jobs a young orphan woman could hope to find if she wished to stay awake at night. Ytoile may not cherish those who toiled during the hours of the sun as much as she did her Stargazers, but far more offensive to

Her were those who used Her holy hours to live a classless life of debauchery.

"I'm sorry, Mother Jehanne." Whatever she might say, the thought of Ava and Malle and the fate that would have awaited me had I joined them only made me more disappointed I'd failed her.

"Enough, child. I'm sure the other mothers are making amends to Ytoile as we speak." It was not Mother Jehanne's duty to attend to the soul of every single child in the tower. No, what we'd shared as I grew up was special. "I summoned you here on another matter entirely. Sit." As my vision grew clearer, I saw her gesture to the stool next to her rocking chair.

We sat in silence for a moment, letting the darkness envelop us. The sliver of light from beneath the curtain was just enough that I could make out Mother Jehanne beside me, her white hair brushing the shimmering silver of her holy mother dress.

"You know that we had some visitors from the city this night."

I nodded, then thought better of it, not sure if she could see me in the dark. "Yes," I said to be certain. For a moment, my chest fluttered. Perhaps I was close to being invited to the festivities with patrons, to stand solemnly in the line of mothers chosen for the task, singing as Mother Jehanne asked Ytoile for blessings for those who would give of themselves to support us.

"We expected two groups. Only one arrived."

I bit my lip. Reality intruded harshly into my dream. "The nomads?" I ventured.

Mother Jehanne cleared her throat. "Most likely." She shifted in her chair, the rustling of the silver fabric sounding a bit like the waterfall. "Thieves and murderers, the lot of them. And desecrating Ytoile's most holy hours with their sinful dancing 'round flames sent from the sun."

I nodded, thinking of the groups of patrons who had been stopped from reaching us before, the number that even now refused to even make the journey.

"We need food, Cateline. And clothing, and books." Mother Jehanne sighed. "I know many of our patrons choose to sleep during the holy hours, even those wealthy enough not to have to support themselves with day labor, but they are beloved by Ytoile nonetheless, for their generosity to Her tower and to the children entrusted to the mothers who love Her."

"Of course." Mother Jehanne would expect my empathy.

Mother Jehanne slammed a fist on her rocking chair armrest. "This cannot stand any longer. Those nomads are the sun demon's children on earth." She took a deep breath. "They must be sent back to where they came from."

I swallowed. To wish a blazing, endless suffering even on a thief, even on a murderer... I could not bear the thought of their pain in fiery torment.

I felt Mother Jehanne's hand on my shoulder. "You will set off for the heart of the duchy, Cateline. Tomorrow, after you sleep. You and one or two of the mothers." She squeezed my shoulder. "Something must be done."

My stomach was a torrent. To be trusted with Mother Jehanne's desperate plea was an honor. To venture forth, before the sun fully set no less, across fields where nomads were known to attack the helpless patrons... I was terrified.

"Of-Of course." It was all I could say. I couldn't bear Mother Jehanne's disappointment.

In the wane light, I took note of Mother Jehanne's weary smile. She patted my shoulder and gestured toward the door. "Bless you, child. Now go. Enjoy your rest. Mother Ermessenda will speak with you in the afternoon."

"Thank you, Mother. May Ytoile bless you." I stood and curtsied, tripping over the stool as I made my exit. I straightened my shoulders and did my best to walk as if I'd never tumbled, exiting quietly on soft footsteps.

Light was breaking, leaking in through open windows and doorways, draping the hallways in shadows. I headed for my chambers, newly chosen for me when I became a mother-in-guidance. They were located at the edge of the dorms for the other mothers, in the room nearest the children's dorms. Someday I'd have a room further in, further away from my past as an orphan.

As I ascended the stairs, I passed a window with its curtains drawn back. I used my arm to shield my eyes from the brightness of the breaking dawn. It'd been a month since I'd seen the light of day properly. A light I'd have to get used to tomorrow. Chosen for more blessed nighttime duties, I slept from dawn until mid-day. I spent the rest of the daylight hours in the safety of rooms with curtains drawn, wondering how much longer it would be until Ytoile won her battle against the demon and would finally bless us with more hours of Her company in the colder months. But even then, I wondered how long I could go without a fire, the cheap imitation of the sun demon. The children never went without one during the winter, but the truly devout mothers, I knew, could sleep and wake without ever relying on a flame's warmth.

Worry about that later. For now, it was the time of the sun demon, the time when his hours were long, and the air burnt with his fiery breath. Amidst the screeching of the cicadas, I heard a woman's lamentation, a scream for absolution, a wracked and heavy sob.

I blinked and shifted my arm a bit up, letting my eyes adjust to the light. I carefully looked up and down the staircase to see if any other mother was watching, scared of being caught paused at a window with its curtains drawn back. But no one was up to rouse the children, and the mothers who did the cooking would have long descended the stairs to start breakfast. They cooked for the children and the day-mothers who sacrificed so much of their time with Ytoile to make sure the children got their education. At least until it was their turn to walk the halls at night.

The window overlooked the meadow and the reservoir. I let my arms fall, my eyes mostly adjusted to the breaking brightness, and felt my heart sink to witness the meadow in the bright light, the green and yellow straw of the grass so repugnant when not bathed in moonlight. Another shriek drew my eyes to the spot where Mother Ermessenda had picked up Durand, a spot awash with daylight, one sure to have hours more of sun scorching its surface. Mother Flore was there, crying and bowing and shrieking. Her silver dress lay discarded beside her, and only a thin shift covered her from waist to torso.

"Scream, child!" she shouted. "Beg for forgiveness!"

Beside her crouched a child, similarly shorn of clothing but for a slip covering his waist. I couldn't make out his face, but I could hear his soft whimpering, the occasional cry of "I'm sorry!" that could in no way match the lamentation of Mother Flore. His dark hair made it clear it was Durand, awoken from his offensive slumber once the sun began to rise. He no doubt had been told he'd have to spend the day in repentance, suffering side by side with the mother who'd had faith in him, the one who'd said he was ready for a night of festivities. The mother who'd thought him ready to know what it was to be among Ytoile's most blessed. *Too soon, perhaps. Even though I was ready at an even younger age.*

I tapped my left thigh with my fingers, searching my mind for any evidence that a mother who'd watched over festivities and failed to keep a child awake had ever joined in the following day's lamentations. There had been from time to time a mother anxious to take her part in the blame and beg of Ytoile's forgiveness. But it wasn't expected of her. She had so many children to watch over, after all. And she wouldn't have been the one who suggested a sleepy child was ready.

I straightened my back and grabbed the hem of my silver skirt, turning to face the top of the stairs. I'd pray for forgiveness in the darkness of my chambers, a venue more likely to reach commune with Ytoile regardless. Perhaps I'd suffer dreams sent by the sun demon as I slumbered, and that would be repentance enough.

I wouldn't think of the pale skin turned red on the fragile child and mother, how the ones out there in the sun would scream and itch and peel away their sins for days or weeks to come.

4

KOJIRO

I hated this time of day more than anything. When the sun edged up over the eastern horizon, the beams of light filtered through the canvas of the doors, rendering my candle superfluous. But the candlelight was my comfort, a friend that only came out when I was safe behind closed doors, when the rest of the palace slumbered, and I was free, if but for a few hours, to revel in solitude.

Of course, candlelight didn't free me to be the person that I was. Candlelight was absolutely necessary if I hoped to catch up, and strive toward being the person I had to be.

I turned the page of the barbarian tome, each letter in their meaningless alphabet like a knife to my eyes, each word a strain to make sense of. I could speak the language—I *would* speak it—but reading and writing it was like some secret message that only barbarians could master. Barbarians and my little sister.

"Pardon me."

Only Tomiko would whisper her excuses, as if afraid to be heard. Mother would have a servant say "pardon" for her, and they'd speak it brashly, as if every decibel louder they spoke would keep them one moment longer from death. Father and Elder Brother Nobutada would... Well, it hardly mattered what either of them would do anymore.

Even though I gave no answer, the door to my chambers slid open just far enough to fit the petite fourteen-year-old princess I expected to find there. "Elder Brother Kojiro," came the tentative whisper. "Are you awake yet?"

I shook my head to stave the drowsiness from overcoming my eyelids once and for all and blew out the candle. Although there was no one in all of Hanaobi I'd rather see than Tomiko, there was no denying that solitude was at an end for the evening. I sighed, pattering over to the door that led to the courtyard and sliding it open, letting the sun, the servants, my family and my daily life free access to the wretch who'd been holed up inside the past few hours, forgoing the comfort of his futon for nothing, no progress made, no sense divined from the non-divinable.

Tomiko walked carefully to my table, each step a small sliding movement forward, in that way that only she, Mother and other noblewomen could emulate. I wondered not for the first time if it had more to do with the constricting way the servants wrapped her many-layered *kimono* around her legs than any conscious effort to walk like a spirit. "Didn't you study this last week?" Her small, pale fingers lifted a page of the barbarian tome, her dark brown eyes moving back and forth in that foreign way to make sense of the text written there.

I took two giant steps across the room—wrapped only in my white *kosode* undergarments, I wasn't encumbered, not that my formal blue *hakama* pants ever kept me quite as confined as Tomiko—to snatch the tome from her fingers. "I'm reviewing it."

Tomiko had a way of smiling amiably and looking like a sun spirit on earth while still conveying her disdain. "I don't think the barbarian views on astronomy will prove very useful to you. You're supposed to be focusing on warfare."

If there was ever a person more intelligent and suited for the throne of the cultural center of the world, I couldn't imagine him or her. Too bad for both of us she was third in line. No, second. Second. I couldn't remember to forget Elder Brother Nobutada.

"It's not just astronomy," I said, trying my best to appear the full seventeen summers old I was, the proper elder brother. "It's their religion." I flipped through the book, stopping at a page with a drawing of a constellation, the star at the center blended into the silhouette of a woman. "Ee-to-wa-ru," I pronounced slowly, pointing to the figure. Most of what I remembered I remembered from Yukishige's lecture, not from the reading. "A deity they think lives amongst the stars."

Tomiko pointed to the word beneath the drawing, a jumble of letters that made very little sense to my eyes. "Ytoile," she said, with what was probably perfect barbarian pronunciation. "All you need to know about barbarian religion is that the holiest stay awake at night, they confuse the sun spirit with some sort of demon, and they're all idiots. It's not even that widely practiced." Tomiko gently took the book from me, closing the cover backwards over the image of the stars. "Mother insists that the duke pays nothing more than lip service to his people's religion. He doesn't even bother to stay awake for any nights other than their holiest."

Unbidden, I found myself there, in a meadow in the night. Yukishige told me about festivals with fireflies, and barbarian women dancing and singing in silver dresses. I felt a flush on my cheeks as I pictured a barbarian woman in one of those loose, flowing dresses I'd seen in illustrations, her skin pale on her exposed neck, her hair golden, her chest jutting out far more than any Hanaobi woman's.

Tomiko stood on her tiptoes and rapped the book against my forehead, almost as skillfully as Mother would. "Whatever fancy has taken over your mind, stop. You know Mother hates how you daydream."

I clenched my jaw and stepped around Tomiko, sorting the barbarian tomes and Hanaobi scrolls back into neat piles. *Daydreams are all I have.*

"Pardon." The voice was loud, and unfamiliar. It was too early for Mother, though, so the pain that tore through my chest really had no cause to squeeze my lungs so.

"Enter," I said, expecting the servants who would help me dress for the day. Nobles didn't dress themselves. Even though I'd wear fewer layers than my sister, it was still a hassle to slip on every piece. I took a deep breath, doing my best to ignore the heat rising to my head. I didn't like all the attention that came with dressing.

It was a barbarian man who entered, carefully sliding the door behind him and bowing with his lower legs, hands and face flat against the floor like a servant. I felt that sudden dizziness, that inability to breathe clawing its way across my chest. I looked to Tomiko, sure she could tell me that this was all a joke. Or a test of Mother's. I was looking to my younger sister for guidance, like the failure I was.

Tomiko's lips danced into that mask of a smile of hers, making her face unreadable. She looked from me to the intruder and back to me again, encouraging me to take the lead. My stomach cramped, and I worried briefly if the sweat accumulating at my brow was a sign I was going to vomit. Vomiting in the palace was an offense to the spirits.

"Who-Who are you?" I sputtered out at last, feeling my tongue go dry. I thought better of what I'd said and repeated the question in slow, careful barbarian tongue.

The man, his hands pale and pink as peaches, moved his blond head slightly. "May I stand?" he asked, in near-perfect Hanaobi speech.

"Yes. Yes." My tongue betrayed me before I could give proper thought to my answer. What if he were an intruder? What if Mother had sent him to me, to see if I'd treat him accordingly? My gaze flew to the katana in its scabbard that sat beautifully in its display in the corner. An object of beauty, so rarely held in these two hands. I could barely swing a wooden sword without making a fool of myself. It'd be an insult to Mother if I dared to touch the real blade.

The man stood, revealing clearly that he was outfitted in a brown Hanaobi *kimono* and *hakama*, the cheapest roughest cloth of the working class. "Prince Kojiro," he said, clasping one hand over his abdomen and bowing his head. "Princess Tomiko." He nodded at my sister, who bowed her head slightly in return. "Your mother Her Majesty has sent me to take over your barbarian lessons, Prince Kojiro." I might have imagined it, but I swore I saw the corner of his thin lips twitch at referring to his own people as 'barbarian.' "You may call this one Tierny." He raised his eyes to meet mine, negating the extra care he'd taken to speak formally only to look into my eyes as his equal. He had deep lines around his lids. His eyes were a startling color, like water, and as I darted to look away, I noticed slivers of white mixed in with the golden strands of his hair.

I stiffened my back, keenly aware that this strange, bold barbarian was looking upon the prince of Hanaobi in his undergarments. I fought desperately not to let him know how light my head felt at the many embarrassments. "Tierny," I said, letting my tongue wrap itself around the odd name. "Yukishige and I never begin our lessons before the servants dress me, and before I've had my breakfast."

Tierny smiled grimly. "Your mother Her Majesty no longer agrees with Master Yukishige's... leniency." He bowed stiffly. "I'm to make sure you surpass where your elder brother left off in knowledge and in talent by the end of the week."

He couldn't have just said the end of the week. I was still sleeping, and this was a nightmare. Only I hadn't slept.

I stiffened my shoulders and took a deep breath. "I must speak with Yukishige." I licked my lips, allowing myself another breath. "There must be some mistake."

Tierny raised his eyes to meet mine again, and what I saw in them was something other than audacity, and something closer to that cold determination that lived in Mother's gaze always. "Master Yukishige is no more." He straightened his back, putting himself a full head taller than me. "He slit his own belly in apology to Her Majesty yesterday evening."

<hr>

THERE HAS TO BE SOME MISTAKE. THERE HAS TO BE. THE REFRAIN KEPT rolling through my mind over the next few hours, as I was told to speak in barbarian with Tierny even as servants dressed me in my full *kimono* and brought in a tray of fish, rice, vegetables and soup. When they cleared the food away and my day of education would normally begin, I'd already gotten a headache on top of the ceaseless feeling of nausea, the tightness in my chest.

I'd escaped the barbarian to relieve myself, but he'd warned me, first in barbarian and then in more elegant Hanaobian when it became clear to him that I wasn't comprehending half of what he was saying—not for lack of skill, but because my mind was wandering—not to dawdle, that our lessons continued from sun up to sun down, and I was only free to bathe and sleep without him at my side, murmuring in that harsh language.

And also to use the toilet. Perhaps he thought it too inelegant to mention that. I shut myself in the privacy of the toilet room, needing fully to use the room as I'd told him, but needing the solitude more than anything.

I clasped my hand against my chest, scared of the pain there, terrified, not for the first time, that I would suddenly collapse and die, like some men had done before me. Much older men, to be sure, but weakness of the heart could inflict a young prince surely, and I could feel my lungs refuse to take in enough air. *Breathe in. Breathe out.* I'd live. I always did. The pain would fade away, if only I could think of anything but the pain. But that was difficult. Too difficult.

Part of me wanted to run to Mother, to plead my case like the educated man she wanted me to be. *Elder Brother Nobutada was eighteen when he died. Plus, he was always smarter, you said that yourself; he was a genius, the ideal heir to the throne. To say that I have to be caught up to where he was when he died, when he was not only so much smarter than I am, but when he had a full year longer to study, is insanity.*

I laughed, even if there was nothing at all amusing about the situation. It was the image of accusing Mother of coming up with a plan that was 'insanity' that did it to me. The words out of the mouth of a lesser man would be the last ones he spoke.

Besides, I imagined adding, *all that genius didn't help him, nor Father neither, with their brilliant plan of infiltration. The duke still rules in his duchy, and regardless, the treasure stolen from Hanaobi will always be stolen. Perpetuating this war in secret even while we take their worthless salt, wheat and wool —'goods' we could do without, and 'goods' we give valuable crops for—is idiotic.*

I wouldn't be surprised if even her own son lost her life for that.

"Pardon me, Prince Kojiro."

There would be no solitude. Not even in this foul place for foul actions, and foul, worthless people. I gave no reply, squeezing my hand tighter against my chest.

"We need to get back to work, Your Highness." Tierny.

I took a deep breath and clenched my hands into fists. Feeling a bit more in control of myself, I slid open the door and stepped out.

Tierny bowed slightly and stepped back, probably waiting for me to take the lead, as if I really had any say in where we'd be going. I straightened my spine and led the way back to my study, with Tierny slipping in right behind me, far closer than any proper servant would dare to tread.

"Prince Kojiro, you'll forgive any of my rudeness," spoke Tierny, as if hearing my thoughts. "I've spent enough time traveling to Hanaobi to learn the language passably, but I never expected I'd... That is, I never thought I'd be honored with a long stay."

I stopped in front of the study doorway, waiting for Tierny to slide it open. I paused and looked at Tierny expectantly, and when at last he comprehended my meaning, he slid open the door, bowed and let me walk in ahead of him. Of course, a servant would have crouched to the ground and avoided my eyes as I entered, but Yukishige would have stood much as Tierny did. I wasn't sure what sort of mix between the two Tierny might be. But he was a barbarian regardless.

"Your culture. I know too little about it," said Tierny casually, almost as if speaking to an old friend. He sat on the floor at the table across from me, crossing his legs with his knees outward, like a barbarian. I slipped across from him with my shins flat against the floor. "But your mother Her Majesty said she'd forgive me my barbarian ways if I could teach you to speak, read and write better than a barbarian."

Then you'll never be forgiven. Maybe if we had a year instead of a week. I sighed. Not even then, not if the goal was Elder Brother Nobutada.

Tierny must have thought my sigh was at him, although I supposed it was in part. He smiled. "We'll do it, you'll see," he said, switching to barbarian tongue. He pointed to an open barbarian tome. "You converse well, Prince Kojiro," lied Tierny, as I knew full well he'd barely gotten me to speak in Hanaobian or barbarian. "You read well enough, too, just perhaps too slowly for people around you to be aware of your ability." He tapped his finger on the open page. "This is a record I kept when I captained my own ship." He grinned. "Bet they found it a pain to do the bookkeeping without it." He ran his finger across the page, pointing to letters and numbers in a jumble that hardly made sense. "The empress told me she'd like you to be able to make sense of the trade records. The *real* trade records hidden beneath the ones on paper anyway."

I stared at Tierny blankly. I got the gist of what he was saying, but if he was suggesting I make sense of a list of goods traded and look for hidden meanings in a language in which I could barely make sense of the surface meanings, he was strangely too optimistic.

Tierny stared back for a moment, and I noticed the lump on his throat jiggle before he turned back to the book, tapping his finger here and there. "10 barrels of wheat for 20 barrels of rice. 5 bushels of wool for 10 bushels of silk."

Even though I didn't mean to make any sounds, a tsk escaped my lips.

Tierny seized on the sign of life and grinned. "Why do you laugh, Your Highness?"

I shrugged my shoulders, but then I figured the poor man deserved something for his effort. It was nice, after all, that one of us had hope for my success. Leave it to someone who hadn't met me before this morning to have confidence in my ability.

I tapped the silky blue *kimono* sleeve on my arm. Then I gestured at the rough peasant *kimono* Tierny wore. "Silk. Wool. Wear them both and you can see which is better, worth more bushels."

Tierny nodded, smiling like a hopeless idiot. "That's right. And much the same could be said of rice and wheat. At least," he turned around and stared out into the garden, beyond which lay a stone wall, "it may be a matter of taste, but you have plenty of rice, and it's easier to prepare than wheat." His gesture must have been meant to indicate the rice fields in the distance that you couldn't see from within the palace walls. "The duchy confused scarcity for value, ignoring the fact that the superior nation will have what it needs in abundance, so that it never becomes desperate."

He must have been pleased with himself, pretending he thought my own country was superior. I let it go, not sure he'd be able to get away with the same in front of Mother.

"If the duchy has a weakness," continued Tierny, his gaze serious, "it's desperation."

I raised an eyebrow and picked up my quill pen. "Mother says the duchy is all weakness." I dipped the pen in ink and pretended to prepare to write on my parchment like a barbarian would, from the left to the right.

Tierny seemed to force a laugh. "That's true. In many ways, it's true." I looked up out of the corner of my eye and saw him pause. I watched his throat's lump jiggle again. He clearly had stopped himself from saying more.

I put the pen down, having written the first letter of the barbarian alphabet and leaving it at that. "Tierny, tell me."

Tierny smiled and pointed to the book again. "Yes, well, the hidden truth in these pages—"

"No. Tell me more about the duchy's weakness." I cocked an ear slightly, listening for any sign of movement from the hallway. "And its strengths," I whispered.

"My lord," started Tierny, using a barbarian custom to address me. "Your Highness. I don't mean to assume that the duchy is in any way superior to Hanaobi—"

I waved a hand to cut him off. "Be careful what you say." The look of terror on the man's face was enough to assure me Mother had had a nice long discussion with Tierny before she sent him to me. I sighed and lowered my voice. "I mean, for Tierny's sake. For your sake. Such things, they don't matter to me. But they matter to my mother."

A little of the fear left Tierny's odd-colored eyes, but his face remained guarded. "Yes, of course." He intertwined his fingers and placed his fists across his ledger. "The truth is, Prince Kojiro, that the empress does want me to educate you the best I can, to teach you what you need to know to take down the duchy. I just didn't want to offend—"

I raised a hand to silence him. "Enough. No offense given." I kept my mouth shut, thinking over my words in barbarian carefully. "First you must tell me. Why would you betray the duchy?" He certainly was never going to be allowed to go home, now that he was spouting off his mouth about how Mother hoped to overthrow the duke.

A wry smile tugged at the corner of Tierny's lips. "The duchy betrayed me first, Your Highness."

I shook my head. I had no interest in the details or the man's petty personal vengeances. Regardless, he was sure to be dead at the end of the week when it became clear to Mother that a barbarian could hardly pull off a miracle when her own respected teacher could not. "Do you know the duke?" I asked.

"Yes." Tierny lowered his voice. "And it's no secret to him what her imperial highness hopes to do one day. Just as it's no secret to your mother that the duke wouldn't hesitate to eradicate Hanaobi in an instant given the chance."

The heaviness of his tone made the few words I didn't understand clear. "But... Desperation."

Tierny smiled again. "Yes. The duchy is desperate not to starve or freeze. It doesn't produce enough to feed and clothe the vast majority of its people, and the trade alliance with Hanaobi might be all that keeps them from dying by the hundreds. The duke, well"—he ran a sun-spotted hand through his yellow and silver hair—"he's plenty comfortable. He'd prefer to let them all rot and destroy Hanaobi. But for now, he stays his hand."

"Because without his people," I said, thinking over his speech carefully, "he'd have no one to rule."

"Very clever, Prince Kojiro." Tierny slammed a palm against the table, causing me to jump in place. *Barbarian crudity.* "So now you know what motivates the duchy, and the duke. What keeps Hanaobi from taking over the duchy, then, and why do they knowingly offer more of their goods for things of little value to them?"

I raised an eyebrow. "The duchy has nothing we want to take." I wanted to add, "so why would we bother?" but I didn't. Instead, I spoke the truth. "Mother would era-di-tate the duchy if she could."

"*Eradicate,*" corrected Tierny, not unkindly. His voice got impossibly quiet, and he leaned forward, and I found myself doing the same, putting my face uncomfortably close to the barbarian stranger's. "The duchy has a superior army."

That was it? That was why Mother kept up with this farce of a trade system, why she insisted we would take the duchy not through frontal assault but through secrets and shadows? "We have a good army," I said, not able to take the insult to Hanaobi in stride, even if I couldn't possibly be as passionate about my country as Elder Brother Nobutada, or even Tomiko.

Tierny nodded, averting his eyes to the table. "Yes, of course. But your mother needs a duchy ship to land, or it'll be blown out of the water before it even gets near the harbor."

"The cannonbulls," I said, thinking of the flying balls of steel Yukishige warned me were stationed everywhere along the duchy harbor. Strange, he'd told me, that the barbarians hadn't thought to use their explosive powder in more practical forms. A mistake Hanaobi did not make.

Tierny chuckled. "Cannonballs, yes."

I felt my face reddening, not even sure what mistake I'd made in pronunciation. I decided to change the subject, not sure since the man was slated to die that it was worth wasting time discussing the duchy's army.

"So," continued Tierny, more cheerfully and loudly, "that leads me to my ledger's secret truth. What else Hanaobi sends the duchy in exchange for paltry goods."

I didn't need to see the ledger or make sense of its jumble of letters to know the truth. "We send people," I said, using my pen to point to the page, as if I was divining the truth from a pattern I saw written. "We sent them my father and my bigger brother."

"I know," replied Tierny. "And the duke sent the two back in ten different barrels."

5

ROHESIA

I threw back my shoulders and put my hand on my hilt, not out of any intention to attack, but as a sign of respect.

"Rohesia, dear. Come in."

Father's library was as unkempt as ever, with stacks of books scattered from the floor to my waist and unfurled maps on the large table at the center. Father sat by the fireplace, one leg draped over the armrest of his cushioned velvet chair, an open book on his lap, one hand cradling his pale face. His eyes met mine briefly before returning to his book. "You had a late night. I completely missed you after I'd turned in. How did you find the new captain, dear?"

I moved closer and clicked my heels together. "Dead, sir." I swallowed, trying to forget the wide eyes on the man's face. "That is, he's now dead."

Father turned a page, the only indication he'd heard me the pointed arch of his dark brown eyebrow. "How many outsiders?"

"The garrison reported a total of six, Father."

Father sighed and shut the book, moving his legs to sit properly as he rubbed his temples with both hands. "They trickle in like termites through a rotted wall." He clasped his hands together and stared off somewhere behind me. "Let's hope yesterday's incident taught them a lesson." He cleared his throat and stood, tucking his chin in slightly to look down and meet my eyes. "I do hope you left me some sailors, Rohesia. It's a pain to hear captains constantly whining about recruitment."

I stepped back to let Father pass. He pored over the largest map at his table. "Yes, sir," I finally thought to answer. "The ones who surrendered. After the initial fight broke out, that is."

Father sighed and shook his head, his fingers running over the map. "How many?"

I stiffened. "Perhaps a dozen left standing."

"Have them sent to me. I'll find a suitable replacement for captain."

"Of course."

Father shifted a paper weight keeping the edges of his map from curling. It was a strange cat-like beast, carved of a pale green marble Father told me was called "jade." He tapped his finger on the paper, inviting me to step closer. "Tierny should still be in Hanaobi."

"Tierny?" I repeated, not sure I'd heard right.

Father nodded, his eyes still on the paper. "The captain."

I bit my tongue. Father had told me he'd probably been killed, had insisted there'd been a letter saying he fell ill. I was expressly told to investigate his death, to get a feel for the new captain. "I assume, then, that the good captain is among the living?"

Father gave me a brief smirk to acknowledge his deceit and then turned back to the map, tucking his long graying brown hair behind his ear absently. "If there were outsiders smuggled on this boat, that means that Tierny wormed his way into her imperial highness' graces and won the right to stay there a spell in exchange for his crew taking back her discards."

I moved my hand from my sword hilt to clasp the other hand behind my back. The muscles in my shoulder felt tense. "You could have told me I was looking for outsiders."

Father stepped forward, clasping my shoulders in both hands. "But you discovered them regardless, my darling." He smiled and patted my shoulders proudly. "You aren't my daughter for nothing."

"Yes, sir." I felt wounded at being told less than the whole truth, as usual. At being tested at every turn, but still being treated like a child.

I hoped it didn't show on my face. I'd had years to perfect a mask, learning not to let any emotion surface.

Father patted my shoulders one last time and turned back to his map, which showed the whole of the duchy, the sea and Hanaobi. The duchy stretched for miles, the most prominent features the hundreds of farms peppering the land, the forest, the two rivers, the tower and the city that was the heart of the duchy. The duchy was surrounded entirely by water, the coast of Hanaobi less than a hundred nautical miles away. There were mountain ranges drawn on the map behind the sliver of the kingdom of outsiders, and then... The lines there were different from the others, done in inky brush stroke, more artistic than practical.

My fingers traced the map canvas and the inky brush marks. Father noticed my transgression and cleared his throat. "No one from the duchy has ever reached that far, beyond the Hanaobi peaks. There are other nations there, some distance away—so I hear tell." He traced the brush strokes with his own fingers, lingering on the lines as if remembering the one who'd drawn them for him. He tapped the map gently. "But the Hanaobi are a fierce, warmongering people. They don't communicate with their neighbors. They have no allies for us to fear."

At the top of the map were other vague land masses, each marked with an 'X' in different hands. Father pointed to them. "My men have tried to find our own allies, beyond the Hanaobi peaks or in any one of these places, but they proved too distant." Father ran his hand across his face, tugging at the sallow skin beneath his eyes. "My father was not an adventurous man. My grandfather before him—well..." He stroked his cheek, his fingers running through his beard, more white than brown now. "He and my father had their disagreements. What my grandfather knew about the world beyond the sea died with him and his men in this castle."

I let my hand fall back to my side. "When Grandfather seized it from him."

Father's eyes met mine, the smirk on his face causing his irises to glisten. "A mistake to be sure. I may be able to speak little to my grandfather's character, kept in the dark as I was, but I can attest that a slug on the throne would have had more spine than my father."

My eyebrow twitched, but I said nothing. Father had ruled the duchy for twenty years before I was born, inheriting when only fifteen, his father long dead before I uttered my first cry. Perhaps it was a tradition for dukes to keep their children in the dark about their grandfathers. Among other things.

My gaze fell back to the Xs, the untold opportunities that lay there. The sea was treacherous, and ships that had been sent to explore the lands beyond Hanaobi never returned, their last messages sent by pigeon telling of crews still lost at sea.

And a silver light. There were three such letters, battered by the storms, soaked and hardly legible. But there was no mistaking the trembling hands that wrote of the light they saw, the last thing they distinguished clearly in the belly of a storm.

If Father found it odd that the duchy seemed doomed to isolation, the only people we'd ever meet our sworn enemy, he said nothing. He watched me, oblivious to the train of thought my mind had taken. "I hope you seized the goods and began distribution to the merchants," he said, breaking the silence.

"Yes, of course."

"Good." Father pointed to the sea between the duchy and Hanaobi. "The Duke's Favor was so late getting here that I had to send The Duke's Pride early. They should return with more in just over a week." Father crossed his arms and gazed at the map. "Of course, after that, we'll be left with little to trade. It'll have to last. We've too many people who don't know how to ration. Or who take more than their fair share." He tapped the sketch of the forest outside of the heart of the duchy. The farmlands, the forest, and even the Stargazers' tower at the waterfall and cliff that met the mouths of the rivers were all part of the duchy, but it was the city around the castle that really felt like home. Even if the city relied too much on the farmers on the outskirts.

I wondered if Father would send me to check in with the farmers again, see if there was any way they could produce more crops in time for another trade with Hanaobi, but Father had more pressing things on his mind. "There's more to be had, Rohesia. We don't have to rely so desperately on Hanaobi." His finger traced the road skirting the woods that led to the tower and back to the heart of the duchy. "Hoarding. Unfair distribution. Upstart powers thinking too highly of themselves, thinking me too stupid to know what they're doing. That I'm too stupid to know all that they've taken from me."

I watched Father's moss-colored eyes as he spoke and saw the angry fire that burned there. Left unchecked, the fire would spread, and there were few who'd be able to stop it. "I'll take care of it."

My offer broke the fire, and Father smiled, reaching one arm over to pat my shoulder again. "Darling, you are my treasure." He seemed genuinely proud of me. "I don't know what I'd do without you."

Perhaps have to lead your own expeditions more often.

"Ah! Supper." He clasped his hands together. I followed Father's gaze to see Sherrod balancing a golden tray full with fish, steak, rice, bread, vegetables, and ale. It was so heavy, and the greasy man so lithe, I expected it all to come tumbling onto Father's plush rug. Sherrod sweated profusely, his face contorted in agony as he brought the tray over to a small table beside the chair at the fireplace. I had to stop breathing momentarily as he passed.

Father smiled. "Won't you join me for the midday meal, love?"

I clapped my boot heels together. "Thank you, Father, but I already ate." I wasn't going to sit on the flowered rug beside Father's table and pick at his scraps. He still thought of me as the child who sat on his lap and gazed at illustrations of a land of bamboo trees and rice paddies. "Besides, I have work to do." I put my left hand back on my sword hilt and brought the other to my abdomen, bowing slightly. "If you'll excuse me."

"Of course. Don't stay out too late again, dear." Father lifted his glass and took a sip. "Or do. More blessings from Ytoile or what have you."

I nodded, clenching my jaw, and retreated. It was an unspoken joke between us, Father's 'reverence' for the goddess of the land.

I'd only climbed down the first flight of stairs when I smelled the rot of manure and fish swelling up behind me. The ragged breathing, the awkward and rushed clomps down the steps told me all I needed to know. "Sherrod, if you have something to say, say it." I was in no mood for his sniveling and groveling.

"My lady." He was already breathless after one flight of steps, but I supposed he'd carried that large tray up three flights before I'd encountered him. "I need to warn you."

I stopped at the top of the second flight of stairs, spinning to face him. "I ought to warn you as well, Sherrod. Put yourself in my father's presence smelling like refuse again, and you'll be lucky to have any skin left to scrub."

"Oh, yes. Yes, of course, my lady." Sherrod seemed taken aback, licking his lips and rubbing a twitching hand nervously down his chest, as if trying to feel the filth he wasn't aware of. He clearly had yet to bathe since the incident at the docks, and I was growing tired of reminding the man that there existed such a thing as hygiene. He looked quite panicked. "Do you think he noticed?"

Father hardly noticed things outside of his books and reports, but I found no reason to offer Sherrod the reassurance. "What did you want to tell me?"

"Oh. Yes." Sherrod ran his hand through his hair and looked behind him before pausing to peer around me dramatically. "There's talk of another heir," he hissed. "*A lot* of talk lately."

I rolled my eyes and started descending the second flight of stairs. "Sherrod, you're telling me nothing I haven't already heard myself."

Sherrod stumbled down a step to catch up to me, walking at my side. "They're probably not rumors," he wheezed. "You know as well as I—"

I stopped and glared down at him. "Four feet."

"Oh!" Sherrod took a few quick steps ahead of me, completely forgetting that him being four feet *behind me* was equally important as him being four feet *away*.

Sherrod started descending the steps backward so he could face me, tripping every few words. He bowed awkwardly. "I just thought it my duty, my lady. To inform you."

We reached the landing and he nearly buckled under his own feet. I passed him, not turning to glance in his direction. "Come to me with rumors of outsiders we don't yet know about. Otherwise, keep the gossip to yourself." We reached the third staircase, and I heard a maid scream and Sherrod's awkward attempt at an apology to the poor girl he'd knocked to the ground as I began to descend.

Sherrod dashed to catch up beside me. "Of course, my lady. But the people on the underground are a bit mum on that one." Sherrod straightened his back, proud as usual of his seedy connections. As if his smell wasn't clue enough, I could easily tell what part of town Father had plucked him from. He whispered hoarsely. "But they are talking about a new heir. Not the..." He pinched his lips and swallowed. "More importantly, a *male* heir. A *non-outsider* heir."

I paused at the foot of the stairs and glowered at him.

"Not that there's anything wrong or illegitimate about your position, of course, my lady." I could count the sweat beads forming at his temples. "I just wanted to let you know what *people* are saying—"

I cut Sherrod off with a hand to his chest. A disheveled blonde woman, her cloak askew to reveal a dirty but attractive frock, her hair limp and ragged, stood at the entryway to the castle, surrounded by some of my men.

"Please!" she screamed, shaking. "You must help me. My servant, my sister..."

"What's going on here?" It took some effort to make my voice louder than the screeching woman's.

The woman's wide eyes met mine and she curtsied awkwardly, a strange contradiction of filth and elegance. "My lady," she said, suddenly serene. "It's an honor."

"Your sister and servant?"

"Oh!" The woman seemed to remember she was supposed to be panicking. "Beset upon by nomads in the middle of the night! Dead! Or they could be! I don't know! I only just got here. I was so scared, I hid with the first farming family that'd take me in. Ytoile was surely angry at my choice to associate with day laborers, but I really *had no choice*." Her nose wrinkled and then she tossed her hair, puffing her chest outward. "It was one of the nomads who saved me. Probably thought me too beautiful to assault."

I couldn't help but raise my eyebrows at the claim, mask or no mask. I turned to the nearest soldier. "See that she's escorted home. And get a garrison together. We ride in an hour."

Just enough time to grab the lunch I'd sworn I'd already eaten.

6

FASTELLO

Waiting. Waiting. I was sick of waiting. To pass the time, I scrubbed the blood from my clothes in the river. Just as I grew used to watching the blood seep into the water, endless, endless blood, my eyelids started failing me. I fell asleep out of sheer exhaustion beside the riverbed and jolted awake with a start to discover the sun high overhead. Dad was still 'in bed,' but I'd had enough. I gave Dad the same courtesy he gave me: flipping his tent flap open and walking in, not caring if I caught him with his grubby hands on the tits and asses of a dozen girlfriends. (My mind wasn't working properly, of course; I failed to consider the number of hands that would require.) Naturally, I was rewarded with almost exactly what I didn't want to see, and I did care: Mina, Gilia and Dad tangled impossibly among Dad's woolen blankets, bare arms, bare legs and bare breasts too keenly on display.

"Ugharh!" The sound that escaped my lips was something like vomiting mixed with coughing with a little sun demon possession thrown in. I had to bury my eyes into my forearm.

"Well, *you're* the one who walked in on us without warning. What did you expect, to find me praying in here with the holy Stargazin' mother?" Dad grunted. "All right. All right. Ladies, can you give us a minute?"

I heard rustling, and against my better judgment, I lifted my head just enough to catch a glimpse of plump and pleasing Mina slipping her dress over her shoulders. Dad, still lying on the ground in his blankets, kissed her calf. "I won't be long."

"See you, handsome." Gilia dragged her sash across my head as she passed, causing me to drop my arm in surprise. She winked at me and tied the cloth around her waist, leaving me not entirely sure whether the 'handsome' was Dad or me. I watched her go, as at least that kept me from looking at Dad, and waited for Mina to follow. Once she passed, I stared at sunlight streaming in through the open tent flap and waited for Dad to say he was dressed. He did not oblige quickly. Waiting, I wondered not for the first time how Dad could spend his entire day in bed, even if he was hardly doing any sleeping.

"You too, sweetheart."

There was that retching feeling again. *He has a third woman in there.*

A jolt ran through my chest, my mind sorting through images of the girls old—not *too* old—and pretty enough to tempt Dad. My heart sunk, knowing already who I'd see crawling out of the mess of blankets beside my father: Luana, *my* Luana, her dark hair dancing across her collarbone as she fastened a necklace around her neck. It had a large blue jewel encrusted in silver and, at least in my eyes, in blood.

"*Luana!*" I cried.

The blue jewel rested snugly atop the breasts she didn't even bother to hide.

Dad chuckled, but I refused to look at him. I tried to catch Luana's eyes instead, but she simply tossed her hair back and grabbed her dress from the ground, her face bored, her gaze drawn anywhere but in my direction.

"I got tired of sneaking around," she said at last, answering my unasked question. She stood, flaunting her entire bare figure, making me burn with rage and desire and hurt, and slipped the dress over her head.

"Sneaking around with me, or sneaking around with all the jewels I let you keep?" I half hoped there was some chance of punishment awaiting her, but I knew now that she'd slept with Dad, there was little chance of that.

"My wives get all the jewels their pretty little hearts desire." Dad laughed again, as if we were gathered around the fire recounting humorous tales, and he walked between me and Luana—with his pants on, thank the stars—grabbed her roughly by the shoulders and leaned in for a kiss.

I turned, fighting the urge to step out of the tent and into the sunlight and into the ocean. I leaned against one of the support beams, crossing my arms tightly against my chest. I wasn't there for Luana. I was there for the jewel around her neck.

Luana passed by without so much as turning to look at me.

"My brother murdered for that necklace." I wanted to see if at least *that* would penetrate her icy, smug face.

She shrugged slightly and tossed her hair back over her shoulder. "The haves will share with the have nots. That's the nomad way." She stepped into the sunlight and walked away, her face perfectly serene.

I felt a hand clamp onto my shoulder. "Hope you're not too upset to lose her, son." He spoke as if it was his winning wit or his rawhide skin that drew Luana to his side instead of the openly flaunting way he peppered women with a cut of our take. "Someday, if you're king, you'll be able to do the same—"

I slithered out of his grasp and spun to face him, self-imposed 'king' of the nomads, a meaningless title putting him somewhere in worth between the duke and the empress of Hanaobi. "*If* I become king, apparently, my future *wives* are still sucking at their mothers' teats at the moment."

Dad laughed, genuinely amused by my attempt to cut him. I should have known to leave any mention of teats out of it. "I've been spurned in love once or twice, Fastello. The pain runs its course." He lowered his voice and grinned mischievously. "Get to be my age, and it won't surprise you why the women you grew up with hardly draw your eye. You'll thank me you weren't attached to Luana by then, believe me." He scratched his head. "They're hard to get rid of after you've been with them so long, though, so you're stuck with 'em."

"I want to go, Fastello. Be happy for me." Sitting at a bedside, a small fire burning. The creak, creak, creak...

I took a deep breath and shook my head to clear it. "I came to talk about last night, not backstabbing girlfriends."

"Good," said Dad, suddenly serious. He was probably impressed with my apparent ability to drop my lover like she was as much a plaything to me as she undoubtedly was to him. If I wanted sympathy about how she treated me, I wasn't going to find it in his tent. "Rento told me he got the drop on 'em." Of course. He was more impressed with the little butcher of a son he'd fathered after me.

I snorted. "He and I will have to disagree on that." Someone had to have given Dad the necklace to drape around the slim neck of Luana. So Rento probably hadn't even washed the blood from his hands. He probably walked right in on Dad in bed, not caring what he'd find there.

Dad shook his head. "Rento said you were no help—"

"Excuse me?"

Dad raised a hand to silence me. "Did you dispose of the bodies?"

"No!" I exhaled sharply. "They didn't need to be killed—"

"So Rento took them down, collected the goods, and arranged for the men to complete the disposal." Dad sighed, as if the mere act of talking to me was exasperation. "And he's twelve."

I jutted a finger at him. "He's a little murdering demon, and I don't know why you thought telling him to kill them was a good idea—"

Dad smacked my hand away. He hit it so hard, he probably bruised it. "Don't you point your finger at me, boy." His chest expanded as he took a deep breath, and then he ran a hand through his ruffled hair. "I told him to deal with them if you took too long. And you *always do*."

I clenched my fist. "Because charming my way into robbing them may take a full twenty minutes." I mockingly gasped. "And we don't have time like that to spare here, in the traveling *kingdom* of lecherousness and languor."

The back of Dad's hand flew across my face. I dodged, but not before feeling the sting of his fingers against my cheek. Dad's face contorted. "What we do, we do for the poor farmers," he lied through clenched teeth. "They toil day and night to feed this kingdom and watch most of their crops traded to another country for some tasteless garbage." He stepped closer, shoving his face uncomfortably close to mine. "Maybe you don't understand that. Maybe it's your spoiled blood."

I clenched my teeth, fighting against the wince I felt as I pulled my cheek muscles tight. "*I'm* not the one who decided to make off with a rich girl, all the while spouting hypocritical bile about hating their very kind."

"No, but you'll *woo* and *charm* them nonetheless, like saying 'please' and 'thank you' will get them to think of others besides themselves." Dad stepped back and pulled out an imaginary skirt to the sides to curtsey as he spoke, speaking in a high-pitched voice in a horrible impression of a noblewoman. "Like they haven't already been warned to watch out for *handsome* strangers in need of help on the road."

I ignored the attempt to hurt me and thought of that poor Cecily and how the women had spoke of the girl volunteering at the hospital, which I knew treated the poor without charge if they couldn't afford to pay. Arguing that the rich weren't all selfish, though, was not the tack to take. "Like they haven't been warned about the rich who leave the duchy and never come back? So what happens when the wealthy stop visiting the tower?"

Dad waved a hand as if to say I was a bother and bent to pick up his shirt. "Leave none alive, and the wealthy won't know what became of the rest, will they?" He pulled the tunic over his head. "But Rento says you let one go back and warn them. Smart move, son."

"Like they won't figure out what happened when their jewels go up for sale in the underground," I muttered.

"What was that?" Dad crossed the tent and leaned in toward me, as if he'd had trouble hearing what I said. "You have something to tell me?"

I put on my most sarcastic smile. "No, sir!" *Nothing you'd listen to, anyway.*

Dad shook his head. "They aren't gonna stop visiting the tower, though, are they? That's the beauty of what we've got going on here." He raised his hands up and glanced at the ceiling of the tent earnestly, mocking a position of prayer. "Thank Ytoile and all her little fairy stars! She tells the rich they can join her amongst the shiny balls in the sky no matter how selfish they are, so long as they visit Her tower at night on occasion."

"Forget it—"

"Davazanto!" A burly man, Nico, walked into the tent, not at all surprised to find the bruised son and the pretend zealot in front of him. He waved a piece of parchment in his hand, shaking a few droplets of water off of the damp edges. "We got a message. A raid today, before sunset!"

Dad clapped his hands together, doing one last raised-hands-to-the-sky act of prayer. "Praise Ytoile! Ask and ye shall receive."

"I'm helping out." The words were out of my mouth before I could properly think them.

Dad raised an eyebrow and rubbed his hands together. "We're going as a group. No time for charm and flattery."

Nico laughed. "That wouldn't work with this lot, anyway."

Dad brushed past me and leaned over to read Nico's note. He sniggered and clasped Nico on the back. "Ytoile asks and we shall deliver, whatever the circumstances."

I didn't care what it had to say. I clenched my fist and fingered the hilt of the real dagger at my belt. "I'm coming."

Dad shrugged and rolled up the parchment, tucking it into his tunic. "All right, then. But you're going to have to do a lot to impress me more than your little brother at this point."

At this point, Dad was going to have to do a lot more to make me care what he thought.

7

CATELINE

"The sun is still up, after all." Mother Ermessenda sniffed for what had to be the tenth time already. It was almost disgusting. I was tempted to offer her my kerchief, but then I'd be afraid to use it after.

Mother Flore sat silently on her horse beside me. She tugged her horse's reins and positioned me between her and Mother Ermessenda, perhaps a clever thing to do considering Mother Ermessenda's attempt to get Mother Flore to admit she'd ended her penance too early.

"The child had suffered enough," spoke Mother Flore at last. "He was shaking, and he was red all over. The sun demon had clearly done his work."

Mother Ermessenda looked out at the horizon, cupping a hand over her eyes to shield them from the bright light. "True devotion requires more than *suffering enough*." She sniffed again. "But then again, it was *you* who thought the boy ready for a night of festivities. Perhaps it's you who should suffer more than he."

Mother Flore bowed contritely, wisely saying nothing to spur the elder woman any further. A disgusting flush had embedded its way into Mother Flore's skin after her day in the sunlight. Red peppered her face and even her hands. I could only imagine the red, peeling skin that would be found beneath her silver dress, skin hot to the touch, burning with the sun demon's wrath. I felt a creeping sensation up my own back, a sympathetic pain for what she would soon be enduring, what I might have endured. What part of me thought I ought to have endured.

The horse neighed beneath me and I loosened my grip on its reins, realizing in my distracted thoughts I'd tugged too hard, almost leading the beast to bump into Mother Flore's.

Although her own horse had not been in danger, Mother Ermessenda pulled up her reins to guide her horse further from me. Her eyes narrowed. "Are you sure you're suited to riding a horse alone?" She pointed an elbow at my hand, as if I needed further explanation. "In your condition?"

"Yes." I scowled. The word had come out too sharply, and disapproval formed on Mother Ermessenda's puckered lips. I made sure my next words were lighter. "But thank you for your concern, Mother. You're always thinking of others."

The compliment relaxed the tense muscles in Mother Ermessenda's face, and I was rewarded with a few more moments of silence.

But not for long. "When we get our audience with the duke, I think we should appear as a point," spoke Mother Ermessenda, referring to one person in front of and between the others, a position the mothers took often in ceremonies as it resembled the point of a star. Mother Ermessenda nodded in our direction. "Since Mother Flore is in penance and Cateline, you're still a mother-in-guidance—"

"You should appear at the head of the point, of course." I swallowed. I was in no hurry to put myself at the head of the point in public, anyway. I had dreams of one day being there for ceremonies, but later, after I'd done something accomplished, a deed to make the people want to see me. Right now, I'd command the room's attention, but their eyes would be focused on my stump, their regard for me either pity or curiosity.

"A mother can command a room with her presence alone. With the way she presents herself." I straightened my shoulders, remembering Mother Jehanne's words.

"We'll remind the duke that his charity to the tower has been better in the past," spoke Mother Ermessenda, ripping me from my thoughts with the sharp edge of her voice. "That he *owes* us."

"Mother Ermessenda—" Mother Flore spoke so softly I could hardly hear her over the horses.

"I have a feeling he'll simply suggest the worshippers make their visits during the day, when the nomads are in hiding." Mother Ermessenda scrunched her nose, as if she could smell the insult her imagined version of the duke might make. "We'll have to remind him —gently, of course—that these are our most devout worshippers, the ones most responsible for keeping the tower well stocked, and that Ytoile will surely prefer them to travel during her—"

"*Mother Ermessenda!*" hissed Mother Flore. I was surprised to see her red face so concerned. I followed her gaze to the edge of the forest ahead and took in the large crowd of people gathered there.

"*Nomads,*" hissed Mother Flore.

Mother Ermessenda stopped speaking at once, her face flushed as if receiving a rebuke. "Ytoile save us!" she shrieked. "We should have never set foot outside the tower during the daylight. I told Mother Jehanne as much, she never—"

"Quiet!" Mother Flore tugged on the reins and pulled her horse to a stop. "Please," she added, somewhat less harshly.

They were still somewhat off in the distance, but it worried me that they made no attempt to conceal their presence, that they hadn't waited for the ambush until we were closer.

"What do we do?" Mother Ermessenda's nervousness influenced her horse, the poor thing neighing and bucking slightly as Mother Ermessenda tugged oddly at its reins.

"We head back—" began Mother Flore.

"We can't!" It was hard to tell if Mother Ermessenda was more panicked about the band of nomads or the thought of not fulfilling her task. "This is a holy quest, commissioned by Mother Jehanne on behalf of Ytoile herself!"

"Mother Ermessenda, you're exaggerating."

"I most certainly am not!"

"Our safety comes first."

"Ytoile will protect us!"

"How can you even want to *see* the man—"

I left the mothers to their bickering and dug my heel into my horse's flank, spurring it forward to get a better look.

"Cateline!" I heard both the shrill cry and the commanding softer voice behind me.

I wanted a closer look. Something seemed off—different than I might have expected. True to my instinct, the forms spreading out on the road in front of me were small or lithe. I felt a swell of relief flood through my body. I turned my head, raising my voice, although the mothers may have been too far behind to hear me. "They're women and children!"

I supposed I thought them less capable of sin, thinking of my home and the women and children who were my family. Men were others, unknowable people more prone to the temptation of the sun demons. The only men I saw—the occasional aristocrat or aristocrat's servant—were like other creatures entirely. I found myself studying them, trying to find some common aspect in their behavior, but I couldn't stare long, lest their eyes caught mine and I felt the flush of shame at being noticed, of their inevitable look at the end of my sleeve.

Mother Flore had perhaps not heard what I had said. "Cateline! Come back! Now! Hurry!"

She turned her horse around as if to head back to the tower but lingered, peering over her shoulder anxiously and waiting for me to join her. Mother Ermessenda, I saw, was already headed back down the path toward the tower.

I tugged on the reins to turn my horse back. I pulled too hard in my panic and unbalance, confusing the horse and nearly jostling off the saddle. A hand reached out to touch my thigh to steady me. "Easy there, silver lady." The small hand patted my horse's flank, shushing it. "Steady, steady."

With another few trots and a shake of its head, the horse stopped moving. I caught the eye of my small savior. A boy, no older than Aymon, ten or twelve at most. His skin was a darker shade than we were used to, just a slight twinge of brown that made him seem as if forever kissed by the sun demon, and without even having the red burns I and the other Stargazers would have to suffer for it. He smiled and released his hand from my thigh, cupping it out before me, as if expecting me to hand him something. "An offering for my people, silver lady?"

"No, sorry. I mean, thank you for before, but…" I gripped the reins tightly in my hand, my eyes darting across the faces of the women and children gathering around me. Even if I could direct the horse backward, I didn't know if I'd be able to dodge all of the sun-kissed sinners. They were women and children—no harm would come to me, surely—but they were family to the rest of the nomads, the very ones we were going to speak to the duke about. "The tower doesn't have enough to share with you, I'm sorry."

"Come on now, silver lady." The boy's smile faltered. "We know you've got something. That silver dress isn't bought with air. We need to eat too, you know."

"Then why don't you try an honest day's work?" I pursed my lips together. They were lower than farmers, sinners who begged and stole, never giving anything—

"Like the farmers, huh?" The boy was no longer smiling, and his hand dropped to his side. "And who feeds the farmers?"

I shook my head and felt the dizzy rush of confusion. All the dark eyes, the leering faces. "The farmers," I sputtered. "They work for their food."

The boy shook his head. "The food they grow is taken away for trade, for the rich." He thumped his chest proudly. "*We* feed the farmers. We give them back what people like you have stolen." His hand flicked toward me and I realized it was now clutching a small dagger. "So give back what you've stolen."

"Mother Flore!" I screamed. "Mother Erme—" I tugged back and the horse reared its legs, sending the boy and the nearest women and children scattering. I squeezed my thighs desperately against its flank, trying to hang on, but I turned the horse at last, barely managing to stay seated. And that's when I saw the crowd of people, a short distance behind me. Right where I last saw Mother Flore—

"Mother Flore!" Her horse was in the midst of a crowd—a crowd of *men*—but there was no rider. I heard a distant scream, the soft, shrill sound fading to nothing. They must have hidden in the forest. The women and children were nothing but distractions.

"Give up what you've stolen!" screamed the boy, launching himself beside me. He slashed his dagger at my calf and I screamed, just managing to scare the horse into stepping out of the blade's reach.

Were the children distractions? Nothing but thieves and murderers, the lot of them.

"Heathens! Sinners!" I spat. "I've got nothing on me!" I pulled, determined to get back to the tower, past the boy and the rest of the crowd gathering in front of me. I couldn't steer the horse correctly. In vain, I slapped my stump across my chest, trying to wind it through the reins so I could communicate to the horse that I was ready to plough right through the screeching women and children. It reared its front legs again.

"Let's go!"

I screamed, even as the horse righted itself. Arms slid around my sides to grab hold of the reins. When the horse had reared, someone had managed to jump on behind me.

I slapped my hand over and over against the sun-kissed arms wrapped around my waist. "Let me go! Help! Mother Flore! Ytoile, save me!"

"Some advice, should you ever find yourself surrounded by an angry mob again." The voice was tenor, deep but melodious. I felt the soft brush of dark hair press against my cheek as he spoke, as the man—the *man*—ignored my blows and turned the horse around, back toward the duchy. "Don't rely on someone in the sky to get down in time to save you." He flicked the reins. "Hee-yah!" The horse went speeding forward, the few women and children remaining in that direction scrambling desperately to flee the pounding of hooves taking me away from Mother Flore and Mother Ermessenda, away from Mother Jehanne and the safety of the towers... And off into the burning ember sun, toward the duchy, a sun-kissed, unknown savior seated behind me.

"Why are there no men in the Stargazers, Mother Jehanne? Why must all the boys leave when they come of age?"

Mother Jehanne stroked my hair, lulling me to sleep with the rhythms of her rocking chair. "Ytoile would not permit their savagery. We take their gifts to the tower, it's true. We might bless them even, if they are devout. But they will never be as dear to Ytoile as are women and children." Mother Jehanne leaned in, whispering directly into my ear. "Men want women, Cateline. They want them in unspeakable ways. If one ever catches you, let Ytoile guide your hand. Don't let him defile you."

I shielded my eyes with my arm at my forehead, feeling the hot burn of the sun demon even through my closed eyelids, taunting me to do what needed doing.

8
KOJIRO

Tierny stood gazing out the open door into the garden. He lifted both arms above his head and clasped his hands together, stretching himself from limb to limb, looking more like an animal than a man, a barbarian through and through. He rested against the sliding door, staring silently at the ember glow of the sky as it enveloped the horizon. He sighed and turned around, so I moved my hand in a flurry and flicked my eyes back to the parchment.

Tierny padded his large bare feet over the *tatami* like a boy crushing ants and bent forward to get a look at the parchment. "Yes, looks good, Prince Kojiro." He leaned across my shoulder to grab the parchment, making me uncomfortable with his closeness. "I was told you couldn't speak my tongue well, but you seem to be quite proficient." There was a note of joviality in his voice, and I had not the heart to tell him I didn't understand what 'proficient' meant. He clasped his hand atop my shoulder, which made me shudder. *He shouldn't touch me.* "I'm sure Her Majesty will be quite pleased."

I laid the brush back carefully on its stand, letting it settle comfortably onto the smooth marble. "Thank you," I said at last. I couldn't tell him that he was wrong. I had to learn what I could from the man before the week was up. Before Mother found his teaching not up to her standards.

And she *would* find his teaching not up to her standards. The man had no idea of the extent of the impossible task that he had been given.

"Now, just remember what I told you about 'the.'" Tierny seated himself on the floor beside me. He slid the parchment back onto the table, not noticing at all how strange I found it that he sat so close to me, his own cushion on the other side of the table. "You used it correctly here, but you wouldn't need it here. '*Ships* carry goods,' not '*the* ships.' We're not talking about specific ships here."

I nodded, even as I slid a bit off my cushion to put more space between us. His lecture continued, but I found myself staring at the ink stains forming on his arm as he dragged his hand over the lines I'd done my best to translate.

"...Still, not bad at all." He slapped the table with his palm and snapped me out of my daydream. "And I don't see how you'd use writing anyway. Reading means you can intercept a note and learn something about your enemy. Listening means you can overhear what your enemy thinks you're too dumb to understand. Not that you're dumb at all, of course, Prince—"

I held up a hand to stop him. "Please. No apologies. Not to me." I really didn't have time for the barbarian's awkward attempts at ingratiating himself to me, although I had to admit, it was nice to finally be around someone who thought highly of me, even if he was so far below me it was hardly worth noticing. And he was probably only interested enough to save his own skin. But the two days he'd spent teaching me had been less stressful than an hour with Yukishige, and I believed I'd learned fifty times as much in half the time. A thought occurred to me, but I was unsure if I should voice it. "Speaking would be difficult, yes? Would not the barbarians strike me down?"

Tierny's face lit up with an easy, friendly grin. He tapped his head with two fingers strangely. "Now you're thinking, Prince Kojiro. You're an excellent student, full of intelligent questions—"

"Pardon us." The loud but insistent voice from the other side of the door belonged no doubt to that of a servant. It was void of the soft cadence of Tomiko.

Tierny clapped his hands together, startling me, and stood. "Dinner, no doubt? We work while we eat, Your Highness, but we can take turns with the speaking and the listening, and I can give you a few pointers…" He stopped suddenly, and his mouth remained strangely agape.

"Please. Do continue, Captain. Think of me as an observer."

The voice sent a shot to my chest, the invisible hand squeezing my heart like a fist. She spoke barbarian almost perfectly, her accent mere light flourishes to the harsh tongue. The servants brought two trays of fish and rice to the table, gently placing them down without disturbing the parchment and books and pouring the tea before retreating just as silently behind me.

"Yes, of course. Welcome, your imperial majesty," said Tierny.

"Kojiro." She said the name sharply, the emphasis on the 'ji' Tierny had put on my name completely absent.

I turned, putting my forearms and my forehead against the floor, unable to see anything but the hem of her flowered *kimono* and the white of the socks cushioning her toes before I flattened my eyes against the *tatami*. "Good evening, Honorable Mother," I spoke to the floor in Hanaobian.

"*Kojiro*," sneered Mother, her pronunciation of the name distinctly Hanaobian, at odds with the rest of her sentence, "we are practicing barbarian here, are we not? Please speak to me like a barbarian."

For the first time in almost as many days as I could remember, I smiled genuinely and was grateful the *tatami* smashed against my face and hid the expression from those around me. "Yes, Mother," I answered, switching tongues and holding back any number of barbaric things one could say. I sat back up, my calves tucked beneath my thighs, my back straight, and took in the figure that had appeared, several servants trailing behind her.

She was beautiful, the type of woman made for the paintings that hung on scrolls around the palace, an empress-turned-legend to inspire the descendants who would know her only by name, by beauty and by deed. The red and blue of her flowing *kimono*, several layers more than even Tomiko would wear. The black hair that hung down to her waist, simultaneously loose and flowing and tied just right at the nape of her neck to keep it orderly and in place. The makeup she wore added just the right touch of vibrancy to an otherwise rigid face but did nothing to hide the lines that appeared around her eyes. My gaze darted to Tierny, who was scrambling up from his own awkward bow, and I noticed not for the first time the lines around his mouth, which Mother did not share. She did not laugh or frown enough to earn them. Her face was a work of art: unmovable, implacable.

"Eat. Please." Mother gestured slightly before her. "Pretend I am not here." Tierny picked up his soup bowl and began to slurp, but Mother was not finished speaking. "I want to hear about the barbarians striking down Kojiro," she said, completely negating her expressed wish to be nothing but an observer.

I took a sip of the tea to calm the shaking of my hands that never seemed to stop whenever I was in her presence—and not for hours afterward, either.

Tierny put his soup down, oblivious to the fear making my mind and vision hazy. "Well, that was a good observation is all." He gestured to me crudely. "Prince Kojiro was thinking on his feet. He won't be able to say a word to anyone in the duchy. They'd look at him, peg him for an outsider—whether a prince or a farmer, they wouldn't much care—and report him to the soldiers. If they didn't just kill him themselves, as the duke gives all his citizens the right to do."

I heard the subtle shuffle of fabric against the *tatami*, the slight footsteps as Mother drew closer. "The *duke*. As if what he says is an act of providence. As if *he* has the blessing of the spirits to rule."

Tierny ran a hand over his bearded cheek. I focused on how soft and strange the fur there seemed, trying anything to distract myself from the dizziness in my head. "Well, there's no one much to contest him in the duchy. Not enough people passionate about it, anyway."

"There are enough." Mother stood beside the table, towering over me. "They just need a leader." I felt without being asked the sudden need to set down my long-since-empty cup, and Mother nodded, drawing a servant over immediately to refill it. "If Kojiro passes this test I have given him, I hope you will take him with you on your ship."

"On The Duke's Pride?" asked Tierny, utterly confusing me. "The Duke's Favor was mine, Your Highness, and it's not due for a while yet—"

"It also had a new captain last I knew, if I'm not mistaken." Mother's eyebrow twitched just slightly, and she looked down at Tierny as if stating a fact and not looking at all for correction. "The price for a few mistakes made."

"Yes, of course, Your Majesty." Tierny's pale face grew even paler, and he darted his eyes to the dead fish staring back up at him on the plate.

Mother looked out the open door into the garden. "The Duke's Pride arrived yesterday, early, said the Captain, because of the delay with The Duke's Favor." The glow from the open door caressed Mother's figure, as if to emphasize that the spirit from the fading sun gave this woman its blessing. "The captain of that ship had quite a few more mistakes to make up for." She turned her head back to gaze at Tierny. "And I wasn't impressed with his plan to make amends. The ship is yours now, Captain."

"Thank you, Your Majesty." Tierny spoke quietly, bowing his head but refusing to look up at the spirit-on-earth that stood watching him from above.

I cradled the tea in my hands. I wasn't sure what Mother's decision—to slay one captain and have need for another—had to say about her threat to Tierny if he didn't catch me up to Elder Brother Nobutada in a week. What penance would there be for the man if he failed? A missing eye, a lost leg?

I actually didn't want the poor man to be tortured. But I certainly didn't want to be at sea in a week, leading some suicide mission to assassinate a man who could no more pose a threat to us here in this castle than he could pose a threat to the sun spirit in its fiery domain. I took a sip of my tea clumsily, feeling the dribble of the hot liquid slip down my chin as I did.

"Of course, if Kojiro fails..." Mother paused, and although she barely did so much as nod her head, I felt her eyes boring into the tea dribbling down my chin, as if it were proof I'd already failed her and would fail her again. "We start again. Captain or no captain, The Duke's Pride can sail. You'll be needed to finish Princess Tomiko's studies and prepare her for the assault."

I choked on the last bit of tea, sounding too much like a cat emptying its stomach of hair, causing a flurry of servants to arrive at my side to take the cup from me. "What assault?" I asked at last, ignoring the wetness streaking down my chin onto my *kimono*.

Mother covered her mouth with a long sleeve, as if my choking on tea somehow reeked and she couldn't bear the smell of it. "The assassination of the duke and traitor once and for all, of course. The decimation of the duchy. What your father and elder brother died for."

"But *Tomiko*!" My heart was thumping wildly, my mouth spitting out words without first thinking them over, my mind a stranger to common sense.

Mother stepped back and turned, nodding to a couple of the servants who swept in behind her to pick up her *kimono* trail. "It is the heir's duty," she said curtly. "For the country. For the family. For her empress. And by the end of the week, Princess Tomiko will no doubt be my heir."

She moved to go, the *kimono* covering her feet entirely, her appearance that of a gliding spirit. She had nothing more to say, but what was left to say hardly needed saying: *There is no disinheritance. At the end of the week, it'll be my son, not Tierny, I have slit his own belly.*

THE CANDLELIGHT COULD NOT SAVE ME, EVEN IN THE QUIET solitude of my room. The small fiery glow wasn't a comfort, but a reminder that the darkness that surrounded me was the reality of the world, and no flame but the sun's would be big enough to fight it. My eyes could barely stay open, but I refused to let them shut for more than a moment because every time they did, I saw myself in the middle of the throne room, the staring eyes, the rigid faces, the pain and the wetness at my abdomen as I sliced the sword across my belly. Part of me choked my throat from the inside, squeezed my chest and wanted to scream that I wouldn't do it—I'd *fight*, damn it, not give the woman the satisfaction to know that at least her son died peaceably—but the other part of me, the one lulling me to sleep, the only one that offered relief from the tightness, said to let it go. Let it all go. It's what I wanted anyway, an end to this life. Why not accept it?

"Elder Brother." The voice was so quiet I almost didn't hear it, so soft I thought I'd dreamed it, and so full of urgency, she skipped the "pardon" and slid the door open.

Tomiko slipped in from the darkness of the hallway, stepping gently into the glow of the candlelight. Her hair down, her face beautiful even without the makeup, she wore only a single *kimono*, affording her greater room to move. Still, out of habit, she glided in like a spirit. She held a small wooden box in both hands and sat beside me on the floor, handing the box over.

"Take it," she whispered. "It was Elder Brother Nobutada's. He left it behind for his assault. I told him not to. I told him it could prove vital to his mission. But he didn't trust it."

My fingers traced the wood of the box, quite sure I knew what I'd find in there. I was there for Tomiko's pleading, for Elder Brother Nobutada's first practice with it, for the startling noise it made when he handled it. For a moment, I felt something, something like *hope*, and then the relief from pain swept through me and I held it out toward Tomiko. "You take it, then. You'll need it for your assault on the duchy."

Tomiko's lips tightened. "I'm not going to lead an assault on the duchy."

"But you'll be heir—"

"Don't tell me you've given up, Elder Brother." Her eyes narrowed. "Because I haven't."

My eyes fell back to the wooden box, and then to the ceremonial sword on its stand across the room, probably too big to be the one that Mother would ask me to use to slit my own belly, but a harrowing reminder nonetheless. My inability to use it properly. The time I hit my own head with the wooden practice blade. The silver glint across the flesh of my belly.

I held the box against my chest. "What can I possibly do? I'm trying to learn, I really am—"

"Mother has no intention of saying you passed the test, even if you write a tome in barbarian yourself."

I nodded. I knew as much. "Then there's no hope."

Tomiko's small hand covered mine still atop the box. "Tierny is leaving tonight."

I met Tomiko's eyes, searching for some mistake, some trick, but knowing I would never find it in those eyes, in the sweetness of her nature. "But why? How?"

She brushed aside my hair and placed her head on my shoulder, the softness of her cheek sinking into the silk of my *kimono*. "To save you, you idiot." She reached her arms across and embraced me before pulling away and standing upright. She reached a hand down to me. The glow from the candlelight wrapped around her slight body, not as strong as the setting sun had done on Mother, but warmer and more hopeful somehow. "Come on," she said, curling her fingers.

I reached up and grabbed her extended hand.

9

ROHESIA

It felt strange putting the heart of the duchy behind me. Life beyond the walls of the city was something foreign, something strange, like one of Father's Hanaobi scrolls brought to life. Our farmers worked nothing like the farmers in Hanaobi, I knew—those in Hanaobi grew food out of fields covered in pools of water—but they were people with whom I'd never before spoken. People who only shrieked as Father commanded his soldiers to take things away. Their crops. Their food. Their babies.

I was used to drawing their attention as I followed the dirt road along the forest to the tower, a garrison of a dozen soldiers moving in tandem behind me. They looked up from their scythes, from their hoes, from their baskets, perhaps wondering which farm we would stop at today. I watched each person as we passed from the corner of my eye, not turning my head, not wanting to give them reason to believe I was headed toward them. I knew if Father were along and turned to face any of them, they would quickly pick up their tools and scramble to seem busy, fooling no one, but having no other choice but to play the fool. No, let them stare. Let them get back to work when we were safely away. I was not here for farmers this day.

We were only halfway to the tower when we saw the path full of people ahead of us. I shaded my eyes to get a better look: small forms intermingled among larger forms, only two horses to be seen. They'd just barely come into sight when I heard incoherent shouting, a murmur of voices, and then the crowd scattered, running for the trees of the forest.

I shifted atop Sunset, the horse given to me by Father, slowing her to a trot, and withdrew my sword, raising it above my head. "Nomads!" I shouted, feeling the word reverberate down my throat. I pointed my blade toward the forest. "After them!"

I guided Sunset off of the dirt road and we shot across the grassy fields in a straight line, to the edge of the forest where the last of the crowd had disappeared. I felt the horses behind me change direction, continuing their pointed formation. We arrived at the spot where I'd seen the last boot retreat into brambles and leaves, and I tugged Sunset's reins to guide her to a stop. "Dismount!"

A quick sheathing of my blade, and I hopped down the side of the mare, patting her mane appreciatively for her speed and focus. I handed her reins to one of the men whose job it was to walk the horses and I drew out the blade again to point at different areas of the forest. "Right flank, west end. Left flank, take the middle. Center, you're with me."

The men scattered, pulling out swords that would double as scythes through the overgrowth. I nodded to the men who formed behind me and raised my boot, ready to scour the forest.

"Lady Rohesia!" The voice was so ragged and out of breath, you'd have sworn the man had run all the way himself instead of lagging behind on a stallion he had little control over.

I stopped but momentarily. "Sherrod, stay here! Watch over the horses."

"There are women on the road!" I heard him say before I stepped into the forest. "Dead women, I think…"

The rustle of the branches and the steeled-toe boots crunching the leafy debris at our feet cut off the rest of what he had to say. I couldn't focus on dead women on the road. Not with live men escaping further into the forest with each breath I took.

I led the men in silence for quite a while, the sounds of the other bands of soldiers breaking into the forest growing more distant with each passing heartbeat. It was easy to track the nomads. The crunched leaves and broken twines ahead spoke of movement, revealing the only path someone could have taken through the maze.

But after several minutes, the minor destruction halted, the forest pristinely chaotic in every direction ahead.

"Lady Rohesia," whispered one of the men, but I raised my free hand to silence him.

The twitter of rodents. The rustling of the leaves in the breeze. The smallest trickle of water from the river that ran through the forest from the tower into the ocean. If I could hear the river, that meant we were still near the forest edge. Too far out to be anywhere near any of the clearings the nomads had made, hiding like wild animals among the overgrowth, in the bushes, in the trees...

Something soared past my ear like a shot of venom from a python and crashed into the leaves below. I spun and let my blade skirt the ground, the air and the branches, stopping the next arrow before it struck against the armor on my back. "The trees!" I shouted, as if the men needed further explanation regarding what was hailing down on us.

Arrows loosened from at least five directions, and the soldiers scattered into the bushes, deflecting some arrows and letting some clank against their armor. One arrow caught a soldier in the small strip of flesh exposed between his chest plate and his helmet, dropping him instantly into the mossy cover, the squishy natural material enveloping the body almost as if eating it.

They weren't bad. For amateurs who would try to fight us without blade and armor.

I ducked behind a tree at which two of the soldiers were gathered.

"Lady Rohesia, a torch—"

"No."

"But it would only take a moment, spark a fire with some rocks while we covered you—"

"No."

"Save the fire. Burn everything, and there will be nothing left to rule." One of Father's lessons. It was why he preferred the water often. *"Wash them all out."*

"Fire should always be the last option, the one you take before death." I wondered if I reminded them that fire was the tool of the sun demon, I might wipe the uncertainty off their faces. But I had no idea how devout the men were. I doubted very, if they were here with me at this instant, fire the first thing that came to their minds.

I looked up the tree that was our cover, seeing no rustle of movement among its boughs. True, he could be still on purpose, thinking of what I'd do next, waiting to greet me face to face, but I doubted a nomad had the patience for that. If one were there, he'd loose whatever arrows he had left at the three of us. I slid my sword back into its sheath and unclasped my chest and arm plates, letting the moss below devour the glistening iron. I let my cape fall with it and slid the daggers I kept around my wrists out from their hiding places.

"My lady," spoke one of the soldiers, reminding me unpleasantly of Sherrod's grating voice.

"Keep them busy," I said, nodding toward where we'd first encountered the barbs of the squirrely hunters. I hugged the tree trunk, stabbing two places with two daggers, and dug my boot toe into the bark, using the metal to dig a small gash into the trunk and take another step up. I got a few yards further up and looked down, watching the remaining men step out into the clearing to deflect an arrow or two and retreat back behind the safety of the trees. I sheathed one dagger with a flick of my wrist and removed my helmet, releasing the short black hair beneath, dropping the hat below and sticking the dagger back into the bark. The helmet made a small clang, hopefully lost in the sounds of arrow-on-sword and arrow-on-armor.

I was making faster progress now that I'd shed all the weight. My arms began to burn with each instant I pulled myself upward, and I swore, wishing I'd sent one of the men up instead, but I cleared my head of such foolishness, fully aware the men had neither the skills nor the lack of weight necessary to make my idea work. At last I reached the lowest-hanging bough, and I sheathed my daggers one after the other, gripping the jutting wood.

I swung my leg up and felt the sting of the cut against my calf even before I heard the spit of the viper and the thunk of the arrow hitting the wood just behind me. I swung again and rolled onto the bough safely, running across its surface as if it were nothing more than the top of a stone wall.

I was running out of sturdy bough beneath me, so as I came to the edge, I ran faster, leaping through the air and grabbing the extended bough of the next tree before I could even think about summoning the courage necessary to make such a jump.

The branch snapped. I had to let it go and heave my body sideways down the bough until I grabbed a piece that wouldn't break off under my weight. I dangled by one hand for an instant, just long enough to swing and dodge the arrow that soared past me. I'd lost the element of surprise. It was time to act.

I swerved and gripped the tree limb with my other hand, pulling my body up to the bough. As soon as I steadied myself, I ducked again, but the arrow went where I went and grazed my unprotected shoulder, like a whip slash. I flicked my wrist, sending the first dagger flying right into the base of the throat of the nomad waiting for me at the tree trunk. He slumped, but before he could fall to the ground, I was there in three great strides, grabbing his body and using it as a shield to deflect the other arrows. I peeked over the nomad's shoulder, taking in the other nomads now at level with me, barely hiding behind the leaves of the surrounding trees. Only two more.

I yanked the dagger out of the man's throat, ignoring the spurt of warm blood that gushed out to fleck all over my arm and face. I aimed at the nearest nomad, watching with satisfaction as it struck him in the chest and he tumbled down to the ground. The other was too far to reach with the remaining dagger.

An arrow struck the chest of the oozing corpse I spun in front of me. I wrenched the bow from the body's hand, finding it difficult to peel the tight grip the fingers had around the handle, but thankful for the man's crazed devotion to the weapon even in death, grateful it hadn't fallen down. I slipped an arrow from the holster at his back. His last one.

It'd been a while since I bothered with bows and arrows—child's play, Father called it. I aimed and unleashed. The nomad at the tree across from me stepped back, but he needn't have bothered. The arrow drooped several yards before the tree into the mossy floor below.

The nomad laughed and peeked his head through the leaves, cupping his hands around his mouth. "Need a little target practice yet, eh, princess?"

He didn't shoot. Perhaps he was out of arrows. Perhaps he intended to stay up there in his tree, waiting to see if I'd climb again or just let him starve to death up in the branches. Nomads seemed to think the trees saved them.

"I'm not a princess," I corrected the nomad, my left hand reaching behind my back to grab the shaft of the arrow that had struck the body's chest. I pulled, feeling the tension rip through my sore shoulder. "And you'll do just fine for that." My second arrow hit the target who so graciously offered himself to me.

I kicked the nomad cadaver down into the moss below to join its brethren. The soldiers left stepped carefully into the area where we'd been ambushed, looking up to find me. "That all?" called one.

I hugged the tree trunk, scraping my right hand's fingernails against the bark and making do with one dagger until I could grab my other one from the body below. I counted the directions the arrows had come from in my head. We were missing one. I looked without turning my head. A small figure near the river dashed out of sight behind the trunk of the tree.

"Yes," I answered and finished my descent down the trunk.

"MY LADY, IT WAS A DEAD END. AN AMBUSH. NO SIGN OF THE CAMP." I nodded at the west flank soldier who joined the rest of my men as he and four others broke through the edge of the forest.

"The same with us, and the other group." I started counting metallic helmets. "How many losses?"

"Three," spoke one.

"One," said another.

"One for us as well."

Sherrod, ignoring the exchange of all the soldiers around him, folded his cape over a woman's body, the rough and dirty black material over the gleaming silver dress like a gilded amulet beneath a used kerchief. His shoulders shook slightly, and in the waiting silence, I could just make out sobs.

My stomach turned, and I tore my eyes back to those awaiting orders. "You, go back with one other to tell my father what has happened." The soldier nodded and gestured to a man behind him, and the duo whistled to summon their horses. I turned back to the group. "The rest of you load the two women's bodies onto their horses. We'll take them to the Stargazers." The men dispersed.

Sunset was near Sherrod, as she was the only horse he probably thought worth actually guarding. I sighed and followed the men heading toward the first body, flinching with every sob that grew louder as we approached.

"She was so beautiful," choked Sherrod, as if answering a question no one bothered asking. "Familiar even." He cried out as men tossed the edge of the cape over the woman's flushed face and grabbed the body.

I didn't know whether to ignore the man or berate him, or point out that even if the woman hadn't been a mother, she certainly would have never bothered to give his unpleasant face a second thought.

"She reminded me of home," Sherrod sniffled. "That must be it." Sherrod had been an orphan who grew up in the tower, I knew. I knew far too much about him, the consequence of an ever-prattling tongue. Sherrod turned, taking me in for the first time. "Oh, but my lady, you're hurt—"

"Just minor scratches." I stuck my foot in Sunset's saddle and climbed onto her back. "Sherrod, go back with the men on their way to my father," I said, gripping the reins.

Sherrod wiped his sleeve over his dribbling face, staining the cloth. "But what about the Stargazers—"

"We're taking them back to their tower."

"Then I would like to come along."

I stared at Sherrod, letting no emotion mar my face. "Back to my father." I'd have none of his bumbling and wailing as I explained my visit.

Sherrod retreated from my glare, bowing. "Yes, of course, my lady." He looked up again. "But what of his lordship's request?"

I shook my head. "Do you really think yourself capable of helping me with that, in your state? Or ever?" Before he could answer, I kicked the horse's flank and sped down the road, leading the remaining men to the cliff and the tower.

10

FASTELLO

The red-headed vision looked as at home among the piles of hay, the sheep and the pigs as the duke himself would have looked in a trough of mud. Every few seconds, she shifted her rear and checked to make sure her skirt was tucked tightly over her knees, which she so desperately clutched to her chest so as little of the silver dress came in contact with the hay as possible. Her pale face was pinched, her freckle-dotted nose squished in an attempt to breathe very little of the air around her. I couldn't help but be drawn to the hand with no fingers she kept tucked beneath her elbow. Not that I could see the lack of fingers just then. It was like a jewel she kept hidden, tucked away. I'd only seen it clearly when she panicked and tried to grip the reins of her horse with phantom fingers.

It was that hand that struck me, reaching deeper into my heart than a slap to the face. The girl had suffered enough. She was the one I was meant to save. And she, a silver dancer, a goddess-blessed daughter, would be the one to save me in return.

"Well?" snapped the blessed daughter, the first words she'd spoken to me since demanding I get off her horse and release my grip around her waist. "Are you going to kill me?"

The thought was so far from my mind, I laughed despite knowing she was in what must be a scary situation for her. Despite what I knew must have befallen her friends.

"You think murder is funny?" Her eyes met mine. Wow, they were gorgeous. A green, leafy color I'd never seen before.

I remembered what had just happened and forced the grin off my face. "No, of course not." I ran a hand through my hair nervously. "I'm sorry. I would have saved the others, too, but..." But what? What excuse did I have to offer?

The girl dropped her desperate grip on her skirt and waved her left hand all around her. "Is this what you call it? 'Saving' me?" She didn't notice that some of the hem of her silver skirt now brushed the yellow hay below her.

I clutched my own knees to my chest like she had and rocked back and forth, thinking. "Well, sure. I got you away from my people and—"

"You murdering *heathens*."

I bit my lip. She was right, unfortunately. Although she strangely emphasized what I considered to be the less offensive description. "There's a chance they let the other women go. We weren't always so quick to—"

The girl snorted and looked pointedly at the sheep butt a few yards beside her. There were flies gathering around its dirty rump. "Death would be preferable to what else they might do to them."

"What else they might do?"

"You know. What men *do*." The girl turned to glare at me, then she noticed her skirt hem had fallen and bent quickly to scoop it back up around her knees. It was the flurry of movement that allowed me to see the fingerless hand, if just for a moment before she tucked it back under her elbow. I hadn't been imagining it. "You men *do* do something unspeakable, don't you?"

"Oh?" I'd been distracted. I didn't fully understand her accusation, but her words were so harsh, I could only imagine what a beautiful virgin silver mother might consider more unspeakable than death and heathenism. "No. I mean..." I thought of Dad, and how he bragged about stealing a voluptuous rich girl away, along with the gold and jewels she'd been wearing. I shook my head. It was just the once. Just long enough to produce... me. "No. We didn't even kill anyone until recently. Not really. I mean, besides self-defense."

The girl shook her head and blew a tendril of wavy red hair out of her eyes with one hard breath. "That's a relief. You only killed unprovoked *recently*. I will count my blessings that I didn't set out earlier, when you might have spared my life."

"Look, we're here because I wanted to save you—"

"Oh, thanks." She swatted a fly away.

"You *could* be more grateful."

"I *said* thanks."

"You know what I mean." The horse on which we'd ridden neighed and shook its mane, butting its head against one of the farmer's pigs and stealing some of its grain from a bucket. This was clearly the wrong path to take.

"I'm sorry." I clapped my hands together and bowed my head. "I really am."

I didn't dare peek to see if the girl was looking at me, if her eyes were softening or if she was glaring at me as hard as ever. But the tone of her voice said it all, even if the words suggested absolution. "May Ytoile have mercy on you. It's Her you'll have to answer to, not me."

Clearly, she was about as hopeful of Ytoile having mercy on me as she was glad to be plunked into a pile of hay surrounded by livestock.

"Look, we got off on the wrong foot."

"Clearly."

"I guided your horse here to a farm because, well, I needed to talk to you before we got to the city."

The girl clutched her knees closer to her chest. "Yes, because then I might scream for the soldiers to rescue me."

"No, no." I stood and began pacing. "I mean, I need your help. Just a little bit." There had to be some way to explain. She was sent to help save me. I knew it.

The redhead stood warily, making her way over to her horse, refusing to show me her back at any moment.

"You don't have to be so scared of me." I clenched my jaw. If I thought about it, she really did have plenty of reason to be scared of me.

She kept her eyes locked on mine as she reached across her chest with her left hand to feel blindly for the horse, leaving her right arm tucked behind her back.

I stopped. "Why do you do that?"

"I'm attempting to get out of here. I thought that was rather obvious." Her hand could barely reach past her shoulder. The horse was right there. She could have touched it with her right arm if she'd used it.

"I mean that." I pointed at her arm. "Hide that hand."

She stopped and clutched both hands behind her back. "I'm not hiding anything—"

"You're hiding a deformed hand."

"Pardon me?!"

"No, I mean..." I took a deep breath. "Sorry. I didn't mean for that to come out that way. But I've already seen it. You may as well bring it out."

I saw the color flood across her spotted cheeks and observed the muscles in her jaw clenching. "I'm not an oddity for display."

I threw my hands up. "I didn't mean that! I'm sorry, okay? You don't have to show me."

She crossed her arms and tucked the hand under her armpit. "Good. Because I have no interest in talking to a stranger who made off with me about my hand."

She had a point. But still. I crossed the barn and patted the horse's rear, sending the girl jumping backward like each blow was going to hit her across the face. "Relax," I said, sliding beside the horse and grabbing its reins. "I just wanted to show you he was right here." I held the reins out to her.

Her lips pursed and I felt a burning in my cheeks, in my chest, in my groin thinking how beautiful she seemed when upset. She reached out her left hand and snatched the reins away, startling the horse.

"Easy." I turned to stroke the stallion's mane and shushed it with quiet soothing noises. "You know, it was that hand of yours that made me determined to save you. At some risk to myself, I might add, so..."

A soft white hand brushed under my arm and slapped across my abdomen with such ferocity, such desperate need, I almost forgot myself. I turned and reached out to grab her, eager to kiss her face and moan "Luana," but as I opened my eyes, the red hair, the pale face, and the silver dress brought it all back to me. As did the dagger hilt she clutched tightly in her left hand before her.

"Stay back!"

I put both hands out in front of me, eager to show her I wasn't a threat. I spoke in much the same tone I'd spoken to the horse earlier. "Easy now, Stargazer."

She walked backwards, stumbling, her nose wrinkling and tears welling up in her eyes as she glanced down and saw the mound of shit one of her small brown shoes was encased in. Her lips quivered just a moment, and I used the chance to step closer, but it was the wrong thing to do. She snapped back to attention and slashed her hand out wildly. "Stay back, I said! I won't let you hurt me!"

The corner of my lip twitched despite the poor girl's obvious fright. "You really think you're going to stab me?"

Her brows furrowed, but her grip on the hilt grew steadier. She ripped her foot free from the feces and took another large step back. "Maybe not," she spat. Her voice quivered despite the anger that formed each word. "But I won't let you hurt me. I won't let you do anything to me."

She thrust the hilt into her left breast.

"SEE, IT SLIPS INTO THIS CRISS-CROSS OF THONGS AROUND MY forearm. Like this." I demonstrated the 'I'm stabbed and bleeding' technique with the bladeless hilt that the girl had tried to kill herself with just moments earlier. "Usually I'd wear a bloody shirt with a whole torn into it, so it would poke through the sleeve."

I looked up to see if she was watching and my smile faltered. She was still huddled in the corner of the pen, curled up into a fetal position, no longer caring about the filth as she buried her cheek into the hay. I yanked the hilt out of the thongs and slipped it back into its fake scabbard at my belt. I cleared my throat. "Um. You all right?"

The bush of thick red hair whipped like a gust of wind through thorny bushes. "No, I am not *all right*." Her eyelids were puffed and red, and tears flooded from each eye even despite the glisten of anger that shone across them. "I just tried to kill myself to escape you, and I failed." She sniffed and looked back at the hay. "I tried to *kill* myself," she said, more quietly.

A sigh escaped my lips despite myself. I had no way to interact with girls other than trying to charm and soothe them. And I'd started off in the wrong position to accomplish that with her, even if she weren't a mother and a prude. "Look, you were going about it all wrong."

She sniffed but said nothing.

"I'm not going to hurt you. I really won't. I won't kill you. I won't do 'unspeakable things.'" I tapped the top of the pen fence nervously. "But I understand why you don't believe me."

She turned her head slowly and looked up, much of the passion lost from her gaze. She seemed waiting for me to say more, so I cleared my throat and crouched down into the hay and muck and feces, coming closer to her level. "Fight. Flee. Fight and flee. Do whatever you can. Never give up, uh... What's your name?"

She ran her sleeve across her eyes and dug her nose into her shoulder. She'd used the right arm and I saw clearly she had not a single finger there. "Cateline," she said quietly at last.

I smiled and reached out a hand. "I'm Fastello. Nice to meet you, Mother Cateline."

She put her arm down, and I was astonished to see something like actual happiness touch her features, if just barely beneath the terror. "I'm not a mother yet," she said, her voice steadier than it'd been since I'd met her. She stared at my extended hand and then looked me in the eyes. At my hand and back to my eyes.

"Oh." I felt the rush of heat to my face. I put my right hand down and held out my left. "Sorry."

She took my left hand in hers and stood with me, keeping her eyes locked on mine for a long, gratifying moment. She pulled back her hand and looked down to smooth the crinkles out of her dress, ignoring the fact that it was now a bit stained and accented with hay. "Despite what your people thought, none of us had anything of value to give."

"What? Oh." I shook my head, tearing my eyes from the white, delicate hand caressing her own chest, abdomen and thigh. "I'm not looking for jewels or coins."

Cateline stopped smoothing her dress, her hand paused atop her right breast. "You said you wanted my help?"

I nodded. "I only ask for mercy."

11

CATELINE

Appealing to the skies, giving offerings to the tower, and praying to Ytoile above us. *That* was asking for mercy.

What this smarmy nomad wanted from me was simple trickery.

"Ytoile does not smile kindly upon liars," I told him, sitting up stiffly on the horse's back. His arms were once again wrapped around my waist, but his hands were clasped together, his thumbs pressing gently into my abdomen. Even with the dress between his flesh and mine, I felt ashamed, a flush of heat rising up from where his hands touched me and taking root in my cheeks.

"She would surely make an exception." He spoke so firmly, it was as if he were the one more in tune with Her holiness, like he were the one instructing me on what was and was not sin.

"Exceptions lead to chaos," I snapped, remembering Mother Jehanne's words. "The more edicts you ask Ytoile to bend, the closer you come to damnation, not realizing the sun demon was atop your shoulder whispering into your ear, guiding you closer to his domain with each exception you asked Her to make."

The sound he made from behind me was something like a small laugh, and his breath tickled the top of my head as he made it. "Thank you for the sermon, Mother."

"Mother-in-*guidance*," I reminded him. Still, the momentary thrill of hearing the title washed all of that earlier shame away. Until I remembered it was nothing more than a thieving, murdering heathen who'd spoken it.

"Of course," said Fastello, as if he completely understood why I made the distinction. He paused and spoke again. "How long have you been 'in guidance'?"

"A few weeks." I realized I was slouching slightly and righted myself again. I cleared my throat after he had nothing more to say. "You can't become a mother-in-guidance until you're sixteen years of age, you know." I felt the heat rising to my face, a little ashamed of my pride, but I spoke more anyway. "I'm the first to be chosen in nearly two decades."

Fastello didn't compliment me. "You're the same age as me, then."

Despite all common sense, I found myself turning my head to peer over my shoulder and get a better look at his face. He caught me looking and leaned sideways to meet my gaze, his smile spreading joy all the way up to the autumnal brown of his eyes. I turned back to focus on the bobbing head of the horse, feeling that heat choking me again. He didn't look my age. The boys who'd left the tower at sixteen were still so scrawny. And pale. The slight touch of the brown in Fastello's skin added both charisma and something like wisdom to his visage, testing my heart in ways the boys at the tower never had... I shook my head to clear it. He was tanned permanently. As if there was any better indication he danced with the sunlight and the flames.

"This your favorite time of day then? The night, I mean?"

It was twilight, and the sun demon still oozed his glow menacingly from the edges of the horizon. "Later," I said. "When it's darker. And the stars are out."

"Oh. Of course." There were a few awkward moments of nothingness. "What were you doing out during the day, then? I mean..." He stopped himself. I don't think either of us wanted to dwell too much on what had happened earlier.

"We were on our way to seek audience with the duke." I rolled my shoulders back, jutting my chest forward. "To ask for help in eradicating the nomads."

"'Eradicating'?! Since when do the Stargazers murder people?"

I raised an eyebrow, even though I knew he couldn't see it. "Since *people* started murdering Stargazers. Or at least the worshippers." No need to add that they'd started murdering Stargazers today as well, I was sure of it. Mother Flore... Even Mother Ermessenda. No. I refused to believe it. Surely they'd made it back. It was up to me now to get to the duke. "We weren't necessarily going to ask the duke to kill you and your people. Just to do *something*. Ytoile would want us to find a merciful way."

Now that I'd experienced a raid firsthand, I had to say my opinion was no longer that we should advocate for Ytoile's mercy. I flushed at the heresy.

I felt the clasped hands press tighter into my stomach, but it was a gentle pressure, more like an embrace than a stranglehold. "I'm sorry, Cateline. I'm... I can't live with them anymore."

I cleared my throat to steady my beating heart and found myself actually disappointed when he loosened his grip. "What waits for you in Hanaobi?"

"Nothing. No one." His voice was quiet, lacking in much of the joviality in which he'd wrapped his sly words before. "I don't necessarily intend to get off there. The sea is destination enough for me."

So he meant to follow through and become a sailor. I'd assumed that was just a trick for reaching another place, a sleight of hand to match his half-formed dagger. My stomach clenched at the thought of that dagger, and what I'd intended to do. I coughed. "I'll take you to the docks, and that's it. You'll have to make your own way."

"And you'll be off to the duke, to tell him what happened."

"Of course." How far did this presumptuous nomad think Ytoile's mercy would extend? "I'll leave you out of it. But we cannot let your people run freely. The tower needs its gifts."

Fastello chuckled.

I whipped my head back. "You think murder and theft is *amusing*?"

The smile dropped from his lips like a fire snuffed out. "No! Of course not. I just meant..." He bit his lip. "The tower isn't as poor as you seem to think."

I turned back. It was my turn to laugh, but I was not truly amused. "We have children to feed. And only our worshippers to rely on to feed them."

"Yes, well, my people feed the farmers. What we steal is only what was stolen from them, jewels in exchange for backbreaking labor, coins in exchange for crops taken from them—"

"I have pity for the farmer that doesn't extend to the thief."

Fastello scoffed. "Pity does nothing. Thieves *do something*."

I smiled wryly. "Is that why you stole from a farmer?"

Fastello dropped one hand from my stomach, and I watched out of the corner of my eye as he re-adjusted the filthy blanket he'd taken from the barn over his head like a hood. "I've probably bought him more food with what I've taken than the old blanket's worth," he mumbled.

I said nothing. We were almost at the gate.

"Show your faces and state your business." A soldier stepped from the side of the gate to the middle of it, his hand extended to stop us. I tugged on the horse's reins gently, slowing it to a halt.

"I'm Cateline, mother-in-guidance of the Stargazers." I brushed my hair from my shoulder to give him a good look at the silver dress, hoping it was not bright enough for him to notice any of the mud stains. "I seek an audience with the duke on behalf of Mother Jehanne."

"The duke's out, but you can wait in his castle." The soldier stepped beside my horse and looked me up and down. I felt a strange, uncomfortable feeling travel down my spine, one only calmed at last when I felt Fastello's gentle squeeze at my belly.

"And who's this?" asked the soldier.

I looked behind me, as if just noticing the man clutching my waist. "Oh," I said, trying my best to make the matter an afterthought. "I stopped to pick up someone who'd like to become a sailor along the way. A request," I added. Nothing was a lie. I just hoped he'd assume the man was a farmer, the request one of Mother Jehanne's.

"The docks are definitely in need of sailors." The soldier focused on Fastello's face, ignoring the rest of the blanket covering what must have appeared to his eyes, I knew, to be nothing more than a shapeless lump. It was finally dark enough to cover the brown in his face, but my eyes traveled to the flickering torches around the gate, worried they might cast their devilish glow and undo our efforts to conceal him.

"Carry on then." The soldier slapped my horse's rear and we trotted on our way.

I hadn't been to the heart of the duchy in years, but this was how I remembered it, bathed in twilight, the pathway lighted by torch and lantern glow. Mother Jehanne used to take some of the children with her to the market—which stayed open at night, to honor Ytoile—to exchange the gifts we received for food. I'd asked once why the worshippers simply didn't bring us food, but Mother Jehanne had laughed, reminding me that food spoiled while coins remained ready to spend whenever needed. It was Mother Flore mostly who brought the children who wanted to go now. Mother Flore—

"The docks are this way." Fastello dropped his grip around my waist and reached for the reins. I heard the blanket slip off his shoulders behind him.

"Hey!" I tried to wrestle the reins from him but had no luck. He'd pointed my horse down the road that took us to the sea. I crossed my arms, doing my best to ignore the way his biceps grazed the sides of my shoulders. "You can just get off here then. I'm going the other way."

"You're not going to leave me now, are you?" He may have been joking, but everything seemed a joke to this heathen. "Just escort me to the docks, would you? Then I'll be out of your life forever. I promise."

Since I was trapped between a horse's head and an ass, I didn't have much choice. I felt my face flushing. A *horse's* ass, of course. A few hours with a nomad and I was forgetting everything Ytoile asked concerning dignity, poise and courtesy. I cleared my throat. "You said you buy the food for farmers with stolen goods, correct?"

"You mean I buy back the farmers' own crops with a little distribution of wealth? Yes."

I wondered if he really only bought what the duchy's farmers grew because there was more rice and Hanaobian vegetables to be had than wheat and potatoes. I knew this from how hard it was for the mothers to find food not from that sinful place. The children had even gone hungry from time to time. I had no desire to get into another argument with him, though. I straightened my back and thought of Ytoile watching over me. "I just meant... I wondered why you needed my help getting into the city if you've been here before."

Fastello said nothing a moment. At last he answered. "We nomads aren't allowed in the front door."

As I suspected. "But then why didn't you take the other way?" I wondered if the duke was aware there was a secret path through which heathens were entering and exiting his city.

"Because then they'd know I'd been here."

"'They'?"

"My people. My dad." He muttered the last word rather quietly.

"You have reason to fear your father?"

"I do now that I rescued you from his raid, don't I?"

I bit my lip. How terrible it must be, to be afraid of your own parent. I was grateful, not for the first time, that mine had been guided to give me to Ytoile.

We reached the docks, and I felt conscious of all the eyes on us as we approached. There were other horses along the path, but not many, and I suppose I stood out with my silver dress. I shifted nervously as I made sure my left arm covered my stump and tugged the reins to guide the horse to a stop. "We're here," I said quickly, *too* quickly.

Fastello's grip loosened as he swung his legs and slid off the horse behind me.

"Need boarding for your stallion, Mother?" The momentary happiness I felt again at being addressed by that title vanished the moment I put a face to the voice. A man so filthy I could hardly make out the patches of skin beneath the dirt on his face stepped forward. I looked behind him to see three horses drinking and eating while tied to a pen. "A fine boy, this one." He slapped the horse's rear and I jumped, spinning to tell him to keep his filthy hands off the tower's property—

"Yes, thank you." Fastello grabbed the reins from my loosened grip and handed them to the walking pile of dirt. He reached up and placed his hands around my waist, hoisting me up.

"Wait a minute! Stop!" I felt like I was going to topple over. Eventually I had no choice but to slide my leg around and latch my arms around his shoulders as he guided me off the horse. My feet reached the ground and my shoulders slackened with relief. I pulled my right arm back and tucked the stump under my armpit, completely flustered. I smoothed my hair out of my eyes with my hand. "I wasn't getting off here," I hissed.

"What? You planned to ride the horse all the way to the castle, all high and mighty on your stallion like a one-woman parade?" I blushed because that was exactly what I'd planned on doing. And what was wrong with that? Simply riding through the city didn't mean I was looking for attention. Fastello grabbed the blanket off the horse and dug into a small pouch he kept at his waist pocket. "Board him here, and pick him up on your way out." He handed the filthy man a coin. "Just for a few hours. Well?" His words spurred the man into action and he guided my escape route away, whispering sweet words into its flickering ears.

Fastello fastened his pouch and put his hands on his hips. "What? You can come say goodbye to me before you go."

I sighed. "I could say goodbye right now just fine."

"Don't be like that." Fastello gestured that I should walk before him, swinging his hands out in the direction of a few men gathered around barrels and a small fire beside a huge vessel. "I need your introduction. Nomad, remember?"

It hadn't occurred to me that the duke's ships weren't in the business of hiring well-known thieves and murderers. But what was he going to do once on the ship? Cover his face for the rest of his life? I sighed. It wasn't my problem. "I've gotten you this far…"

"Just repeat the story you told the guard. Only this time specifically say that I'm a farmer. They'll think I tanned from the work in the sun." He swung the blanket around his shoulders and wrapped it over his head again, like a shoddy cloak.

"I don't lie," I mumbled, but he wasn't listening. I bit my lip. If I could just get him on the ship, all of this would be over. I straightened my back and walked toward the men at the docks. They were laughing, but the closer I got, the more I suspected the mugs they had in their hands were amusing them far more than any tales they had to tell. Their faces were red, and not the red from the sun demon's kiss.

Their smiles vanished almost as soon as I stepped beside them.

"Can we help you, Mother?" asked one, clunking his mug down on the barrel he was using as a seat. "The market's in the other direction."

I cleared my throat. "I know where I am. I'm asking for work."

Apparently what I said was just as amusing as whatever it was that had had them in raptures beforehand.

"For him," I added quickly, squeezing my arm tighter against my chest and nodding sideways.

Fastello jutted forth beside me, awkwardly waving a hand at the sailors. A moment passed in which the red-faced men did nothing but look at Fastello and pass awkward glances between themselves. Why now, of all times, was Fastello suddenly bereft of words?

"He helps farmers," I spat. "I was asked to take him here," I added, carefully thinking over my words. "While on a mission for Mother Jehanne." Not a lie in that sentence. Not that Ytoile would forgive me for twice now misleading people. *"Lies are spoken with words, but they're also understood through false intentions."* Mother Jehanne's words flashed through my mind.

One of the other sailors nudged the man who'd spoken to me. "He's a mute or something?"

"No," said Fastello quietly. "Hello." He nodded at the men.

One of the sailors raised his eyebrow. "Well, we are in desperate need of a crew." He cleared his throat. "Quite a few got slaughtered the other day by the duke's men."

Ytoile help them. If he hoped to frighten Fastello into giving up, I wasn't sure it was working. Fastello said nothing, but I saw the muscles twitch in his cheek.

The man shrugged and picked up his mug. "You'll have to wait for The Duke's Pride to get in. We're thinking of consolidating crews. And we're still bereft of a captain." He took a swig.

"And when will that be?" Fastello's voice was steady, but the slight quiver betrayed something close to panic.

The man smacked his lips together. "Another week yet." He gestured around him, one hand still clutching his mug. "It's why we're so terribly occupied. No sense in getting attached to a new sailor." He waved a hand dismissively.

"A week?" I started, visions of walking away from the heathen once and for all vanishing.

Fastello grabbed me lightly by the arm. "I'll be back then. Thank you. Come, Mother." He guided me away from the men, who sat silently a moment more before retreating back into laughter.

We'd just slid down an alley leading toward the market when Fastello's grip finally slackened enough that I could tear my arm away. "Just where are you going?"

Fastello looked around. We were a few yards from the street, and people passed on their way to and from the market. He lowered his voice. "I need a place to stay until they set sail."

I shook my head. "Well, then this is where we say goodbye."

He looked as if I'd slapped him. "You can't leave me now!"

"I most certainly can and I *will*." I stepped back to avoid his outstretched hand. "How is any of this my problem?"

"You're a woman of the goddess, surely you have it in your heart—"

I felt my blood boil. "A proper Stargazer wouldn't bother to *talk* to one of your kind, let alone help him!"

He pulled his hand back. "I need a place to hide. My people will find me here. Or the duke's men."

"Might I suggest a barn again? You seemed so at home among the pigs and the manure." I picked up my skirt, realizing with disgust that the silver hem was dragging along the mud- and water-strewn tiles of the alley.

Fastello let the comment pass. "Is there any way you can take me with you, to the tower?" He looked about to say more but stopped as I shot him what I hoped was my most obvious look of disdain.

"You mean, after I report the crime your people committed to the duke?" I took a step toward the road. "No, I intend to go home escorted by a garrison of soldiers, soldiers looking for nomads to pay for the acts they've committed, so I suggest you find some other—"

Everyone in the street had stopped moving. They all looked up, facing the same direction. A woman dropped a basket of cucumbers to bring her hands to her face, doing nothing as the precious vegetables tumbled out and mixed in with the dirt and horse's droppings that littered the street.

"What's..." Fastello laid a hand on my shoulder.

The crowd began murmuring. I heard two words clearly, over and over: "tower" and "smoke."

"The tower is on fire!" shouted one woman at last.

I turned my head to face the direction they were all staring, my heart thumping so loudly in my ears, I could no longer hear them. I said a prayer over and over under my breath. "Ytoile, please let them be mistaken. Please watch over your tower. Protect it and your children from the wrath of the sun demon—"

Words were ripped from my tongue, and my hand clutched at my throat, as if I could squeeze them out of me. The tower, only the very spire of which could possibly be visible from where I stood behind the city walls, was replaced by black smoke, an ember glow burning against the new night sky. The smoke could be from someplace nearer, blocking any view of home, it had to be a mistake—

A man appeared from that direction down the street, running, ringing a bell and shouting as he passed. "The tower is burning! The Stargazers are traitors to his lordship! Burn your religious artifacts. Being a Stargazer is now punishable by death!"

The herald moved on to spread the law to other avenues. The frozen crowd burst into life, more baskets and wares forgotten, people running toward their homes. I gripped my throat tighter.

A blanket fell over my head, smelling of hay and sheep.

"This way," hissed Fastello, gripping my right arm tightly.

I let him lead me in silence, my hand still wrapped around my throat.

12

KOJIRO

I'd lost count of how many times I'd vomited into the bucket I pinched between my fingers. I felt a splinter digging into my skin, but still, I squeezed harder as I let more empty liquid loose.

"You know, Prince, there's an entire sea you can use to empty your stomach into." Tierny looked up from parchment at his desk, seemingly unconcerned about the fact that he tipped one direction and then the other. He shifted a jade paperweight to stop some parchment from sliding. "It's generally a cleaner practice."

I looked up from my bucket, fully aware of the thread of drool hanging from my lips. "Barbarians care about clean? I learn more from you every day." I tilted my head back toward the bucket and dry heaved.

Tierny laughed and walked over, remarkably keeping his balance even as the floor beneath him swayed. "Well, some of us do, in any case." He reached out a hand. "I'll empty it and get you some food."

I clenched the bucket tighter against my belly. "Not hungry. No food."

"I think you need some." Tierny grabbed the bucket first with one hand and then, finding he could not pry it from me, with two, at last overcoming the fatigue in my muscles and lifting the bucket away. "I'll be right back."

I reached vainly after him as he took my new friend away. I felt the nausea ride up from my stomach to my throat and flailed my hands desperately to find something with which to replace the bucket. My hands touched the small box Tomiko had given me.

My fingers caressed the wooden surface, and like a charm, stroking the engravings on the box washed away the urgency for vomiting. Dyed black into the wood, the lines resembled the sun and a whip of flames.

"All right, so here's dinner." Tierny returned, a plain wooden bowl in his hands, my lovely bucket nowhere in sight. He held it out to me, first with just one hand in the barbarian way, and then with two, remembering proper manners.

"Act like barbarian. It is all right. I need to know now," I said, taking the bowl from him with only one hand as if to prove I were serious. My face fell at the small bowl of rice topped with one chopped-up radish. And a wooden spoon instead of chopsticks. "We will eat like barbarians, too."

Tierny laughed and walked back to his desk, his hands dancing over the piles of papers. "Rice is something new for the duchy," he said, still staring at his desk. "Somewhat new, anyway."

I nodded, thinking of Yukishige's history lessons. "Hanaobi began trading it just eighteen years before. Ago," I added, thinking of the proper word. "The duke's wheat was... broken."

"*Tainted*," corrected Tierny, absentmindedly stroking his beard. "A bug infestation. We had so little food that year, the duke had no choice but to send us searching for countries with which to trade."

"Even though he had nothing to offer." So he made sure he had something to take.

The rice was helping settle my stomach, even if each bite tasted like the bile that coated my mouth. I wished desperately for tea.

Tierny sat down at the desk and clasped his hands together. "We should arrive at the duchy in five more days, winds willing." He tapped the desk. "I didn't have the chance to discuss anything with the previous captain. But it looks like he got a letter by bird while still at sea." He picked up a piece of parchment. "The Duke's Favor checked heavily immediately after docking. Outsiders found. Mutiny suspected. Most of the crew slaughtered."

I stopped chewing, a bit of radish and rice still sitting in my mouth.

Tierny tapped the letter and let it fall back to the desk. "Decent men, most of them." It had been his crew, I knew, just a few weeks before. "I knew what would happen if I didn't return with them. What the duke would think it meant."

I swallowed. "So why didn't you? Return?"

Tierny sighed. "Your mother offered me a job as your tutor, and I didn't feel right refusing." He gnashed his jaw awkwardly. "I'd wanted to retire someday regardless."

I put the bowl down beside me, half-eaten, but I had no room for more. "But now you can never return to Hanaobi."

Tierny smiled weakly. "If we succeed here, I don't see why not." He left the rest unsaid. That it was unlikely we'd both be setting sail again.

"What means this word?" I stood, almost falling but gripping the table just as Tierny reached out to steady my arm and help me keep my ground. I took a deep breath and then searched the letter and the jumble of words to find the one that had confused me. "Mu-ti-ny," I said at last, pointing.

Tierny gave me the Hanaobi translation before switching back to barbarian. "I told my first mate to report I'd died at sea." He ran a hand through his hair and blew out a breath of air. "I'd hoped the duke would actually believe it. I didn't think the duke would suspect the crew had betrayed me. If I was sending a message, he was supposed to hear that I'd *chosen* to stay. Hearing I'd died instead maybe made him look closer at the ship and—"

"The Hanaobi people, they were killed?" The letter hadn't said.

Tierny nodded glumly. "That goes without saying." He stared at me, evidently reading the confusion on my face. He gave me an encouraging smile. "Yes. Any outsider is killed on sight in the duchy. There is no hesitation. That's... The official policy, anyway."

A wave sent the ship tilting again, and for a moment, I almost lost my grip on the table, my knees buckling beneath me. Tierny stood to help support me, but I straightened my back and shook my head, gripping the table's edge tighter. My eyes darted over the parchment, settling on what seemed to be a map of the sole city in the duchy. I turned to look at Tierny, who seated himself again. "So where are the Hanaobi people in the duchy?"

Tierny grinned and tapped a finger on his nose in a strange gesture that did nothing but confuse me. He moved a paperweight and shuffled some parchment, laying a map of the entire island of the duchy beside the one of the city. He pointed to the fields outside the walled city that rested opposite a great forest between a cliff and the city. "Mostly here, at the farms. They come to the duchy knowing how to farm anyway, most of them. They've proven quite helpful to the farmers willing to take the risk of hiding them. The duke knows how badly he needs what little the farms are able to produce, so he doesn't spend much time searching for outsider farmers."

"Farmers?" I didn't understand.

Tierny stared, his eyes meeting mine, and chewed on his lip. Then he sighed. "I think the time for telling you only what your mother ordered me to tell you has passed." The corner of his mouth twitched and he averted his eyes to the table. "I don't smuggle Hanaobi soldiers into the duchy, on the order of the empress. Not usually."

I didn't understand. The floor shifted beneath me, but this time I barely faltered. "Explain."

Tierny sighed and placed the map of the city over the map of the isle of the duchy. "I smuggle Hanaobi slaves."

"Slaves?" I pinched my nose, repeating the word in Hanaobian.

"Yes. Oh." He cleared his throat. "I suppose you think of them as servants."

I scoffed. "It is an honor. A great honor for a poor citizen to be chosen to serve the imperial family—"

"Perhaps so," interrupted Tierny. "Some do accept it. But many are not happy to be forced into labor, as most Hanaobi people—"

I found myself slamming a hand on the table, heat rising to my face. "Tierny, you insult Hanaobi. You insult its people—"

"All right." Tierny gestured with both hands, waving them up and down with his palms turned downward. "All right, Prince Kojiro. I didn't mean to upset you."

I could feel Tierny studying my face, and I turned to stare at the map, breathing in and out deeply.

"Regardless," said Tierny after a moment. "Your mother wasn't happy with what I was doing. I offered these people passage without her permission."

I found myself examining Tierny's face. "Why?"

His eyes didn't falter. "For a small chance of freedom."

I shook my head and tapped the map. "Freedom? Here? In the duchy?"

Tierny shrugged. "For slaves, maybe."

I let out a breath of air sharply. "So Hanaobi farmers travel on the boat," I let go of the table and gestured around me at the dark and dank accommodations, "risk death at the dock, to escape farming? And then they farm still regardless?"

Tierny stacked the parchment neatly so no corners stuck out of the pile. "Farming is different in the duchy."

"Yes." I crossed my arms and dug my heels into the floor, daring the tilting ship to knock me over. "That is why your barbarians are starving."

Tierny shook his head and sighed. "It's not simply a matter of the duchy farmers not working until they collapse, Prince, and letting their hands take breaks for rest and water. The duchy's lands aren't as fertile. They don't have as many hands to help tend the crops—"

"That is still not—"

Tierny raised a hand to stop me. "Let's put that aside for now. I just wanted you to know, well..." He returned to looking at the desk, a strange sort of blankness on his face. "The job I accepted from your mother came a little earlier than I was prepared for. But it was very generous, considering how angry she was at her lost servants. She'd warned me before, and I'd tried to placate her by taking a few soldiers. By arranging passage for your father and elder brother..." He clenched his jaw and stopped. Then he sighed and ran a hand over his face. "It was the last straw."

"Straw? Did you steal hay?" I laughed, thinking of rolling the barrels inconspicuously onto the docks.

Tierny grinned and did his best to explain the idiom in Hanaobi. He switched back to barbarian. "I like seeing you laugh, Prince Kojiro. I like seeing you feel *anything*. You're much more expressive here, away from Hanaobi."

Of course. Knowing Mother would have me kill myself no matter what I did, realizing that death was actually what she wanted for me, even more than terror and disappointment, was almost like a burden lifted from my shoulders. Nothing I did, and nothing I said now would get back to her. Nothing but defeating the duke, succeeding where Elder Brother Nobutada had failed, and that's all she needed to remember.

"So how do we get me from dock to farms?" I asked, a number of plans already forming in my mind. "I do not want to climb in one of those." I pointed to a barrel crammed into the corner, shuddering at the image of what was left of Father and Elder Brother Nobutada, what Mother had insisted I see with my own eyes. *"The price of failure."* All the words she'd had to comfort a devastated child, the future of Hanaobi now resting heavily on his shoulders.

Tierny tapped on the map of the city. "We travel via the underground."

13

ROHESIA

I awoke to the screams of children and the smell of burnt flesh.

I shot up, reaching for a blade at my waist. Finding nothing, I flicked my wrists to try to bring missing daggers to my hands. Nothing. My shallow breaths grew deeper, and I used my forearm to wipe the oozing sweat that had accumulated at my brow. I swung my legs over the side of the bed and padded across the rug and tile to the open window, sliding my arms through the silken robe I grabbed off the chair as I passed.

The fire had died several days ago—there'd been a bit of rain, even though by then there was so little left for the fire to turn to cinder—but I swore the broken stone and ashes still radiated smoke into the sky. It filtered the moonlight and masked the stars, leaving the night sky in almost total darkness.

Darkness. The figure sat in a rocking chair by the window in total darkness.

"You are the holy mother, are you not?" I left the door open behind me, but so little of the setting sunlight filtered into the room. All I was certain of was that there was a form rocking back and forth, the wood of her chair creaking softly with each movement.

There was no answer. I stormed across the room to the window.

"My, uh, my lady, you cannot—"

"Stop! This is heresy!"

The silver-clothed women who had reluctantly allowed me this far into the tower now screamed behind me, but I did not hesitate. I threw the curtains aside.

There wasn't much light left in the day, but the soft glow of twilight was enough to finally bring the rocking woman into focus. Wearing a silver dress just like the other women in the tower, there was nothing remarkable about her on the surface. She had long silver, wavy hair to match the dress, and a pale face sagging and stretched at the corners, but her face was only lightly touched with creases. She didn't regard me. She kept on rocking, her eyes squinting at the window.

I laid a hand on my sword hilt. "I'm the duke's—"

"I know who you are." The woman opened her thin lips at last. Her voice sounded like paper crinkling. "Ytoile is strong today. Can you see the moon out already, even when the sun demon is still fading? The stars will soon follow."

I rarely noticed the stars or moon. Father put little store in the Stargazers' religion. I only bothered to look when... There was something I didn't want to see. But it'd been years since I turned to the moon for solace. I clenched my jaw. "We need to talk."

"You need to listen." The woman kept rocking and shut her eyes. "Close your eyes and hear Her voice, guiding you. You, tainted with the blood of heathens. Even you might be saved."

If she tried to wound me, she failed. I knew what the people thought of me. Still, there were few who would be so bold as to say such a thing to my face.

"Two of your mothers are dead—"

"Hear Her!"

"It was the nomads. I thought you should know before—"

One of the women at the doorway screamed. "Mother Jehanne! Mother Jehanne!"

She stared out the door behind her, her pale face grown even paler. I recognized the terror in her words, and I drew my sword as I crossed the room to enter the hallway.

Smoke, pouring from the stairwell. Smoke, seeping through the windows. Heat and flames. Screams, high-pitched and shrill. A scent of something cooking. My vision was clouded, and I grabbed my helmet off my head with my free hand to see more clearly.

One of the soldiers appeared at the bottom of the stairs, torch in hand. "My lady, we—"

The jolt of pain to the back of my head sent me staggering. The last thing I remembered was the cold stone of the floor smashing across my cheek.

My head still ached, and the tossing and turning I did in bed only aggravated the bruise on my cheek and the lump at the back of my head.

It was such a short moment. A moment of weakness. Of underestimating those around me. And as I'd vanished completely into the darkness, I'd never expected to wake from it.

The black sky reminded me too much of the woman in the rocker, and the last window I'd spent time gazing out of. I lit the candlestick on the table beside my bed and went for a walk in the castle. I didn't grab my sword or load my daggers. Where I walked I was sure no one else would dare enter.

Only Father and I occupied the rooms on the third floor of the castle, but there were many rooms, undusted, unopened. The entire wing at the end of the hallway, the furthest from the stairwell, was the concubine corner.

It wasn't a formal name. Just a title I heard in whispers before I came around corners, usually followed by giggles or sly chuckles, and smiles that vanished from faces as I came into view. It was where Father kept his consorts before I'd been born—a practice his own father did not share, I heard tell, otherwise there might have been other heirs. It was where he'd housed my mother.

There was no mistaking which room had been hers. I'd first explored the area as a child, and I'd found it almost immediately: the door closest to Father's, the one behind which another world existed.

I carefully turned the knob, eager to minimize the sound of the unoiled brass as it squeaked and allowed me to push open. I stepped inside and brought the candle over my head.

Cream white and faded, the soft squishy floor coverings absorbed each step I took. Instead of a bed, there was a mattress on the floor, a small dust-coated cushion on a raised pedestal serving as the pillow. A simple oak table so close to the ground you had to sit on the floor to make any use of it. A lack of chairs. Stone walls covered halfway with thin, papery screens.

And a cat-like beast made of jade to match my Father's, the only thing left on a table encrusted in dust so thick it resembled grey fur. I stepped closer to the table, my eyes drawn to the demon-like cat. There were fingerprints peppered throughout the dust, smaller ones growing slightly larger, evidence that I'd been here at different stages of my growth, always reaching for the statuette for some imagined comfort.

I noticed the large handprint in the dust, the one twice the size of my hand even now.

"I wondered how often you must come in here."

My hand faltered in the air above the jade creature. "Father," I said, snapping my feet together and bowing.

Father padded across the room in a silken robe more colorful than my own. It looked strange against his pale skin, an ill fit that hung loosely at his shoulders.

"There is no reason for formality, my dear, at this hour." He put a hand on my shoulder and curled his lips slightly. "I wondered if you came here for this." He picked up the jade statue and stared at it, running a finger across its smooth belly. He swallowed and then held it out to me. "No need to be so secretive. You can have it. She would have been glad to give it to you."

I took the cat-beast carefully, feeling the cold, smooth otherworldly stone under my fingers, not sure if the statue would bring me as much comfort once I took it out of that room. My head still ached considerably, but the movement of my fingers across the jade proved something like an antidote to the throbbing.

"Momoko gave me a twin statue of that lion," Father said, for the first time giving the creature a name, "and kept this one for herself when we set sail for the duchy. She said they would symbolize how we were always as one, how our hearts were one and the same, even if our outsides were different." Father swallowed and turned, suddenly interested in staring at the dust-covered mattress. "Perhaps it was she who warned me to set off and go after you when the men told me you'd gone to return those bodies to the tower." His face soured as he turned to face me. "The Stargazers say the good shine in the night sky, and the bad burn in the sun. But Momoko told me that her people believed that everyone remained behind, hiding invisible behind the shoulders of those they loved, flitting in and out of everything around us." He gestured to the nearly-empty room, as if to point out my mother's lost spirit somewhere beside us.

I clutched the lion to my chest tightly, not sure what to believe, thinking of the men I'd slaughtered. Was not hate a more powerful emotion than love? I had more reason to believe spirits would hate me than love me, so thinking of them as everywhere around me instead of off somewhere they could never reach me was unnerving.

"Your mother was the last woman I took as my own." Father crossed his hands behind his back and stiffened his shoulders to appear taller. "She asked me to set the others free, and I did."

I knew as much, but I'd never known it was my mother's request that led Father to keep only one woman. Part of me hoped it was simply that he loved her so much more than the others.

Father cleared his throat. "Of course, Momoko didn't quite understand that they weren't slaves like her people, that they were women who volunteered to join me." A flash of something unreadable passed across his eyes. "But she was so grateful that I listened to her plea. She was quite used to her controlling brother, who never paid attention to her desires, who treated her more like a doll for display than the princess she was."

I nearly dropped the jade statue. "Mother was a princess?" I'd assumed she was a slave, like most of the outsider people.

Father laughed, and a small spattering of red brushed his pale cheeks. "Yes. I met her the one time I traveled to Hanaobi, on the pretext of peace. She played hostess, introducing me to all there was to know about her country."

I didn't know what to say. We'd never had this conversation. I'd been too afraid, like acknowledging the outsider blood that heavily featured in my face would be like asking to be executed along with the rest of them. It was why I'd only snuck into Mother's room before. Why I'd been so careful to put the jade lion back exactly where I'd found it.

"Her brother and father would say she told me a little *too much* about their country." Father started pacing back and forth across the room. "She so hated that her people suffered. She wanted to know how the poor were treated in the duchy and was so glad to learn I didn't watch them like hawks, demanding they work until they collapsed." Father ran his tongue across his lips, not mentioning the food he demanded as tax from the farmers. I supposed he never really punished the farmers for not producing enough, so long as they gave him something to trade to Hanaobi. Father cleared his throat. "I was afraid her brother would punish Momoko for the thoughts she'd put into my head because my talks with their father went worse the better I got to know the princess." He shrugged. "The only thing to do was to take her with me."

The question formed at the base of my throat, but it took so long to find the courage to ask it. The heaviness of the lion in my hands at last spurred me forward. "The outsiders. In the barrels. In the farms—"

Father waved a hand. "Soldiers, not escaped slaves. Once safely here herself, Momoko offered refuge to her people at first, but her brother sent trained assassins along with the farmers, slaughtering outsider slaves and the people of the duchy alike." Father shook his head. "Now that's all we get. Soldiers. And traitor sailors who knowingly bring them to us."

A lie. You know about the farms. "But the infants..." I felt my throat grow dry.

Father's eyes caught mine like a predator catching sight of its prey. "An outsider killed your mother when you were an infant. Someone she *loved*. A soldier through and through." He put both hands on my shoulders and gripped me, his eyes widening wildly. "An outsider tried to kill you in your crib."

I let my eyes fall. He'd told me as much before, but—

The little hand dropping below the river, the cries suddenly stopped.

Joined now with the screaming, the flames, the charred meat.

Father embraced me, pushing the jade lion deeper against my chest. I hesitated, not sure if I could let my face rest against his shoulder. Not sure if I should.

"When I saw that tower burning, I thought I'd lost you forever." His voice faltered slightly on the last word. "Then the men brought you out, claiming that demon woman had clonked you over the head and had ordered the whole tower set ablaze herself, the silver-dressed women running about the place setting fire with torches..." His voice was hoarse. "Madwomen. Every one of them. Them and their mad religion. Dancing in the darkness. Sleeping during the day," he muttered. He pushed back on my shoulders gently, putting a small space between us. His eyes danced with tears he refused to let fall. "But at least we can be done with them, too. Another ridiculous upstart power."

I thought again of the children I'd passed as I made my way through the tower. Orphans praying. Orphans reading. Orphans playing. And the silver-haired woman in the rocking chair had ordered them all rounded up, trapped as the tower succumbed to smoke and fire.

No child was safe in the duchy, no matter who offered them shelter.

I forced a faltering smile across my lips, the feeling strange and uncomfortable. "Thank you, Father. For this." I raised the jade lion slightly, so he wouldn't confuse my gratitude for anything else. "Good night."

"Sleep better, my dear, with your mother watching over and protecting you."

I stared at the jade lion as I made my exit. *Sleep better*. As if I deserved to ever sleep well, with all the invisible, hate-filled spirits that I created in my wake.

14

FASTELLO

I took three footsteps to table nine, the mug of ale and the bowl of stew in my aching arms, and immediately turned around, retreating to the kitchen.

Meggy looked up from the potato she was peeling, the knife halfway down the spud's skin. "Table nine!"

Like I'd forgotten her instructions twenty seconds after she'd given them to me. I put the mug and bowl down, my eyes falling on the redhead kneading the dough in the corner. "Cateline, you'll have to take it to her."

Cateline wiped her hand over the apron Meggy had provided, a dingy white draped over a plain, roughspun brown dress. I remembered how her emerald eyes welled over as she watched the silver one burn, giving the last trace of her life in the tower up to the very culprit who'd taken that life from her. Cateline's eyes fell on the mug and bowl. "I can't carry both at once."

She's limiting herself again. I brought the bowl over to her and nodded at her right arm. "Bring it out and tuck this between your elbow and your abdomen. Then you can take the mug in your hand—"

"Oh, for crying out loud, boy, I think she knows better than you considering she's lived that way her whole life. She takes the orders, you serve them. That's what we agreed was best." Meggy shook the knife she handled in my direction.

"I'd rather he took the orders, too," said Cateline softly. She tucked her right hand—which had almost been extended to receive the bowl from me—into her apron pocket.

Meggy shook the potato at her. Nice to know it was only *my* complaining that deserved the blade. "And have spying busybodies whispering I'm keeping a pretty young lady all secret-like back here in the kitchen? No, I'll have none of that kind of talk. No rumors about Meggy's Tavern." She sniffed and went back to peeling. "And it's about time my temporary guests were able to do a little more than eat me out of business."

My gaze fell upon the bags of flour and rice in the corner, thinking of the trap door Meggy had shown us concealed there. I thought of spending the week in the darkness below the kitchen and shuddered. Then again, maybe Cateline would be there with me—

Cateline stumbled a little as she turned back to the dough, and I practically dropped the stew bowl in order to offer her support. She didn't thank me, but she didn't rip her arm out of my grip, either. Her pale skin was punctured heavily by purple bags beneath her glazed eyes. She wasn't used to waking at dawn and working until midnight, collapsing into the cot in the room we shared above the tavern and sleeping through the hours she considered the most holy.

The room we shared. Too bad I slept on the floor.

"Meggy," I said, letting Cateline's arm go, "could you take this one out? Just this one? I promise."

Meggy slammed the potato and knife down on the counter, placing her hands on her hips so quickly, I barely had time to prepare for her glower. "What's this nonsense all about?"

I cleared my throat. "I know her."

Cateline stopped kneading, but she jumped and started working again as soon as I turned to face her. "It could be bad," I said. "For us."

Meggy sighed and ripped the bowl from my arms, grabbing the mug off the counter before sauntering out into the crowded dining area.

I watched Cateline knead a moment more, but she was hardly

putting any force into her movements. "How do you know her?" she asked at last, her tone too carefully nonchalant.

Briefly, I hoped she remembered the blonde woman in question since she'd taken her order, and that the stiffness in her movements might be because the beauty had sparked a bit of jealousy. I leaned back with my elbows on the counter, gazing up to look at her face. "She was a lover of mine," I teased.

And that's exactly how I'd hoped you'd react. Cateline's face grew red, and her brows furrowed, her pace slowing with the dough. I watched her pretty face a moment and felt the familiar kick in my gut as I thought of Luana, so different from this strange little mother, so much more beautiful... But lacking, perhaps, in being so perfect to tease. "For about forty seconds," I added.

Cateline stopped, her mouth open in a perfect little circle. "Should I ask?"

"We didn't get far." I looked away, guiltily, remembering when I'd last met the woman. "I tried to steal from her."

"Of course." Cateline smacked the dough against the counter.

I didn't want to tell Cateline what had become of Agnes' servant and possibly sister. "She came from the tower last week. Didn't you recognize her when you took her order?"

"No," replied Cateline, pushing her knuckles into the dough. I was glad to see she pressed the knuckles of her right hand into the dough as well, as if the permanent fist was made for the task. "If she was a worshipper, I wasn't yet present at any festivities with her there." She chewed on her lip a moment. "I'm surprised, if you assaulted her, that she still lives."

"I didn't *assault* her—"

A hard whack at the back of my head. "Don't lean on the counter where I prepare food."

I turned, rubbing the soreness, searching newly-returned Meggy's hand for the rock she must have used to beat me, when she stepped aside to reveal the blonde in question.

"*You!*" hissed Agnes. She slapped me across the face.

I couldn't believe it. I turned to Meggy, still rubbing the back of my head, the other hand caressing my sore cheek. "What did you bring her in here for?!"

Agnes grabbed me by the front of my tunic. "What did you do with Bernard and Cecily? What did you do with my sister?!"

I put both hands on Agnes' small arms, trying to gently pry them off me. She had my clothes gripped so tightly, I was afraid the tunic would turn to dust in her fingers. "Let me explain." She looked up at me expectantly. My throat grew tighter. I had nothing more to say.

"I don't know if you want to know the answer." Cateline slipped beside me, laying her hand on Agnes' arm. "But you can trust Fastello to have done all he could have to stop it." Her words hurt me like an arrow to the chest. Only because her compliment—so sorely wanted—was misplaced.

Agnes' lips trembled and her grip slackened, her eyes drawn to Cateline's right hand, which she hadn't hidden when she'd come to my aid. "Who are you?" she asked. "You don't look like a nomad."

I gently pulled away from Agnes and stepped back slightly. "No one—"

Cateline rolled her shoulders back and jutted her chin forward in that way she did every time she seemed to think herself better than the people around her. "A Stargazer. A mother-in-guidance. At least I was."

I slapped a hand to my cheek and jumped when I felt the sting worsen. "Cateline, you'll undo everything we've done, put all the people on the underground I contacted to find us this safe place in danger, if you go around proclaiming that freely."

Cateline raised an eyebrow. "You said this woman was a worshipper."

"Yes, but—"

"She asked me for help," interrupted Meggy. "Not too many places she could go. Says the duke's soldiers are after her."

Agnes pinched her lips together and clenched her fists. "I don't really care about the Stargazers. I never did. Just seemed the thing to do, and Cecily liked what they did for the orphans..." She choked on her words slightly, and I noticed a single tear escaping from eyes welling with water. "But after we were *assaulted*, I went to the castle and the duke's soldiers wound up escorting me home." She sniffed. "So as soon as the edict went down, banning all trace of that infantile religion, they remembered who they'd brought home just hours earlier and stormed my house, taking *everything*, claiming it only right since I was a worshipper of *Ytoile*." She spat the name of Cateline's goddess rather harshly.

"*Heathen*," Cateline hissed.

I laid a hand on her shoulder. "Cateline, you can't defend the Stargazers, not when there's a manhunt—"

Cateline spun, wrenching her shoulder from my grip. "There is no *better* time to defend my deity! There is no better time to prove to Her that I, at least, remain faithful!"

"Cateline, we've been over this! Now is not the time for preaching—"

"I can't just *forget* my religion! I can't *forget* who I am!"

I threw my hands in the air. "I'm not asking you to forget it, I'm asking you to keep it quiet until you're safely out of the city—"

"*Quiet*," muttered Meggy. "That might be a good idea."

Cateline crossed her arms, ignoring our patroness. "And to where exactly? Where will I ever be safe? Plan to take me with you to Hanaobi? To the land where the sun demon's most strong? I'd rather *die* here."

I cleared my throat. I knew too well she meant it, too. "I'm not going to Hanaobi," I whispered.

Cateline's mouth opened slightly. "But the ship is due tomorrow—"

I shrugged. "I don't need to become a sailor. I just wanted to get away from my people. And I can get away with you."

Meggy put one hand on my shoulder and the other on Cateline's. "Okay, if you've done enough flirting for the evening—"

"*Flirting*—" Cateline clenched her jaw.

"—I thought you could explain to Lady Agnes how things run around here. At least until you all take off in a couple of days." Meggy went back to her potato.

Agnes peered around Cateline and me to look at Meggy. "You can't mean you're expecting me to *work*?!"

Meggy cocked her head. "Of course, young lady. Why not?"

Agnes bit her lip. "I…" She gestured to her dress, and then seemed to remember that she wasn't wearing a stunning gown and water started coating her eyes again. "I'm not *used* to working."

Meggy pointed the knife in her direction. "When those soldiers came, young lady, how was it you came to be wearing those clothes? How was it you found your way here, and who sheltered you before you plopped that fancy ass of yours down at my table?"

At the sight of the knife aimed unintentionally at her heart, Agnes jumped back in fright. "One of my servants—"

Meggy nodded and turned back to her potato. "Yes, a good *working class* citizen." She peeled a long layer of skin from the vegetable. "Got me three such folks not used to working now, don't I? You need help from the likes of us, you'll make yourself useful." She eyed us each in turn. "And you better be helpful to those farmers who offer you shelter from those you're running from."

Cateline darted out of the kitchen to take orders, and I took her place at the counter by the dough. After a moment of kneading, Agnes stepped awkwardly beside me. "We're going to the farms?" she whispered, her hand trembling as it picked up a knife on the counter.

She plunged it into a tomato haphazardly, the red juices flowing everywhere on the counter. I thought of the blood flowing from the chest of her sister, a sight I'd spared her, but maybe a sight she needed to see.

"We are." I cleared my throat. "And we'll be damn thankful for it."

15

CATELINE

I didn't see how staying in the kitchen would arouse suspicion. I wondered briefly if Meggy just liked to watch my embarrassment. As if hiding my stump in my apron pocket wasn't difficult enough.

"Sweetheart! Another round!" There was no pretending I hadn't heard the raucous cries that followed the clink of metal mugs.

I approached the table, my eyes down, and collected as many of the empty mugs as I could handle. I felt more confident when they weren't filled with liquid, and I remembered Fastello's suggestion and tucked a few extra into the crux of my arm. Something burned inside me at the man *suggesting* anything, though. As if he understood what it was like.

"Think we could get some spices in the next round, sweetheart?" The man placed his filthy fingers on my right arm. "A touch of cinnamon? Or how about a little bit of your sweetness?" The rest of the table laughed.

"*Pardon me.*" I rotated my shoulder to flick the man's hand away without moving my arm. The mugs I'd balanced clinked together, and I had to rebalance them against my abdomen to keep them from falling.

"Whoa!" The man bent forward and reached a hand under my arm. Instead of catching anything, he jostled one of the mugs, sending it and the one next to it tumbling to the floor with a crash. The last drops of ale from the mugs soaked into my apron.

One of the men at the table clapped and cheered, as if I'd just performed a trick for him. I put the rest of the mugs back on the table and bent to grab the fallen ones, wiping my eyes with my forearm as I retreated safely from view.

"All right, all right, enough, gentlemen." No more than a minute had passed before I heard his voice, but I half expected him. He took an overly keen interest in my most discomfiting moments. "We'll get you your refills." He crouched next to me and tossed down a rag before scooping the mugs up with one hand. "Just leave it," he whispered. "You can get the rest."

I grabbed two of the mugs from the table in one hand like Fastello but left the rest where they stood. I was done opening myself up to the embarrassment. I padded across the room, swerving between tables, tuning out the chatter and laughter, and slammed the two mugs next to the large barrel.

"They want cinnamon added," I snapped at Fastello as I filled the second of the mugs, ramming my stump against the tap as I held the mug beneath it. "You can take them back to the kitchen. I take the orders. You bring them out." I flicked the tap off and rubbed my arm over my eyes to keep the tears from falling.

Fastello unloaded the five mugs he was precariously carrying in his arms onto the counter beside the ale and sighed. "You don't think Meggy would just let me bring the cinnamon out here to add it, do you?"

I exhaled sharply and slammed the filled mug down beside the empty ones, not caring that the liquid sloshed over my hand and onto the counter. "I don't think Meggy's looking for any suggestions on how to run her place." I grabbed another mug and jabbed my stump against the tap.

"'Spices are worth more than ale; can't leave the gold out for taking, now can you?'" mocked Fastello, doing a poor imitation of Meggy's voice, but a rather accurate portrayal of her tone.

I laughed despite myself, choking on the sound as a sob became a hiccup.

Fastello put a hand on my shoulder. "You doing all right?"

"Wonderful," I spat, trying to keep him from prying. I almost told him the truth. That I would never be all right again. That I had lost my home, lost my family, that I had lost the ability to tell the world about everything I stood for, but I knew it would lead to an argument, and we'd just had one of those. He'd claim he felt much the same. *But running away from a family of heathens isn't the same as knowing your family was lost to the flames.*

I got into the rhythm of filling the mugs, not even caring if any of the customers noticed it wasn't a fist I was making. But no one said anything. The laughter and murmuring continued unabated, with me lost in the background, just as Fastello had planned. Just as I'd never wished for. Not like this.

The swish of the silver dresses. Sparkling like stars reflected in the water. I squeezed Malle's hand and we watched, enraptured. The mothers towered over us in the meadow, singing and dancing.

"All right." The clink of the metal mugs snapped me out of my memory, and I watched as Fastello balanced two mugs full in each hand, supported between his chest and his arms. "I guess I'll take two trips," he said.

I nodded, shut off the tap, and placed the last of the mugs beside the barrel. I leaned back against the counter and let my eyes roam the room, looking for customers with their hands raised or new customers entirely.

So this is what it comes to. Toiling away as the sun is still setting. Filling my mind with useless thoughts of who needs food and ale.

But still, in some ways, checking on the dining area was more relaxing than staying in the kitchen. The kitchen with bossy Meggy, nosy Fastello, and now another ungrateful heathen, betraying Ytoile at the first sign of trouble. As long as I kept my head down, I could go unnoticed in the restaurant between orders. I could shut my eyes a moment and pray.

The door to the alley opened, ringing the bell Meggy hung atop it to signal the flow of customers. My eyes snapped open and fell upon the scraggly man who entered, sweat or oil stains glistening atop his large forehead and poking through the wispy straw-colored hair. I slipped my stump into my apron and stepped around the counter to follow him to his table, my nose curdling with what I had to be imagining—at that distance—was the odor of the man's filth. He was dressed plainly, but well enough, and his greasy face looked misshapen atop the fine black tunic and cape. He seated himself in a dim corner at the table recently vacated by Agnes, my new snobbish heathen companion in hiding.

I cleared my throat, jumping back at how quickly the man snapped to attention. "Welcome to Meggy's," I said, almost as quiet as a whisper. "Do you know what you want to order?"

"Yes." The man interlocked his fingers and rested his arms atop the table, his eyes darting quickly between me and the door. For a moment, he just repeated the rapid glances and then he threw his shoulders back suddenly. "Oh. Yes. An ale. Please. Not too full."

I nodded and turned but stopped as I felt a tug at the back of my skirt. I turned around to see the greasy man's hand wrapped tightly around the fabric of my dress.

"Actually, two please. Ales, that is." He opened his mouth widely, showing off two rows of yellowing, overly-spaced teeth. One of the front ones jutted out a bit too far. I shuddered instinctively and then nodded and left, practically ripping my skirt out of the man's grip and running across the room as if there had been a cockroach crawling over my dress. I filled two fresh mugs three-quarters to the top and kept my eyes peeled for Fastello.

"Not sure that table needs another round." He appeared beside me, scooping up the remaining mugs from the previous order. He nodded at me. "That a new order?"

"Yes." I put the second of the mugs on the counter.

Fastello balanced his third mug against his chest, giving it a boost with an awkwardly raised knee. "Just two? No spices?"

"No, but—"

"Bring it to them, please!" Fastello stepped around the corner and called over his shoulder.

"Fastello—"

He grinned, squishing the too-full mugs tighter. "You can do it, Cateline."

Holding two mugs at once wasn't the problem. *Ttoile, give me the strength to keep going. Speak to me. Let me know that You're still watching.* I gripped both mugs in my hand, balancing them in front of me carefully.

The greasy man's guest had arrived. A lady. Her brown hair was rather puffed and gaudy, hanging over her shoulders in several loose curls. Her dress was a beautiful blue color, but I noticed as I stepped closer that it was rather dingy and ill-fitting on her broad shoulders. I put the mugs down quietly and slid the first one to the man. He nearly elbowed it—no wonder he asked for it not to be too full—as he reached across the table to squeeze his companion's pale hand.

"All will be well," he whispered hoarsely. The grin he gave her was the exact opposite of reassuring. A shiver ran down my back as I pictured what may lay in store for the woman, what kind of woman would show up at a seedy place like this in a failed attempt to seem classy, with a man who had probably at least half tried to appear seemly.

"Cateline!" The soft voice startled me as I slipped the mug in her direction. The woman jumped back, taking her hand from the man, and I saw her face for the first time.

"*Malle.*" The name slipped past my lips and the hand that moved to cover them before I could even think.

The man pulled back his now-empty hand awkwardly across the wooden table, wrapping it around the mug I'd slid before him. He displayed his terrible set of teeth at me. "You two lovely ladies know each other?" His voice cracked, as if each word were difficult for him to admit.

My eyes fell upon Malle, and she looked away, linking her hands together across her lap. I studied her profile. She was still a bit pretty, but the months had washed away much of her bloom already. If she'd found work as a woman who did most heinous things in the night, an affront to Ytoile far greater than working in a tavern in the daylight...

Malle cleared her throat. "We did once."

I glanced around the room, eager to know if anyone was looking at us, but everyone still seemed lost in their conversations.

You asked Ytoile to send you a sign. This is your chance to show Her you still believe.

I stepped around the table and slid into the third seat. I couldn't tell if it was joy or disappointment that flashed over the greasy man's face before he covered it up with a swig of his mug. I reached across my body to lay my hand on Malle's lap. "What are you doing here?" I whispered.

"Nothing—" said Malle.

"Looking for Meggy," answered the man. I examined him, and he wiped a hand across his mouth, collecting foam onto his fingers. He gestured toward his companion. "For her. Not me." He sucked the foam off of his forefinger.

As if that explained exactly why Malle would be interested in Meggy.

I thought of that blonde, snooty heathen in the kitchen—

"You need..." I started, speaking as if my throat were hoarse. I squeezed Malle's fist, a wash of comfort flooding through my body. "You need help. Because you still believe."

Malle whipped her head sharply to meet my eyes again, and she yanked her hands out of my grip. "I most certainly do *not* care about that crazy religion," she hissed quietly.

I drew my hand back as if her words had been fire. "You're just scared," I said, more to convince myself than to convince her. "Ytoi—"

The man's mug tipped all over the table, sending half of what was left tumbling into my lap. "Shhh!" The man's wild hands flapped two index fingers across his mouth. "Don't say that name! Be careful, the both of you!" he spat, more loudly than he probably intended.

His hysterics drew more attention than anything Malle or I had said. I stood and smiled at the two men a few tables over who'd bothered to look over, tucking my stump beneath my armpit and shaking my apron free of the dripping wetness as if I'd simply been there to clean a mess a drunk pervert had made. The other men went back to their conversation.

The greasy man ran a hand through his hair as if to calm himself and then reached out to grab my apron. "Sit," he said, more sternly than I'd expected of him.

I did, not because of the man's command, but because I was sure that Ytoile had told me I had to save Malle, turn her back onto the path.

"We came for help." The greasy man cleared his throat. "My name—"

"*Lord Sherrod*," said Malle, keen to get his attention.

"—is not important," said 'Lord Sherrod' sharply, his dull blue eyes sending an unspoken message to his companion across the table. He leaned toward me, lowering his voice yet somehow still exuding arrogance with each sentence. "Suffice to say, I had much the same past as my, uh, *friend* Malle here." He righted his empty mug and set it aside so he could lean in even closer. "Of course I don't still believe. I know dear Malle doesn't believe." I chewed my lips, stopping the hiss of "heathens" that was about to escape from them. "But soldiers are demanding that children of the tower prove that they left their beliefs behind when they left the tower behind, and pretty little Malle has only been gone a short while. There have been inquiries after her in the night ladies' quarters."

I turned to look at Malle, and her eyes dropped immediately to the floor. "It's not even been half a year," I hissed, "could you find nothing more respectable to pay Her back for all She'd done for you—"

"What did *She* ever do for me?"

Lord Sherrod pounded the table with a fist. "Enough!" He smiled, but the upturn of his lips faltered. "I risked a lot to come here. A whole lot." He leaned forward to glare at Malle, all trace of friendliness wiped from his features. "And you'll be grateful and quiet and meek for it, won't you?"

"I *paid* you already," Malle said. Her lips quivered.

Lord Sherrod raised what he seemed to have forgotten was an empty mug to his lips. "Yes, well, maybe I found the payment somewhat *lacking*."

I studied Lord Sherrod and Malle, trying to understand everything that had passed between them. That greasy disgusting man kept pretending to drink his ale, his eye shifting sideways to regard me. His gaze traveled down. To where I'd rested my stump atop the table without realizing. He lowered his mug just enough that I saw his tongue run over his lips slowly.

I jumped up and tucked the arm beneath my armpit, spinning to grab Malle's arm. "Thank you, *Lord Sherrod*." I emphasized his name, saying it perhaps a little too loudly.

Lord Sherrod slammed his mug back on the table. "Don't call me that *here*—"

"You've gotten her where she needs to be. I'm sure she's grateful."

"Yes," stuttered Malle as I dragged her around the table.

"The ale is on the house," I spat, using the term Meggy had taught me quite expressly *never* to use. "Thank you, you can go now."

I weaved skillfully through the tables, dragging a meekly protesting Malle behind me. *Lord Sherrod* said something more, but I ignored it, tugging on Malle so she wouldn't turn to respond.

"*Cateline*," she whispered hoarsely, "you can't make that man angry. He's the du—"

I brought Malle around the corner and into the kitchen, three staring faces greeting us as we entered.

"Who's she?" asked Fastello, the ladle with which he was scooping stew from a pot now dripping onto the floor.

I tugged on Malle in her gaudy lady of the night dress and positioned her in front of the remaining dough, using both hands to steer her shoulders.

"Meggy," I said, looking over my shoulder. "You've got another worker for the next couple of days."

I could hear Meggy's guttural laughter, the chop of a hatchet into a flank of meat. "Every able hand is needed."

Hand. Not *hands*. I wondered if she'd been careful with what she'd said. I rolled my shoulders and showed Malle how to toss the dough. I leaned over her shoulder and whispered, "Just don't mention I gave the ale away for free."

16

KOJIRO

Knock. Knock knock knock. Knock knock.

I heard the cadence of the knocks that Tierny had told me was code for the underground. Still, with no way of seeing who stood above me, my shoulders tensed and I clutched at the weapon I'd tucked beneath the sash around my hips. It was ready to go, but I'd have only one chance. My chest squeezed, my head pounded, the nausea fled up from my stomach to my throat—

"Jiro," he said, using the shortened form of my name which we agreed seemed less regal, "I'm letting you up."

My shoulders relaxed. I hadn't even realized I'd hunched them.

The trap door in the ship cabin swept aside and Tierny reached a hand down to help me. His face darkened slightly with the effort, but I held on to the sides of the opening and scrambled up. Tierny laughed, the redness receding from beneath his gold and gray beard. "You got some heft on you. That's good."

"'Heft'?" I repeated, and Tierny laughed again, waving a hand.

He stepped across his cabin and tossed me the cloak that hung over the chair at his desk. "Keep the hood up. It's dark, but people are already on alert."

I swung the cloak around my shoulders, but at his words, my hands froze as I was about to lift the hood to cover my head.

Tierny saw my look and waved dismissively. "Not for outsiders. They didn't even bother to do more than check the barrels this time, not that there was anyone else to find, and not that I'd be stupid enough to keep hiding outsiders in barrels. No. It's Stargazers who are currently victim of the duke's wrath."

Stargazers. The people who believed in the night sky goddess.

I finished sliding the hood over my hair, smoothing the cloak to cover more of my body, even if I was wearing barbarian sailor attire. "Are not you all..." My mouth grew dry, finding it hard to pronounce the goddess' name. "Followers of the star goddess?"

Tierny shrugged. "Most people were. On the surface, at least. Not anymore." He scraped his neck with his fingers. "Death to any left claiming worship. No hesitation." He dug a cloak for himself out of a chest in the corner. "It's better not to think too hard about the duke's whims. Just be sure to keep track of them."

I shook my head. As if one would simply stop believing in the sun spirit and all the spirits around us if Mother had told them to. Not that she would ever tell them to. It was the spirits that made our family divine, even if she believed too fully in her own divinity.

Tierny stepped in front of me and gestured after him. "No time to adjust to not using your sea legs, Jiro. I only have a short time, and I need to get you to a safe place that can get you out of the city."

I followed Tierny onto the deck of the ship, relishing the cool air as it brushed my face, but quickly bringing the hood down further despite the brief moment of peace the fresh air had allowed me. I scrambled down the plank, stumbling as I adjusted to the ground no longer swaying. True to his word, Tierny didn't wait for me to right myself, leading me down a blackened alley, dodging the glow provided by a hanging torchlight.

Despite the lateness of the hour, there were people everywhere. I quickly lowered my face so no one would see it, but I felt my throat constrict when I saw the muck in which Tierny and I were stepping, the puddles across the strange stone roads either water or piss or blood. I took broad strides, dancing from one almost-clean stone to the next several paces away, until Tierny stopped suddenly and I slammed into his back.

"Walk normally," he hissed. "The people here get their feet dirty."

I gulped. And dragged that mud and muck and feces into their homes and shops, I knew. I'd read it all in *Denunciation of a Primitive Culture*, one of Yukishige's essays.

Tierny picked up the pace and I took a deep breath, feeling the calming freshness of the air caress my lungs. I stepped forward, one foot after the other, ignoring the shot of dizziness I felt each time my foot stepped into something soft or squishy.

"Hey, you!" Someone grabbed my arm. "Got plans for the night?"

I spun, almost dropping the hood, my fingers dancing across the top of the sash. Thin arms encased in ratty, rough red fabric had my arm in a tight grip; something soft and flower-scented bumped into my shoulder.

Tierny stepped in front of me, prying the arms off. "Not tonight, sweetheart. Me and him already have company."

"Not just each other, I hope." The woman giggled. "Although *I* might pay *you* to see that, handsome." The soft timbre of her laughter was joined by echoes of similar giggling voices.

Tierny grabbed me by the elbow and pulled me onward. "Avoid the ladies of the night." We stopped moving, and I noticed a slight twitch at the corner of his mouth. "At least when there are rumors the soldiers are combing their chambers."

He dropped my arm and guided me onward, through one alley and the next, through more puddles and muck than I ever imagined could exist.

At last he turned a corner and stopped again. No one was in this alley, and there was no torch to light our path. Something pulsated in the dark beneath me, like the heartbeat of the city, buried in mud and feces. I lifted a foot and shook it, suddenly feeling like I was covered in rats and insects.

Knock. Knock knock knock. Knock knock. Tierny's fist pounded on a door I hadn't even realized stood partway down the stone wall. He pounded the pattern again. And then once more.

"All right, enough." A woman's throaty voice called back from the other side of the doorway. I waited patiently, bouncing my knees and reminding myself that even a city as filthy as this one couldn't possibly have as many spiders and vermin as I pictured now crawling up my leg.

The door opened, revealing a squat and stocky woman holding a candle in my face.

I looked down and saw my foot squished into the pile of what I hoped was horse excrement and all the maggots and worms squirming in it.

I shook my leg, uttering as many curses as I could think of as quietly as I could manage before I slammed one hand into the wall, fighting the nausea. Breathing in, breathing out.

"Sure, why not? I've got a full house already, but what's another?" The woman grunted. "Haven't gotten an outsider in some time."

It was the Hanaobian curse words that had given me away. Since she already knew, I ripped the hood off my head and leaned against the wall, looking up, letting the cool air soothe my flushed face. You could hardly see a star in the sky.

"This one is special." Tierny leaned in toward the woman and whispered something, and the stout woman's scrunched-up features softened. Her eyes met mine and I felt her searching for something. Perhaps some semblance of royal lineage.

Finding nothing, as I expected her to, she shrugged. I was no Elder Brother Nobutada. No Tomiko. No Mother. But maybe that was better, to blend into this world of filth and darkness.

Tierny put his hands on both my shoulders. "Jiro, this is Meggy. She'll get you to the farms." He turned his head slightly as if to wait for Meggy's confirmation, and she nodded and stepped back inside the building. Tierny leaned in closer, his voice dropping, his language switching to his lilting Hanaobian. "I cannot accompany you further. The duke expects me, and I've spent enough time away. I'm already being suspected." He patted my shoulders and stepped back. "Remember the plan." Tierny tipped his hat and stepped away.

"Tier—" I stopped, not wanting to speak his name loudly in this place. "Teacher. Thank you."

Tierny smiled and ran a hand across his beard.

"Come along then!" Meggy's voice hissed from inside the building.

I stepped inside into the candle's warm glow. Meggy shut the door behind me and pointed to a piece of metal set up beside the doorway. She stared at me expectantly. "Well? Put it in then, would you?"

I scrambled to heave the rod up, not sure what to do until Meggy indicated the metal studs on either side of the doorway. To keep the door shut. In this land of barbarians, there were locks and rods and secrecy. When the city was so dirty, it was no wonder people were eager to hide behind closed doors, shutting the rest of the barbarians away.

"This way," said Meggy quietly. I followed her, taking in the hallway and the wide open room with empty tables that we passed, only just visible in the darkness under the dome of candle glow. "Up here." She put a foot on a wooden stairway. I followed, eager not to let the candlelight leave me behind.

"You've got company," said Meggy as we reached the top, and I wasn't at all sure I understood her. She spoke too quickly, and her voice was rough. "It's rather crowded in the room I have to spare." She stopped and slid the candle above her head in order to stare into my face. "And you'll have to go in the cellar tomorrow, I'm sorry. Can't close up shop, and I can't risk any nosy drunkards wandering back into the kitchen."

I nodded meekly. I at least picked up the important part: I was going to hide in a cellar, cut off from light, trapped under ground like vermin in a filthy, disgusting place.

"But," said Meggy, turning back around. "You won't be there long. Escort's picking you all up tomorrow night. And I figure you should meet who you're going with." She stopped in front of a door and knocked in the same pattern Tierny had taught me. "It's me."

"All right," called a voice from behind the door. I waited a moment and this time I heard the metal clink of a rod being moved from the door. It swung open, and Meggy's candle revealed a young barbarian, the top of his head almost a full hand-length taller than my own. His light brown eyes almost immediately began to study me. "Who's this?"

"What is it?" I heard a soft voice from inside the room. It was a dainty voice, almost as ethereal and lovely as Tomiko's.

The man turned his head behind me. "Stay there a second, Cateline."

I could feel my face flushing. Had we walked in on them... It was night, and I'd read about how people become parents.

Meggy slapped a hand on my back and I almost fell over in

surprise. "This here is...?" She stopped, turning, as if waiting for me to speak.

"Jiro," I spat uncomfortably, mimicking the way Tierny said it, with a hard emphasis on the 'ji.' He seemed to think it would be easier for barbarians to pronounce, and he worried if any of them had heard of a Prince Kojiro. I didn't think to point out that surely if my name reached across the sea, a shorter form wouldn't do much to disguise it. Maybe I was expecting too much of barbarians.

"Another one set for the farms tomorrow night," said Meggy. She pushed me forward. "May as well get to know him. He'll be in the cellar come dawn and all day tomorrow, so make use of what time you've got." She turned to go. "But get some sleep, all of you! I've got plenty of work for you tomorrow."

Someone groaned from inside the room. The man stepped aside and I shuffled inside, awkwardly moving out of the way as he lifted the bar back over the doorway. I heard him take a few steps and scratch something against rock, and then he appeared before me with a lit candle in his hand. He was.... Maybe it was just the effect of the dim candlelight, but his face was darker than I expected for a barbarian. His hair was brown instead of the golden color I'd more often seen on the sailors.

"I *must* be dreaming," hissed a woman, a voice much lower than I'd heard before.

"Oh *no*, I'm not risking my life traveling with *him*." Yet another woman's voice.

A gasp. "Ytoile have mercy." It was that first voice, the small and dainty one.

"Cateline, what did I tell you about that name?" The young man again.

"Ytoile, my mother, my shining star. Watch over us and bless us from the night sky—"

"*Cateline!*" A second woman.

"I must have angered *some* deity. I cannot believe my life has taken this turn. I won't go!" A different woman. So many women. How many women?

The man with the candle brushed past me and stepped toward the center of the room. "All right, ladies, please. Let's let, uh, Jiro say hello."

The candlelight revealed *three* young women, one in a barbarian-style raised bed and two on beds made of, I believe, empty sacks of flour on the floor. An additional sack lay crumpled up as far as possible on the other side of the room, but there was so little room, the man was basically sleeping with both of the women on the floor. I flushed, my eyes taking in the women's faces under the candlelight, each lovelier than the last.

"Do you understand us? Do you speak the language?" asked the man. I nodded, and he switched the candle to his left hand and extended his right. I knew I was supposed to take it in mine and bob it up and down, but after what I'd seen in the city, I was in no mood to participate in more unclean barbarian practices. The man raised his eyebrows and pulled his hand back, wiping it on his tunic. "I'm Fastello."

"*Fastello*," hissed the woman on the bed. She had the yellow hair I'd associated with barbarians, the flattened ringlets hanging loosely out of a half-finished bun. "I'm *not* traveling anywhere with an..." Her voice lowered. "...*outsider*."

"Then you're welcome to turn yourself in to the duke's soldiers, Agnes." Fastello cleared his throat. "It might make for a more pleasant trip for the rest of us that way."

"You—You *barbarian!*" The word was strange coming from a barbarian herself. Agnes threw a floppy pillow across the room, which Fastello dodged easily. Agnes pulled a sheet over her head and then flopped back onto the bed. "I'm not staying awake for another second. I've never worked so hard in my life!"

Fastello scoffed and shrugged his shoulders. I turned to the other two women, on the floor. The one nearest Agnes seemed to feel my eyes on her, and she faced me, smiling gently. "I'm Malle." Her long hair was brown, like Fastello's, but her face was much paler. She turned to the woman beside her expectantly. My eyes followed.

And for just one moment, all pain vanished from my chest, a warmth spreading from my fingers to my toes. She had hair the color of flames, wild and wavy, and the palest face I'd ever seen, as white as a swan's feathers. It was peppered with small brown marks, like kisses from the sun spirit. I longed to see her eyes, but they were closed, her hands clasped together before her throat.

"Ytoile, my mother, my shining star..." I just realized that she hadn't stopped murmuring the chant since she'd first started.

Fastello leaned forward, blocking my view of the sun spirit maiden. "This is Cateline," he said sharply. His nose scrunched up. "I have a feeling she might have a bit of a problem getting to know you." He cleared his throat. "She probably thinks you're a demon."

The warmth vanished, the pain choking its way back up my throat again.

17

ROHESIA

How Sherrod expected me to walk down the filthy streets unnoticed, I could not say. Perhaps he thought I would have no need for cover, using my face and Father's soldiers to demand cooperation from every seedy merchant and bustling tavern keeper I passed. But some people would rather die than talk. Father had shown me that, too, at an early age.

Better to wait here, in a filthy alley on the outskirts of the slums, waiting for Sherrod to consort with all his favorite people. I watched a group of maggots feeding on the massive pile of dung someone had dumped right outside the back door of a tavern. At least I had no interest in eating there.

"My lady!" called Sherrod as soon as he turned the corner. He trotted awkwardly, as if attempting to run, and by the time he reached me, I could smell the foulness he exhaled with each pant.

I flicked my wrist and let a dagger slip into my palm, extending my hand and stopping it just short of the man's neck.

"Lady Rohesia..." Sherrod whimpered. He licked his lips.

"Don't shout my title. Don't say my name. Not here." I stood up from the barrel I'd used as a seat and slid the blade back into my sleeve. The look on Sherrod's face was something like strained gratification, but if he thought he hid the anger well, he was mistaken.

"Of course, my—of course." He cleared his throat and wiped his sweaty forehead with the back of his arm. A new suit, I noticed, wondering briefly what sort of activities required him to look several stations above himself. I shook the images away. Ill-fitting, just like the suit itself.

I adjusted the hilt of the small dagger into the scabbard I kept stored beneath my sleeve. "Well?" I asked at last, when no information was forthcoming.

"Oh. Yes." Sherrod clicked his heels together. "A merchant was willing to accept my price. I mean, *your* price. He gave up a farmer, and he told me where he lives."

I nodded. "Bring our horses to the gates. You'll take me there."

"Today?" Sherrod seemed as puzzled as he'd be if I'd asked him to accompany me to Hanaobi.

"Right now," I answered sharply, and he was off, dashing through the dung and puddles as if afraid he'd catch my dagger in his back.

"Men like Sherrod have their uses." If Sherrod was so useful, I wondered not for the first time why Father had entrusted him to me. *Or entrusted me to him.* I'd seen as much, probably more, of the walking pile of grease growing up as I had Father.

For the first time in years when outside the castle, I didn't wear my full armor. To be honest, I hadn't worn my leg guards since almost as soon as I tried them on and realized they turned me into someone with half the speed and twice the noise. But walking the streets of the city without my chest plate and helmet made me feel strangely weaker somehow, even if I knew the daggers were at my wrists and my blade at my waist. I switched the cape for a cloak to offer some cover for my face, but the only things I didn't leave behind were the steel-toed boots that had proven so useful when climbing tree trunks. *That, and the jade lion.* I patted the pouch on my belt, where I'd stored the small statue, useless dead weight I somehow couldn't bring myself to leave on my bedside table. I'd even left the silver flute behind to make room for it.

Mother has spent enough years left behind in that castle.

And maybe that was why I'd seen so much death every time I set forth from that place.

I made it to the gates without being accosted, just another hooded figure hiding someone someone else might want to slay, with a hand on her hilt and an eye on the ground. That said, if they'd noticed I was a woman, it would be clear who I was. But there was a way of walking that would keep me from drawing attention. When I got to the gate, I threw back the hood and instructed the soldiers to let me pass, and to tell Sherrod to catch up with me on the road. Despite having the horses, he took longer to show than I had patience for.

There was a pounding of hooves behind me. "My la—My—I'm here!"

I raised an eyebrow as Sherrod appeared breathlessly on horseback, as if he'd run himself instead of leaving all of the work to the horses. "My title is acceptable out here." I would already stand out, no matter what I did, and I wondered if it would be so bad if some people knew I was looking for them. I stuck a boot into the stirrup and swung my leg over Sunset's back, patting her neck and gathering her reins in my hands. I stared at Sherrod. "Well?"

"Oh! Yes, of course. My lady." Sherrod shook his horse's reins rather awkwardly and led the way.

We did not speak for all the time it took to travel the road and then to cut across the fields, past crops, between livestock, and among curious farmers. Everywhere we turned, the charred remains of the tower loomed down on me. It had stopped smoking, but I would always smell their flesh.

Sherrod stopped at a hilltop and pointed at a small cottage some distance away. "That one. I didn't think we should ride up any closer." He cleared his throat. "It might draw attention."

Clever Sherrod, good boy, I wanted to say, but I stopped myself just short of treating him like a man whose obedience and intelligence were equal to that of a dog. My hand brushed the pouch at my hips. "Yes. Thank you, Sherrod."

I dismounted and handed the reins over to Sherrod, who took them after a moment, his mouth agape. His mouth flapped at last. "Pardon, my lady?"

I cleared my throat, reminding myself annoyingly of Sherrod. I averted my eyes, not acknowledging his request that I repeat it. "You may return now."

"What? No, I couldn't—"

I glared up at him. "But you will."

Sherrod seemed aghast. "My lady, but if his lordship knew I'd left you here *alone* and for what purpose..."

I patted his horse's neck. "Then I suggest you come up with some other way to explain my absence. I won't be able to accomplish what I set out to do unless I can observe without being noticed. And that means I do it alone."

Sherrod swallowed perceptibly. "Very well, my lady, but I do not advise—"

I waved a hand and set off down the hill. "Come back for me in the morning."

The wheat yet harvested provided more than enough cover to make my way closer to the cottage. I settled comfortably among the stalks for the long wait ahead.

IT WAS DUSK BEFORE THERE WAS ANY SIGN OF UNUSUAL MOVEMENT at the cottage. I'd counted the farmer, his wife, and two young sons coming and going throughout the day, spending most of the time in the fields or the small barn but returning for food or water. No sign of outsiders. Perhaps this farm didn't have need of them. I snacked on a piece of bread I'd tucked in along with the jade lion, fully intending to spend most of the day watching. My instinct told me nothing unlawful would happen while under the light of day, but I had to be sure, as the nomads were certainly becoming bolder in recent weeks.

While watching, I made sure to collect as many details as possible. The farmers' clothing was in rather good shape for the work they did. There was plenty of food for just four people—I could see into an open window—when the price of crops was soaring and farmers were required to purchase their own crops back from the duchy in exchange for using Father's lands. They hadn't failed to give their crops to the soldiers who had collected it, or they wouldn't be so brazenly out here in the open. *A small farm. No need for extra hands. So how do they have enough money to afford all this?*

The farmers settled at the table after dinner, after they'd put the dishes in a bucket and put all food away. Except then the mother set two new places at the table, scooping her rice and stew onto two recently-cleaned plates.

The rustle of the stalks beside me caught my attention. I crouched down further, watching as two shadowy figures disturbed the fields. *From the direction of the forest. Sherrod, you and your "connections" did it.*

Two men came out of the field, the first dangling a small pouch in his hand. They knocked on the cottage door. Knock. Knock knock knock. Knock knock. That wasn't a random pattern.

The door opened and the farmer let the men in, greeting them as dearly as bosom friends. Their voices were muffled inside the cottage, but I watched as the men stepped clearly into view, their ever-tanned skin apparent in the glow of candlelight. The first man handed the farmer the pouch, and the two sat down to dig into the meal awaiting them.

The farmer emptied the pouch into his wife's hand. *Jewels. Coins.* Enough to sell and enough to buy whatever they needed for months to come. *Maybe even years.* The thought startled me, a stark reminder of the state of things for those outside the city. I caressed my jade lion through the pouch and waited, watching.

It was some time later that the nomads finally went on their way, and the family they left behind blew out their candles and went to bed. I waited until the men were almost completely out of sight, mere rustlings in the field of wheat, to creep out from my hiding place and risk skirting around the field, intending to catch them as they came out at the side nearest the forest.

They didn't disappoint. By the time I reached the edge of the field, they were already up the hill and crossing the road, sure to lead me to their campsite. I hung back, waiting as long as I dared, darting out as softly as I could, ducking behind trees or stones or whatever would provide cover. There were moments when there was no place for me to hide, when I knew that even under the cover of darkness, I'd be seen if either man turned, but they never did. Their speech was unclear, but the tone of their voices so relaxed, so trusting. They thought they had the world to themselves, that what they did was as natural as the flow of the river. The men skirted the trees and ducked inside, near the forest's end.

I hung back a minute more and followed, placing my foot in the worn brush with such care I was afraid I'd lose sight of them entirely. But there was no mistaking this path. The trodden brush shot off in different directions—perhaps different paths the nomads took, to appear from the trees in different locations—but they all merged in one heading straight for the river. I could hear the men's voices languishing on the air behind them, mixed in with the steady trickling flow of the water. I paused before the river, not sure where they might have gone, before noticing the soft glow of firelight poking through the leaves and brush. But I hadn't seen the smoke outside the forest. We never did—that was why they were proving so difficult to track. *Not that Father ever bothered to take the stealthy route.* "Run them down, like the rain from the sky. Wash them out. Let them know they have no hope of beating you."

I drew my sword from its scabbard and rested the hilt atop my head, one hand balancing it flat against my hair. I waded through the river, which reached up to my waist, grateful I'd left the armor behind, and slipped the sword back in its scabbard as I cleared the other side of the water. I kept my head low to the ground, sneaking closer to the light, until I reached the edge of the forest, stopping abruptly behind a bush.

Their camp was in a cave. A cavern in the side of the cliff that housed the waterfall back by the tower. A great fire roared, and people moved to and fro tents that surrounded it. Some of the tents boldly stood outside of the cave, hidden by the cliff wall from those who might pass several miles away on the road to the tower. No, it was just the fire they wished to hide, the smoke that might signal where they were stationed. The fire and the music, soft but echoing deep inside the cavern.

So many people. I'll need to come back with soldiers. I didn't dare move the branches of the bush, so sure I was that the rustle might call attention to the forest. There were children playing a mere arm's length away. Two little boys who ran into the arms of the men I'd followed, each insisting their fathers put them up on their shoulders. The boys rode the men like upright horses, laughing as their fathers neighed and skipped and weaved their way through the crowd of people.

"Wash them out."

Infants floating down one of the rivers into the sea.

Once I told Father, there would be more blood spilt. More children...

One man at the fireside, his arms draped around two busty women on either side, a third woman rubbing his foot, shooed the woman holding his foot with a slight kick in the air, and stood as the two men and their boy riders approached him.

He clapped his hands together. "They were grateful, no?"

The man nearest bent down so his child could climb onto the ground and the other followed suit. He was still laughing. "As ever. Had one of the finest dinners I've had in years."

"Did you bring us any?" asked one of the boys, his hand extended.

The man patted his belly. "Yeah, in here." He bent down and tickled the boy, who screeched and squirmed away, his friend tagging after him. He stood. "They say we're welcome any evening, in small groups."

The man who'd risen from the fire raised both hands in the air and spun around. The music stopped. "Hear that? Another poor family fed, and kind enough to share the booty!"

There was a loud cry of triumph around the camp, a shouting that wove itself into laughter. One of the women who'd sat next to man who'd started the cheer brought him a large wooden cup, which he immediately took and brought up his lips. He wiped a ring of foam that lingered on his brown beard and grabbed the woman roughly, pressing himself against her. "Davazanto!" I heard her say playfully, as he peppered her cheek with kisses. Davazanto raised the cup up. "To life!" he shouted.

"To life!" echoed his voice, repeated again and again as the crowd screamed into the cavern.

"To sharing the wealth!"

"To sharing the wealth!"

"To our mother!" Davazanto stepped back and gestured his cup at the fire.

A woman sat before the fire, not on the ground but in a chair. She rocked back and forth, the silver hem of her dress brushing against the dust on the ground with each movement. She nodded at the cups extended in her direction, a small smile forming at her lips.

"To our mother!" echoed the crowd. They hugged their neighbors or flung an arm around them, and the rustle of all the movement fluttered the rocking woman's silver hair like a breeze.

Davazanto held his cup out again and waited for everyone to quiet. "Thanks to you, we will never have to steal again." He smiled at the old woman, took a long sip and tossed the mug on the ground before sweeping the dark-haired woman into his arms.

The crowd screamed and the music started up again, people rushing to grab their partners. I slithered backward, using the cover of the noise to mask my rustling. I pulled myself out of the bush, ready to crouch and waddle back toward the river. I turned slowly.

"Who are you?"

The boys who had ridden their fathers like horses appeared in the forest behind me.

Recognition seemed to pass on the taller boy's face. "An outsi—"

I flicked my wrists and gripped the handles of my twin daggers.

18

FASTELLO

My teacher couldn't have been taller than my abdomen. Her small fingers rubbed the kernels off the wheat stalk, and she stuck out her basket to collect them. Then she stopped, pointing to my basket and then to the wheat in front of me.

I tried to do what she did, sliding the leaves between my fingers, and some of the kernels snapped, the rest tumbling to the ground. The little girl grunted, said something softly in Hanaobian and bent down to collect the fallen grain.

"I'm sorry," I said, crouching down to join her. I held out a hand, pointing to it. "Big fingers."

The little girl pursed her lips and kept pinching the fallen grain between her fingers and dropping it into her basket. She muttered something, and whatever it was, it was clear I'd disappointed her. Her and every other female I'd encountered these days.

"She says you waste the crop."

I put a hand over my forehead to shield my eyes from the sun. Jiro slung a scythe handle over his shoulders and wiped a forehead beading with sweat with the back of his hand. I looked back to see his handiwork, a line of jagged clump of stalks, all still too tall, all uneven. "Did she say you couldn't handle a blade if your life depended on it, too?"

Jiro's lips hardened into a straight line. I still wasn't sure he understood everything we said, but I had a feeling it wasn't hard to understand the sentiment. I sighed and stood, stretching my arms over my head. "Switch with me." I held a hand out for the scythe. Jiro studied me a moment and then handed over the scythe without a word. He swept past me to grab the basket I'd left on the ground besides the Hanaobian girl.

I took a whack at the stalks the farmers had finished gathering grain from, standing back to marvel at the clean straight line I made below where Jiro had hacked rather irregularly. "Do you know any of these people?" I whacked again. "Jiro?"

Jiro turned slowly, his hand still crushing a stalk. "No. Why?"

I shrugged and brought the scythe back. "I just thought you might be running from home to join somebody you know."

The little girl shouted and stepped behind Jiro, looking at me and pointing to the perfectly straight line I'd made in the stalks.

It was the first time I'd seen even a brush of a grin appear on Jiro's face. "She says you cut them too tall. Way too tall."

I ran a hand through my hair and leaned on the scythe like I might on a walking stick. The girl crouched at the stalk in front of me and reached back, yanking at the scythe handle. I let her have it and she pulled at the stalks near the ground, almost completely felling them.

"Like this," Jiro translated.

She didn't seem to care when Jiro was the one hacking at the tops. I raised an eyebrow and took the proffered scythe from the girl, crouching where she had. It was more difficult for me to balance on the balls of my feet in order to grip the stalks near the root and pull the blade across them. "How come she didn't fall over when she crouched?" I panted.

Jiro laughed and crouched next to me, putting the basket between us. "You, uh..." He waved his hands. "...*crouched* strange."

I looked at Jiro and the girl, both crouched with the entirety of their feet on the ground and far better balanced than I was. "How do you..." Jiro waved a hand at his rear end. "...if you can't stay upright?"

I couldn't help but grin. "Did you just ask me how I shit, Jiro?"

Jiro's face, the strange oaken tone of his skin, blushed with slight redness. "Forget it," he said, but not brusquely.

We both laughed, but the little girl didn't think we were very funny. She gestured and spoke in her native tongue.

"Work more. Talk less," said Jiro, grabbing his basket and standing. A child could put us both in our places, and it was only the second day since we'd started working.

I gripped another bunch of wheat in my hand. But maybe neither of us was really in our place. I cut the grass, wondering if I'd ever find my place.

"Fastello!" A basket practically hit me in the face. I peered up, my hand over my eyes, to see the crossed arms and the pinched mouth that could only belong to Agnes. "I've had it! You need to talk to the farmer and get me out of here!"

I stood, feeling the aching warmth in my thighs as I stretched back up. "I'm not sure why I need to do anything for you, Agnes."

"You jest, surely!" Agnes clenched her fists to her side. "Need I remind you what you did to my servant and sister—"

I coughed. "It wasn't me."

"No, I'm sure you did everything you could to save them." Tears welled up in Agnes' eyes, but I couldn't be certain if they were there because of her loved ones or because her pale skin had started to burn despite the kerchief the farmer's wife had given her.

I sighed and leaned the scythe against the stalks, turning to Jiro. "I'll be right back." I nodded at the girl. "Don't let the boss work you too hard."

Jiro looked at the girl and took in the serious expression she wore before bursting out laughing, threshing a stalk for another bunch of kernels. The girl said something to him and he spoke back sharply, seriously, and I wondered if he'd be tasked with twice the work before I'd return.

Agnes seized my arm, digging her dirty nails into my skin and dragging me away. "Why are you getting so friendly with *them*?"

I scratched my head and let Agnes lead me toward the cottage, beside the barn we now called home. "Maybe because we're all going to be living here together?"

"Speak for yourself," spat Agnes. She'd slipped her arm through mine and we strolled down the path, like a rich man escorting a lady. Old habits died hard for Agnes.

"What do you propose then? Where do you hope to go?"

Agnes bit her lip. "I'd rather go back and work at the ridiculous tavern than do this."

"Huh. Because you worked there all of a day and a half and you kept moaning how you couldn't *wait* to get out of there."

"That was before I knew I'd be sweating like a peasant and tanning like a nomad!" She slipped her arm from mine and gestured to her filthy dress.

I didn't bother pointing out that she was as good as a peasant now. Or even worse off than one, since she was relying on others and in hiding. "I thought you didn't really believe in the stuff purported by the Stargazers," I said, tackling the jab at a nomad's skin tone instead. We tanned just as much as other people who spent time in the sun. We just started off a tad darker.

"I *don't*," Agnes snapped. "Which is why I shouldn't be in this mess to begin with!"

Oh, to have her problems. Although the only thing she had going for her was that she so quickly adapted to a world without Stargazers.

Cateline and Malle sat on the stoop of the porch of the cottage, shucking corn for dinner. Agnes crossed her arms as she towered over them. "Now doesn't that look *exhausting*? Isn't it nice to be put on cooking duty?" She looked around at the fields, at the near and distant forms of people at work. "To be on the only task where you're not surrounded by outsiders?"

Malle looked at me as if to ask what was wrong with this woman. Cateline stood, jabbing a finger at her. "Perhaps if you'd been more faithful, Ytoile would have prevented you from being burned by the sun demon!"

"*Cateline*," began Malle, a hand reaching over to tug on her skirt.

Agnes jutted her chin out. "Oh, don't attribute your luck to some distant star! The farmer took one look at that deformed *stump* of yours and had to find some way to make you useful!"

I put a hand on Agnes' shoulder. "*Agnes*! That—"

Cateline gestured to Malle seated below her, using the fingerless hand that Agnes had just mocked her for. "Then how do you explain my companion? Ytoile blessed Malle with this task in the shade as well."

Agnes sneered. "She's your friend. The farmer saw it, and—"

"Ladies, please—" I felt as if I wasn't even standing there between them.

"Enough!" called Malle, drawing everyone's attention. She turned to Agnes. "Farmer Mason and his wife have been kind enough to offer us shelter. I suggest you take advantage of that kindness, Agnes, and ask them for a more suitable task. The wife is in the kitchen—" She hadn't even finished before Agnes stepped up the stoop, brushing her skirt over Malle's head, and went inside the cottage.

Malle stared forward blankly, as if determined to ignore Agnes' rudeness. She swallowed and looked up at Cateline. "Cateline, *please* stop saying that name. I told you, I no longer follow that religion, and for your own good, you must remember all it did to you. All it *failed* to do."

Cateline slid back on the stoop beside Malle and took Malle's hand in hers, the two of them holding onto a corn cob together. "You have lost your way, Malle—"

"I have not!" Malle tore her hand away, throwing the cob into a basket with many others. A tear slipped out of her eye, and her lips wavered as she battled an onslaught of them. "Maybe *this* is the sign you need, Cateline!" She gestured around her. "Maybe there is a deity out there, and maybe being stuck here is Her way of finally getting you out of that tower!"

Cateline pulled her arm back as if slapped and cradled her fingerless hand against her chest. "I can't believe Ytoile would kill the mothers, and all those children for something like that. Ytoile—"

Malle shot up. "*Ytoile. Ytoile.* Enough! You're just as bad as the rest of them. I thought I could stay with you, Cateline. That we could be friends like we were long ago." She looked over my shoulder. "But you won't believe me. And I'm done." She bit her lip. "I'd rather go back to the city."

"It's settled! I'm going back to the city." The door banged open and Agnes stepped out, her hands flat against her hips. She took a deep breath and appraised the scene before her. "Mason's wife said I might be suited for city work on the underground. Since I don't look so *obviously* suspicious." Her nose wrinkled as she surveyed the fields and the Hanaobian farmers who toiled there.

"I'm coming with you, then." Malle cleared her throat.

"*Malle*," said Cateline softly.

Agnes looked Malle up and down. "I'm not sure the underground has need for whores, though."

"*Agnes!*" I couldn't believe the words coming out of her mouth.

Malle shook her head at me. "No, it's okay. She's right. I won't need to work on the underground, though. I just want to travel with her when the transporter next arrives."

Cateline stood, grabbing Malle's arm tightly. "Malle, you *can't*! That kind of work is sinful—"

Malle peeled Cateline's fingers away. "Enough preaching, Cateline. Remember what we talked about."

Cateline bit her lip. "But they're looking for you there."

Malle took a deep breath. "Not me specifically. They knew the women in the night house had recently taken in some grown orphans from the tower."

"Not Ava too?" Cateline's eyes were wide.

Malle reached out to pat Cateline's shoulder. "She's dead, Cateline. They got her the first night the duke proclaimed his order." She scoffed. "I told her to forget Ytoile. She wouldn't listen. Even after all those months. After what we'd become."

I sat down on the stoop, my legs suddenly weary. Agnes shrugged and went back inside the cottage, clearly uninterested in those who considered a couple of days working in a field more like a blessing than suffering.

"But then..." Cateline swallowed. "You can't go back there. What if the other women told the soldiers there was another?"

Malle sighed. "They did. I'm not going back. I—"

"Someone's coming!" I jumped to my feet, curling my hands around my eyes as if it would somehow let me see better. I whipped the door open. "Mistress Mason, there are two men on horses approaching!"

Agnes sat munching on a roll at the table, not at all perturbed by my news. Mistress Mason dropped the spoon she was using to stir a pot over the fire and rubbed her hands on her apron, dashing across the room to join me. She stepped outside. "Ring the bell!" she called back. "They know to hide."

The bell. How foolish I'd been. The Masons had told us if we ever heard the bell, we were to hide, the Hanaobians especially. Cateline jumped up and reached out to ding the supper bell that was certainly not for calling and would warn the field workers to stay away.

It did call one man, though. As most of the figures in the fields suddenly vanished, crouching beneath the crops, Farmer Mason jumped out of the fields onto the dusty road, running toward the men and horses. Or, as I took a better look, the man and the horses. One man, two horses.

The farmer's wife didn't once let her eyes wander from her husband. She gestured her hand behind me. "Girls, you can stay. Be our daughters. Fastello, you probably ought to go in—" She raised a finger. "Wait," she said, even though my hands were already on the door handle.

I supposed at this distance the stranger might wonder why someone had run inside at their approach. I pulled the kerchief I'd worn around my neck over the lower half of my face.

Mistress Mason let out a sigh of relief and smiled weakly. Farmer Mason was making strange gestures with his arms. "No, it's okay. It's okay. I thought it was odd. They don't usually come just by themselves. And they usually leave us be most days, this far out." She crossed the porch and rang the bell, in a strange practiced pattern. Ding. Ding ding ding. Ding ding. The figures appeared back in the fields and started working, as calmly and naturally as if this was simply the way of things. Which I supposed it was.

I noticed Cateline looking forward, her shoulders slumped and her fingerless hand tucked under her armpit. "Are you all right?" I asked, sliding in behind her.

Cateline looked up at me and nodded, but I didn't believe her. Her eyes darted from the approaching Farmer Mason and horses to Malle. "Malle, is that—"

Malle bit her lip and nodded. Then she straightened her shoulders and stepped forward.

"My lord!" she called, suddenly quite a different person. She seemed cheerful, although I swear I saw her smile faltering.

The man's horse trotted faster, as did the other horse, which he guided by clutching the reins. "My dear girl! I'd hoped to find you here, and so I did!"

He let go of both reins and swung his leg around, dropping to the ground and stumbling, kicking up dirt beneath him. He leaned on his horse to regain his balance, and then straightened and dusted off his tunic. "What are the odds?" he said. He smiled first at Malle and then at the farmers in turn. "I knew this was a safe place for those on the underground, and I was nearby—"

"What were you doing nearby?" I spat, removing the kerchief from my face. There was something about the short and greasy man that rubbed me the wrong way, and there was really nothing much out here. Nothing but some farms, the ruin of the Stargazer tower and... The edge of the forest. I clenched my fists.

The little lord examined me as if seeing me for the first time. He squinted his eyes and ran his tongue over his lips, but he said nothing. Even if he knew I was a nomad, he wasn't here for me.

"Malle," he said, stepping forth to grab the young woman's hands in his. "This has to be fate. You wanted to try the farming life, I know, but surely you can see that I made you a better offer."

"You've been most kind, Lord Sherrod." Malle bent her head and looked downward.

"I know your options are limited, but I can give you a good life, a safe life. I will get you your pardon and there will never be any question—"

Cateline ran down the stoop, her skirt clutched tightly in her hand to keep the hem from slowing her down. "You can't mean to *marry* this man, Malle! You told me he was one of your"—she gulped—"*customers*."

The lord's lip twitched. "Ah, your young friend is still with you."

Malle met Cateline's eyes and bit her lip. "Yes, but I'm done here," she said to Sherrod, although she was facing Cateline. She turned her head and slipped her arm through the lord's. "Yes, I will accept your offer, Lord Sherrod. Please take me back to the heart of the duchy."

"Malle!"

I watched the scene unfold before me, the puzzled Farmer Mason and his wife watching silently as the greasy little man awkwardly helped Malle up onto the second horse. Cateline looked on with horror, and I wasn't that sure Malle felt much differently, but her lips held firm in a steady line. The only one clearly overjoyed was the lord himself, but the look on his face turned my stomach, as it did whenever I saw it on Dad's, and he at least had the handsome features to make it somewhat pleasing. On the little lord's face, it looked more like he intended to devour his hostage bride rather than please her.

"That lucky whore." I jumped and noticed Agnes standing behind me, having opened the cottage door. She tore into what had to be her second or third biscuit. "A man like him will give her all she's ever wanted."

"A man like him?" I repeated, incredulous that the haughty and pretty blonde could watch the pair trot away on horseback with anything at all akin to envy.

"That's one of the duke's most trusted advisors," replied Agnes, finishing another bite. "Practically raised the duke's daughter. He's not really supposed to go anywhere without her." And then, as if all she said made perfect sense, she stuffed the rest of the biscuit into her mouth and stepped back into the cottage.

I watched the two until they disappeared over the last hill. He'd come by chance, with an empty horse. *One of the duke's most trusted advisors.* Then what was he doing, clearly involved in the underground?

"Agnes." I opened the door and stepped inside. "If you don't want to wait any longer, I'll escort you back to the city come nightfall. I know the underground."

So long as Cateline was safe, I'd risk getting caught. Agnes was of little concern to me.

19

CATELINE

"*The mothers were cruel, Cateline. You were so mesmerized by them, you seem to have forgotten.*"

It'd been hours since Malle had left with her slimy soon-to-be-husband, a man she'd told me repulsed her, even if he treated her better than many of the other men who'd shared her bed. I heard Mother Jehanne's words as if they were meant for me and not young women like Ava and Malle. "*Ytoile thinks most harshly of those who chase after wealth by selling their souls in the hours most sacred.*" Farmer Mason had called an end to the work for the day, although much of it continued into evening, like feeding the livestock with whom we shared our new home. I suppressed the nausea that I felt at the stench of the place—animals, feces and a dozen or so sun demon worshippers—and buried my head into my knees.

"Did you eat? Are you not hungry?"

I raised my head just enough to see Jiro crouched on the hay beside me, both of his hands cupping a chipped wooden bowl of rice he held out to me. I hit my forehead against my knees again. First the nomad. Then the outsider from the land of the sun demon. Ytoile was certainly testing me in this new life, after the sun demon took my family away.

"The mothers set the fire themselves, Cateline," Malle had insisted. "To burn the duke's daughter."

I scoffed into my knees. Heresy! And last I heard, the duke's daughter had survived the fire. She and her men, most of them, survived just fine. It was the mothers and the children who'd burned, so it was clear to me it was not *them* who invited the flames—

"They locked the children inside. The duke's men tried to knock down the door with furniture, but the flames burned too hot, and they had to escape, not a single child saved. They passed women in silver dresses singing, clinging to pillars as they caught fire, refusing to be carried away."

I'd asked her how she knew all this. Her 'Lord Sherrod,' of course. Like that vulgar sinning heathen could be trusted, especially when he was so keen to make her his bride. Keen as soon as he realized he'd be able to offer her something she couldn't refuse. I supposed if he got there before Ava was murdered, he would have made her a similar offer. They were probably all the same to him.

"It is good. Not bad for a servant's meal."

I snatched the bowl from Jiro before I had to hear another word and balanced it atop my knees. I dug in with the spoon, not at all hungry, but then I paused. The rice was sticky but seemed to melt in my mouth. It wasn't at all hard or like porridge. I covered my mouth in surprise.

Jiro grinned and sat beside me, tucking his calves beneath his thighs. "The Hanaobi people here, they cooked this. Much different from rice at the tavern, yes?"

I swallowed and brought another spoonful to my mouth, not sure I wanted to admit it was better even than anything I'd had back home. *Home.*

The gentle rocking of her chair as she stroked my hair. "The duke lay with a woman of the sun demon worshippers. That child he calls 'a lady' is nothing but an abomination." But to burn the tower down... Impossible. Mother Jehanne was not fond of the duke, but she told me Ytoile would take care of his punishment. Yet she died for the sake of burning the duke's daughter. And she failed even to do that.

I choked, alarmed at the brief sense of pain I felt in my stump. *Ytoile would have taken care of them. It wouldn't have been worth the sacrifice of the children. I'm in a barn full of sun demon worshippers, and I could never imagine hurting them myself. Ytoile would never ask that of us, no matter how misguided they are.*

Jiro extended a hand cautiously and lightly patted me on the back. "Are you all right?"

"Yes." I forced down the morsel of rice and stabbed the remainder with my spoon. I ate for a while longer, listening as the strange, harsh murmurs in the barn faded to silence, the burning candles blown out one after the other as the heathen outsiders settled in for the evening.

Jiro was not one to sleep. I stirred my rice absently. "Don't you all sleep when the sun is down?" I asked, hoping he might leave me be. "When your god is not watching?"

Jiro cocked his head slightly. "My... god?"

I wrinkled my nose and gathered the last bite on the spoon. "The sun... demon."

Jiro laughed. "The sun spirit? She's just one spirit. A special one, but just one. One of many."

She. I didn't say anything, carefully placing the bowl on the hay between us.

Jiro gestured around the barn. "There are spirits everywhere. In the animals, in the plants, in the..." He picked up the wooden bowl. "Even in things people make."

I couldn't stop myself from gasping. "Ridiculous!"

Jiro shrugged and turned the bowl in his fingers. "This bowl was once a tree. It was given new life by someone like you or me." He met my eyes and smiled, pointing out a chip in the wood. "It's lived long like this. Enough time to welcome in a spirit, to carry on a spirit left behind from the tree."

I rolled my legs sideways to face him. "Do you believe in the spirit in the stars?"

"Of course!" Jiro placed the bowl down on the hay gently, with both hands. "There are many spirits there, watching over you and me."

I bit my lip. "The children. Burned alive in the tower. They're there, accepted into Ytoile's arms."

Jiro clasped his hands together on his lap. "My people would say... We believe the dead spirits are here." He moved his hands wildly. "Everywhere. Invisible, but always with us."

I thought of Durand and Mother Flore getting sunburnt in the courtyard. Of Oriabel and Malle, their hatred so evident for the home we were blessed with. I stroked my stump. "I'm not sure I'd want to believe the children are still here. A place in the sky with Ytoile. That is a much more peaceful place."

Jiro nodded, biting his lip. I studied his strange and compelling face. He didn't make my chest tighten or my cheeks flush quite so vexingly as Fastello, but he was alluring in his own way. *The sun demon is alluring....* I swallowed. "My friend... Malle told me the mothers burnt the tower down themselves."

Jiro regarded me blankly, so I tried to better explain. "The Stargazers." I pointed to myself. "The women there I left behind. They killed the children there. And themselves."

Jiro's eyes widened. "Why?"

My stump was hurting. No matter how hard I rubbed, I couldn't massage the pain away. "Because a child of the sun demon worshippers walked into the tower."

"Demon worshippers?" Jiro pronounced the second word carefully, as if unsure what it meant.

"Outsiders." I cleared my throat. "Your Hanaobi people."

"We do not worship. Spirits, not demons." Jiro's mouth closed, and he paused, trying to form his words. "We love the stars. We love the sun. We love the sky. We do not think of it."

I clutched my hand and stump to my chest. "But Mother Jehanne said your empress has the sun demon's blessing."

Jiro laughed and shook his head. "No. Mother is not of the blood chosen—" He stopped.

"Mother Jehanne?" I asked. "'Mother,' to the Stargazers, is a title."

"No." Jiro shifted to face me, his calves still tucked strangely beneath his thighs. "*My* mother. My mother is the empress."

My response caught in my throat. My mind went blank. The empress' son? "Are you a prince?" I hissed at last.

Jiro nodded curtly, clutching his thighs with his hands. "I am Prince Kojiro, heir to the imperial title of Hanaobi." The words were so stiff, so perfect, like he'd practiced the line over and over.

My eyes darted around the room at the sleeping outsiders. Ours was the last candle lit. "But do they know? That you're here?"

Jiro raised a hand to stop me. He thought a moment and then

spoke quietly. "They do not know yet. But they will know soon. I will need their help."

"With *what*?" The words escaped through clenched teeth. For a moment, I feared for the Stargazers, and what a house of heathens would mean to them, but then I remembered. There were no Stargazers. None but me.

"I must era-di-cate the duke." He said one word slowly, each syllable carefully. "He stole from Hanaobi."

"What?" My hand—my *stump*—was hurting more than ever. I searched the barn helplessly for Fastello. I hadn't seen him in hours. Where could he have gone to? I shouldn't be the only one hearing this. *But why am I thinking of Fastello?*

"The Stargazers." Jiro gestured toward me. "You were never our enemy. Only the duke is our enemy. He stole my aunt, many years ago."

"The duke's consort..." I chewed my lip. I knew little about the history of the duke, so unhappy was Mother Jehanne with him and his poorly pretended piety. But I knew at least that he had long ago taken many consorts—*"a wicked, heinous man"* Mother Jehanne had described him. He returned with an outsider woman from the land of Hanaobi, and then his daughter Rohesia was born, just about a year before I was. (Not that I was sure when I was born, but I celebrated my birth the day I'd arrived at the tower.) The duke sent all his other wives away a short time later. *"He was ensnared by the sun demon himself!"*

"Did you say she was your *aunt*?" I asked Jiro, my thoughts chaotic.

I saw Jiro's jaw tighten. "Yes. She was the true heir to the imperial title of Hanaobi. Older than Father. So she—and her children—were supposed to rule."

"But that means..." I rubbed the shattered knuckles of my stump harder. "The duke's daughter, who will one day be our duchess, is the empress of Hanaobi..."

"The day the duke dies, the sun demon wins. He'll gain the rule of the duchy." Mother Jehanne pulled my arm so I had no choice to patter after her. It hurt. My shoulder ached, but she would not listen. She pulled and tugged me onward.

She stopped and bent down to slap me across the face. "Quiet, child! It's what you want, isn't it? The sun demon ruling over our land? Then you'll see how much fun you'll have in the hours of his greatest power!"

She pulled that arm even harder and then my hand hurt. It hurt so much. It hurt, and I'd never felt such pain, never knew it could exist. I screamed—

"*Ytoile! Have mercy on this sinner!*"

—drowning out Mother Jehanne's frantic prayer and watched as my hand burned in the fire. My fingers blackened, the flesh peeled away. And then I passed out, wrapped in Ytoile's blessed darkness.

I spun around and vomited into the hay behind me. It would not stop, the feeling of sickness. The flashes of memory, of Malle crying at my bedside. Of Mother Jehanne trying to soothe me, even while she explained why she had to do it—and then why she had to *cut* the fiery rot away. Of that first night I unwrapped the bandages and saw the small stump that had once been my hand. I couldn't have been more than a couple of years old. All I remembered was laughing and playing in the meadow, feeling the warmth of the sun shining down on my face. And how much I told myself in the days and weeks after that I had sinned to play outdoors in daylight, to show such joy. I told myself again and again until I finally forgot it ever happened.

"Cateline!" The way he spoke my name was odd, like he were calling someone else entirely. I felt his hand touch my back tentatively and start rubbing it.

At last I felt a break and turned back to face him. Crying. Laughing. It all felt so surreal. "And here I am, comforted by the prince of Hanaobi."

Jiro's head turned behind him and I followed his gaze. Fastello's face loomed in the dim candlelight. His eyes were a little wide, but he seemed less surprised at the revelation than he had been to discover my fingerless stump.

"Hmm. That makes things more interesting." Fastello crouched beside us. "You all right?" he asked me.

I wiped my mouth with the back of my sleeve. "I'm feeling better about one thing, anyway." *Malle was right. One person deserved to dance in the flames and succumb to the light.* "Ytoile damn Mother Jehanne!"

Fastello raised his eyebrows, unsure whether or not to ask. He didn't. "There's a bit of a crisis back in the duchy."

My chest tightened, thinking of Malle. And belatedly of Agnes.

"The duke's daughter has gone missing," explained Fastello. "And I think I may be the only one who knows where to find her."

20

KOJIRO

"The princess is lost. There was no hope for saving her. We go now to finish what I started years ago. To end the shame of the lost princess, and to remove what she left behind."

Father had no last words for me before he set sail for the duchy. But these were the words he spoke to Elder Brother Nobutada, one hand atop his favorite son's shoulder, before they stepped onto the dock. It was never said explicitly, but I had no need for clarification. My family's mission hung above our heads like the vengeful spirit of the aunt I'd never known, the one who gave birth a world away about the same time I entered the world: destroy the duke, but destroy the princess and her progeny, too. Leave no question that we were the heirs to Hanaobi.

And now I was on my way to save her, the cousin I'd never met, the one I'd have to kill if I ever hoped to go home. *A villain's blood runs through her veins.*

"We can thank our greasy lord for the information." Fastello strolled across the fields ahead of Cateline and me, his hands clutched behind his head and his elbows stuck out sideways. "It took me a bit to track him down now that weddings are no longer the domain of the tower..." He stopped and waited for us to catch up, looking at the beautiful deformed Stargazer as if waiting for her to react. She kept walking, the candle in her hand, her head down. Fastello shrugged and joined her. "Anyway, marriages are made official in a soldier's barracks outside of the castle. I had to wait a while for the couple to emerge, but I managed to, uh, *pull* him aside with the help of this." He pulled a dagger out of his belt and then laughed. I didn't understand what he found humorous until I saw the hilt gleam in the moonlight and noticed that there was no blade. He seemed to think Cateline would understand, but if she did, she said nothing. He put a hand on her shoulder. "He was awfully scared the duke had sent me, Cateline. Told me he was the last one with Lady Rohesia, and the duke would have his head."

Cateline froze. "Malle...?"

Fastello sighed. "She was already his wife by then. I don't know whether her lord had gotten news of the ransom before he dragged her to the barracks for his wedding regardless, but now he can't provide her with that home and protection he offered her."

Cateline's shoulders slumped. "But then she married him for nothing. I should have gone with her. I should have *believed* her—"

"This has nothing to do with you." Fastello drew her eyes toward his, and I wondered if there was something more between them. "He promised to keep her hidden. To keep her safe. They were headed back to the underground." He let his hand fall off Cateline's shoulder. "And if we get the duke's daughter back unharmed, surely she will vouch for her little lord wet nurse. He insisted she forced him to ride back without her, and that she would protect him from her father's wrath."

If you get her back unharmed. I knew what much of his words meant. My hand touched the steel weapon I kept at my belt, as if to remind myself that I could be terrible at sword fighting, but I had all I needed to follow through.

Cateline handed me the candle, so I took it, only to watch as she threw her arms around Fastello and rubbed her face into his chest. I felt that tightness in my chest returning, a hot flush of dizziness rush to my head.

"I've been a fool," sobbed Cateline, although her voice was muffled by Fastello's tunic. "The mothers burnt down the tower themselves. They killed... They killed the children."

Fastello was clearly surprised for a moment, but he embraced her back, squeezing her tight against him and murmuring soft assurances. I had to look away.

"So," I heard Fastello speak after a moment. "Your mothers were terrible. My dad is too lazy to do his own dirty work, preferring to leave that to the children." I turned in time to see Fastello point at me, and Cateline step away from his embrace, rubbing her eyes. "Your mother keeps her people as slaves."

I clenched a fist and opened my mouth to speak, but I closed it shut again. I thought of the little girl at the farm, who'd told me she was happier in the duchy. Who worked from dawn until dusk but said it was still less strenuous than it was in Hanaobi. She'd thought I was another escaped farmer. Another escaped slave.

"You're the last blessed mother of Ytoile left in the duchy." He patted Cateline's shoulder and then nodded toward me. "You're a Hanaobi prince, and I'm the duke's grandson. May as well save the duke's daughter and see if we can make sense of this mess together."

He spoke so quickly, I couldn't be sure what he'd said. But I had no idea of the reaction his words would cause in Cateline. I wasn't sure I understood what Fastello was exactly. The word 'nomad' meant nothing to me, and the girl at the farm had just told me, *"He's one of those. They steal from some but give to others. They live amongst the trees."*

"You're *what*?!" Cateline pounded her wounded hand against Fastello's chest. She shouted so loudly, I looked around to make sure we were still alone in the field. We weren't too far from the dirt road that led back to the city, and the forest loomed before us.

Fastello tenderly gripped her wounded hand and pulled it away. He shrugged. "Dad kidnapped a rich woman seventeen years ago. Turned out she was the duke's daughter, told to leave the castle because the duke had settled on staying true to his Hanaobi consort. He snatched her up on her way to the tower to see if she could become a mother with the rest of them."

Cateline stepped back from Fastello, the anger clear on her features even in the dim moonlight. "You said your people didn't *do* those kinds of things!"

"Well, *I* don't anyway!" Fastello tossed his hair roughly, reminding me somewhat of Tierny. "I think my mom was the only one, really.

Most nomads prefer to pair off amongst themselves. Dad was just..." He stopped and cleared his throat. "Don't blame me for something he did before I was even born."

Cateline, still ranting, didn't respond to his remark. "And what do you mean *with the others?!*"

Fastello put his hands on his hips and looked at the ground. "I heard the rest of his consorts and daughters became mothers at the tower. Mother Jehanne took them all in. The duke had no sons, so it seemed fitting."

Cateline's mouth dropped open. "And just how many *consorts and daughters* did he have?"

Fastello shrugged and took the candle from me. "I never asked, and Mom died when I was pretty young. Illness," he added as he looked from Cateline to me and back again, as if either of us might accuse him of murder. "I think one time Dad said Mom had six sisters, and four moms between them?"

Cateline looked faint, and since Fastello had the candle, I was able to beat him to her, propping her up under her shoulders. "There were ten mothers," she whispered. "Besides Mother Jehanne. I was the first mother-in-guidance in years."

I didn't really understand what was upsetting her, but I felt such comfort to have her light, soft body in my arms, even if she was drooping with each moment. Fastello cleared his throat and held the candle over us. "They get to the part in your training where they tell you about their deal with us yet?"

Cateline clutched my arm with her hand, but her attention was entirely on Fastello. "What are you talking about?" she said, quietly, urgently.

Fastello exhaled sharply, sending a gust of air to blow a strand of his brown hair out of his face. "I guess not." He gestured for us to follow him. "I'll tell you on the way."

❧

When we reached the river in the forest, I wasn't at all sure I could cross it. Not without taking out what I'd slipped into the pouch at my belt, and I wasn't sure I should reveal what I was carrying and risk all the questions that came with it.

"How..." I struggled to come up with the word, raising my hands up and down. "How deep?"

Fastello shrugged and tossed the candle into the river, extinguishing its flame. There was just enough moonlight trickling through the leaves of the trees above us that I could still see him. He waded in and turned around, pointing to his waist. "This deep. Not too hard to walk through."

It wasn't the difficulty I was concerned with. I nodded and shifted the belt higher, pulling it tightly like Tierny had showed me around my midsection. As my foot hit the water, a hand clutched my arm. I turned back. Cateline's lips were trembling, the skin around her eyes swollen and red. "Do you think he was telling the truth?" she whispered.

I glanced over my shoulder to watch as Fastello climbed out of the river and shook his legs dry. "I do not know. I do not know him well." I didn't add the truth of what I thought of the matter—I didn't care if he was telling the truth or lying. I just needed him to lead me to the duke's daughter.

Cateline's grip on my arm loosened just slightly. "He said the mothers told the nomads when worshippers were coming, especially if they were the types to bring along jewelry and coins and not give them all to the tower. He said the mothers took some of the stolen items in exchange for the warning. But I never saw anything so fancy in the tower outside of the donation plates. *Never.* Anything donated was immediately sold for food." She spoke softly toward the end, like she were doubting every word.

I followed Fastello's example and put both my hands on her shoulders. "He is a good man?"

Cateline's eyes watered. "Yes. Maybe..."

I smiled. "Then follow the good man. He wants to do good things, yes?"

"Come on!" Fastello's voice was hushed but clear behind us. "And keep quiet from now on!"

I guided Cateline toward the river and gave her a nod of encouragement. She slogged through the water and I followed, readjusting my belt as I shook my boots of the excess water on the opposite bank.

Fastello put a finger to his mouth—something Tierny unintentionally showed me had meant "to be quiet"—and we walked slowly through the forest, eventually crawling on our hands and knees at Fastello's example. I heard the voices first, the laughter. Then I heard the music, a bizarre melody on strange rough instruments. There was clearly a fire going as we approached, sliding on our bellies, using our arms to drag us forward. Cateline's nose twitched as we slid along the dirt and leaves, but I found it a rather refreshing filthiness compared to that of the rancid mess in the city.

Fastello stopped at the edge of a bush and waited for us to slide next to him. He pointed at the glowing light.

I saw men and women dancing, the swish of the dark beauties' skirts not silver like I'd imagined in my visions of the Stargazers, but bright and colorful, like accents to the flames behind them. It took a while for my gaze to wander from their wild faces, wet with perspiration—but a happy sweat, not one from a day of labor. But when Cateline gasped and Fastello's hand shot out to cover her lips, I turned to follow her widened eyes and saw a woman entirely out of place. While everyone else danced or stood or sat on the ground, she was in a large duchy chair that held her a short distance off of the ground. It let her rock back and forth while sitting. She had silver hair and was somewhat old, pale and not without a sort of worn-down beauty. But when I realized she wore a silver dress that sparkled with the reflection of the flames as she rocked back and forth, I knew immediately why Cateline had caught her breath.

"Stargazer?" I whispered.

From behind Fastello's hand, Cateline nodded.

Fastello pointed again with his free hand, lower. I looked back and saw that one of the people on the floor wasn't bouncing to the music or enjoying food and drink. She sat cross-legged, her arms tucked behind her back—a rope wrapped around her chest twice, I realized. Her face was Hanaobian for the most part. Except perhaps her eyes were a bit wider. Something someone from the duchy probably wouldn't notice.

My cousin. I felt for the weapon I kept at my side. It was still there.

Fastello pulled his hand back from Cateline's mouth. "Jiro," he whispered. "Keep her here. Stay hidden. If things don't work out, then the two of you go get help at the farm." He slid slightly back. "Time for a little family reunion."

That was never a good thing in my family.

21

ROHESIA

The boy's fingers stroked my jade lion as he stuffed a piece of bread into his mouth, the crumbs tumbling all over his lap. He was seated some distance away, in the edges of the firelight, but there was no mistaking the way the flames gleamed off of the smoky green surface of the statue.

"You sure you don't want anything to drink, Mother?" My attention was drawn to the figure towering over me. The man called Davazanto fancied himself some sort of nomad leader—their *king*, he called it—but Father had told me that there would always be people wanting to kill leaders, so leaders must be careful how much they drink and eschew opium entirely. The nomad leader was either unaware of his stupidity or didn't consider that someone who wanted to kill him was nearby.

"No, thank you. The fresh night air, and the bounty of Ytoile is enough for me." Mother Jehanne. There was no mistaking that rocking figure, even if I hadn't seen her as clearly in her darkened room. The silver hair, the strange, almost trance-like way she rocked staring forward. She'd ordered her own tower burnt down, my soldiers told me, and while the orphans and her fellow mothers were turned to ash and bone, she sat beside a fire in the nomad camp, as naturally as if she truly belonged there.

"What about you, eh, good sister?" Davazanto crouched and rubbed his arm against my shoulder. He'd spoken of sisters I'd never known, mentioned something over and over about a woman's bosoms and rear quarters, stating my sinewy frame couldn't be further in resemblance from hers. I said nothing, as ever.

"Maybe she only speaks outsider!" shouted a man.

Davazanto stood and raised his mug, cheering. "*Hai, hai, domo domo*! Thank you for jewels. We do farming!" he called, bowing his head exaggeratedly with each made-up word. The performance seemed to amuse the crowd, but as full of drink as they were, I imagined even my blade through Davazanto's neck would cause an unbridled uproar. My eyes fell to the belt and scabbard hanging loosely around Davazanto's waist, my pilfered daggers tied haphazardly around his wrists in mockery of how they'd found me. *You won't be able to slide them to your wrists like that. Assuming you could do anything once you had them in your grip anyway.*

"*Wash them all out.*" As I watched the revelry around me, I was starting to wonder at my hesitation when the boys caught me unawares. A second flick with each wrist and—

No. I swallowed. I'd done it to *save* them. I thought I could go back and ask Father to spare the women and children at least. Maybe task them with working for the farmers. The music picked up and the lazy, thieving upstarts went back to their dancing, Davazanto tossing his mug on the ground and swirling a woman into the fray circling the fire.

"I don't know which part of your blood is more tainted." Jehanne's voice was so soft, I could hardly hear her but for how close she rocked behind me. "The blood of the sun demon worshipper or the blood of the heathen sinner, the foul man who thought of nothing but sins of the night, the most heinous kind of sinning there is."

I wanted to ask exactly what kind of sins she was referring to, but I was in no mood to encourage the woman to proselytize more of her religion. At the very least, her attempt to kill me had done away with their grip over the duchy once and for all. With the rest of the mothers and children gone and no innocents left to hurt, I was glad Father had outlawed the Stargazing religion.

"Oh, his blood walked my tower," said Jehanne, probably certain I was listening. She rocked and rocked in her chair. "Six mothers, your sisters, six times more deserving to be duchess."

"Then why did you kill them?" I asked sharply, not at all interested in the truth of her words, but more in the truth of her actions.

Jehanne rocked a bit longer, then squeezed her dry lips together a moment before opening them. "They wanted to burn. They were ashamed of their blood. They were ashamed to share any of it with a heathen like you."

I faced away from the madwoman, but she continued. "But we would have taken the castle, the moment your father died. Everyone knows you aren't the rightful heir. Everyone praises Ytoile. They would have joined us, put one of your sisters in her rightful place."

"Yes, well, now no one who praised Ytoile is allowed to live."

"You think you've won then, do you?" Jehanne sounded oddly proud, even though, until she'd tried to murder me, I didn't even know we were battling over anything. "My mothers may be gone, but there is still an heir who outranks you. A seventh sister of yours married Davazanto, and the next duke will be one of my people."

I raised an eyebrow and studied the woman, despite myself. She was so pale, but then I saw it, something I'd mistaken for the slight discoloring of age and years gone by. A slight touch of tan to her skin, washed out by discolored whiteness. I turned back around. How much did Father know about the Stargazers and the madwoman who'd run them? Did he know his old consorts were there, his other daughters? Is that why he told me to eradicate the nomads but mentioned nothing about the tower? If only I hadn't taken the bodies of those women back to the Stargazers...

The bodies. I wondered if either was my sister. What they'd thought when Mother banished them from their home. Was Mother so obviously jealous? Did she know what fate awaited them if she turned them from the castle? Did Father really think he could erase his past just by willing it?

"Did you know that the nomads slew some of your mothers?" I asked, unable to hide the way I hoped the words would hurt her. "Before you burnt the rest of them? Before I'd defiled your sacred tower and you had the need to kill them?"

"Yes. Yes, of course." Jehanne's chair creaked even on the dirt ground. "One mother who was getting rather full of herself, if I do say so. Her daughter was the first in line to be duchess, you see. And her daughter was rather too soft and weak for the job, so I sent her off with her. The other..." She shrugged. "A new addition. I thought she held promise, but she disappointed me after all. It was harder for her to work with her deformity anyway. I could have sent her back to her parents, but she'd be no use to them. Besides, I took her as payment for them stealing from the tower's kitchen that year the famine was harshest."

A spark flew out from the roaring fire, but Jehanne didn't falter. She'd been expecting three bodies. But she'd never bothered to check. I, for one, was glad at least one had been spared. Although I wondered what had become of her. Neither body I found was deformed as far as I could tell.

Davazanto and the woman twirled and came to a rest before me, my sword clanking loudly against his thighs.

"Phew!" Davazanto wiped his brow with the back of his arm and, noticing the dagger strapped there, began untying both from his arms hurriedly. He laughed. "You really walk around like this?" He dropped the first dagger on the ground and then began working on the second. He nodded sideways, shouting over the music. "Rento!"

The boy who'd taken my jade lion got up slowly and made his way closer to the fire. My statue hung lazily in one hand.

Davazanto dropped the second dagger on the ground and began fiddling with the belt holding my sword scabbard around his waist. "Why don't you take these? They're made for a smaller hand regardless." He looked at me as he held my blade out to the boy Rento, as if the size of my hands were somehow an insult. He tiptoed and snuck up behind a different woman than the one he'd been dancing with, a woman who'd stopped dancing by herself to grab a drink of ale from a barrel. "Luana!" he seized her from behind, and she screamed, dropping her mug and spilling the nearly-full contents everywhere. The liquid soaked into the dirt, but not before spreading a few feet over toward me, pooling around my legs.

Davazanto spun the new woman, took her hands in his, and the two joined those circling the fire, the sweat already soaking their clothing. I watched with mild interest as the woman he'd left standing by me regarded them painfully for a moment and then turned to the boy playing with my things like toys. She smiled gently. "Now isn't that nice of your dad, Rento? Such great weapons for a great boy—"

"Shut up, hag." Rento finished tying my blade around his waist and bent to gather one of the daggers he'd left on the ground beside the jade lion. He watched me even as he bent, and I knew from experience that there was something more in his eyes than childlike wonder.

The woman cleared her throat and stepped aside, walking toward the barrel of ale without another word.

"Dad thinks the duke will pay pretty for you," said Rento to me, even though I'd said nothing. "But don't be mistaken. We don't intend to hand you over." He slipped one of my daggers out of its scabbard and held the blade into the firelight, watching the red and yellow flicker off of its metal.

I stopped myself from raising an eyebrow, settling for a slight adjustment, moving my legs out of the spilled ale and sitting sideways to better face the rocking madwoman. "My nephew?" I asked, drawing her out of her trance.

Jehanne studied the boy, who was sliding the dagger back into its scabbard and tying it tightly around his wrist, leaving no room for the dagger to slip out if he flicked it. "No. Not this one."

Rento bent to grab the other dagger almost as if he were slapping the ground in anger. "Yes, but *I* will be king, not my brother." He stood and shook his head. "We *told* you, Grandmother, Fastello is gone. A traitor. Dad's heard he's been working the underground, but when he finds him, Dad won't be in the mood for forgiveness." He finished tying the second dagger scabbard around his right wrist. It was loose, perhaps because he had no strength in his left hand. "Or at least, I'll make sure he isn't." A bit of his *grandmother*'s face flashed across the boy's, something that made it easier for me to forget he was but a child. He had nothing of the curious innocence on the faces of the boys who'd found me.

Jehanne slammed her fist on the armrest of her rocking chair, causing even me to start unexpectedly. "Wicked child!" She leaned forward to stand, kicking the jade lion dangerously close to the fire. My heart lurched. "The sun demon dances too strong in you—"

"Grandmother, stop!" Rento bent to reach for the jade lion. "That's probably worth a lot—ow, damn it." The second dagger had slipped out of the loose scabbard at his wrist as he bent to reach for the statue. Not having the skills or preparation necessary to flick his hand just so to catch the hilt, the edge of the blade slashed against his palm. He stood up, holding his hand out, the jade lion forgotten. "I'm bleeding!"

"You've been poisoned, too," I added, calmly. It was fool's luck, perhaps, that he'd chosen the one dipped in poison to tie on loosely.

The boy's face paled, his lip trembled. He clutched the bleeding hand to his chest. "You're lying."

I shrugged. "It makes no difference to me whether or not you believe me."

Rento screamed. "I won't wait to kill you!" He pushed Jehanne aside and grabbed for my blade at his waist, first with his bleeding hand and then awkwardly with his left. He fumbled as he struggled and only succeeded in bringing it out halfway.

And that's when I figured it was as good a time as any to stand, since they'd failed to bind my legs in any way. I felt the fire rush through my muscles as I stood, scraping my feet through the mud and dirt and kicking the mixture high enough to plaster the short boy's face.

"Bitch!" He groaned angrily and went to wipe the muck out of his eyes, his bleeding hand dripping red into the brown and black that covered him. I spun around him and kicked the jade lion and the poison dagger he'd dropped away from the flames. He turned, his eyes framed with mud like a mad raccoon, and bent to tackle me, but I'd moved and shaken my shoulders enough to loosen the rope around my torso, spreading my arms apart and sending the coil flying over my head. I snatched the dagger and turned, ready to fling it and put the wide-eyed boy out of his misery, but my hand faltered.

The boy was covered in flames, writhing in the bonfire and screaming. Jehanne stepped backward, leery, disappearing around the other side of the fire. I used the opportunity to scoop up the jade lion and slip it into the empty pouch at my waist, tucking the dagger into my sash without a scabbard, regardless of the danger of poison. Then I pushed past screaming women and men with glazed-over eyes and grabbed the barrel of ale, lifting it over my head with two hands.

"No, that's alcohol—" The woman Davazanto had left standing

darted out in front of me, her eyes flickering between me and the flaming boy.

I shrugged and slammed the barrel on the ground, spilling its contents everywhere. The noise in the camp was deafening now, the chaos of men, women, and children running hither and thither. Most running away from the flaming boy. My ears picked up some sort of screaming around the other side of the camp, but I had other matters to attend to. I kicked the flailing boy into the dirt, wiping the heat from my steel-toed boot in the dirt to cool it. The woman screamed and the boy, unable to scream now, continued to flail limply on the ground. I tore my cloak off and covered him, pushing him back and forth in the wet dirt with my foot until the flames subsided.

I kicked the cloak off of him. He was charred. Too far gone, even if his wide eyes were still rolling, torn from their eyelids, and focused entirely up at me.

"Oh! My baby!" The woman slid into the dirt beside him, touching him and pulling back at the moan the creature before her made. She glanced at me. "Thank... Thank you..."

I shook my head and pulled the dagger from my sash, flicking it with ease into the boy's neck. His eyes rolled upward, and a trickle of blood spilled forth from the cracked blackened lips as Rento settled into death. I pursed my lips and bent, retrieving my thrown dagger. I looked at the woman whose mouth was stuck open, her hands faltering at her cheeks. "He was too far gone. I did him a favor." She screamed in response, so I gave up, using the dagger to gently pry the scabbards off the boy's wrists and waist and retrieve my second dagger and blade. They were hot, and the leather was wrinkled and scarred, but they'd survived better than the flesh on which they'd been so inexpertly fastened. I kicked the scabbards out of the way of the body, picking up the discarded barrel and pouring the last drip of ale over the leather to cool them enough to grab them and fasten them on me. I didn't think I'd have much time.

I looked around. The woman was the only one left nearby, the sounds of the screaming coming from farther away in the camp. I stepped around the fire—

"Rohesia! This way!" I turned at the sound of my name, so strange without its title. A redheaded girl, too pale to be a nomad, waved a hand—no, a fist, a fingerless hand—and beckoned me toward the bushes in which I'd spied on the nomad camp earlier. I looked at her and then back in the other direction. A crowd of nomads had gathered there, and there was no one here to mourn Davazanto's son. Peculiar.

The girl came closer, and I whipped my head around at the sound of the second set of footsteps making their way through the brush. An outsider. My hand reached for my blade's hilt, and the jolt of heat made me pull my hand way. The young man watched the movement, his own hand clutching at the pouch at his waist. We looked into each other's eyes. I saw the anger, but he did not sustain it. His gaze faltered.

The girl clutched my arm with the hand she had that worked. I studied her curiously, uncomfortable at the touch, fighting my initial instinct to flick my hand and send a dagger into it. But the girl wasn't looking at me. Her attention was caught on the crowd a short distance away. "Fastello." She spoke quietly and her hand dug into my arm with what light force she might be able to muster. "He's in trouble. I know it."

"Fastello?" I pulled my arm easily away and gripped my sword hilt, not caring about the heat that lingered. I pulled the blade out of its scabbard. "I can't leave without meeting my nephew."

I stepped toward the crowd, disregarding the soft calls of my name that beckoned me back.

22

FASTELLO

"May I cut in?" Really? That was my plan? Dance with a former lover, somehow cause a distraction?

The swinging bodies, the laughing faces, the smile that vanished the moment they stopped dancing. They both stared, as shocked to see me standing there at the edge of the bonfire as they may have been to see the duke.

I felt my own smile faltering. I extended a hand. "Luana, you're looking lovely."

Dad and Luana exchanged a glance, and then Dad turned back to face me, guiding Luana over, his arm wrapped snugly around her waist. "Fastello, my boy!" He gestured with his free hand. "You've picked quite a night to finally join us. We caught us quite a catch, and we're sure to soon have enough riches to spend every night carousing!"

My lips twitched. "Isn't that what you do regardless?"

Dad chuckled and patted his hand against Luana's waist. "Your grandmother is here to see you—"

"Ah. Grandmother." At the mention of my grandmother, I thought of Cateline, how I'd yet to tell her. I cleared my throat. "How was it that she survived the tower fire exactly?"

Dad laughed. "Mom had her little bitches carry her out, rocking chair and all, before they jumped back into the burning tower!"

I clutched nervously at the dagger hilt at my waist. Cateline knew now that her Mother Jehanne was still alive, after she'd just realized what the woman had done. She'd been shocked. Scared. If she found out that woman was my grandmother... But whatever Cateline would think of me, I wouldn't let that woman threaten Cateline. I'd threaten her with my dagger if I had to.

Dad stepped beside me, letting Luana go at last and slipping his arm around my shoulders. "Come! Drink! Speak with the woman who's come to see you."

"No!" I meant to swivel out of his grip. I pushed a hand against his chest. Strangely, I found the dagger hilt in that hand, the one without a blade. I hadn't meant it for him.

Dad looked down, his face paralyzed in surprise. Then a grin danced on his lips. "What's this? You 'stabbed' me?" He snorted. "Nice work, son. Keep practicing with your dummy dagger and maybe someday you'll work up to a real blade." He grabbed the bladeless hilt from my limp hand and reached over to tuck it back into its holster, smacking the back of my head once he finished. I felt numb. "Now don't go scaring your grandmother with your asinine tricks."

"Fastello." Luana's sultry voice was quiet, cautious. She slipped a hand on my arm and I met her eyes. There was none of the confidence there. She looked at me now like she was unsure who she saw standing there before her.

I slipped a hand around her exposed waist, fighting the rush of heat that traveled down my arm to my groin at the soft touch of her flesh beneath her short tunic, and then I heard my name, screeched and unpleasant.

"Fastello! Fastello!"

I turned to find her, the murderous bitch who'd condemned children to die even as she made her escape. The crazy woman I'd hardly seen my whole life, but who made every creak remind me with a shiver of the rock of her chair. And I found my blade hilt against Dad's chest again. Only this time his face's frozen features didn't falter. Until he choked up a bubble of blood, and slumped to the ground, my real dagger in his chest.

The blood on my right hand. The supple flesh beneath my left. The body on the ground, the blood pooling around it. My dagger in his chest.

"What have you done?!" Luana wriggled free from my light touch on her hips and beat her fists against my chest. Her beautiful eyes brimmed with tears and looked from me to the body that lay bleeding at our feet. To Dad.

My hand trembled. I held it away from me, as if I could separate it from myself, as if that could undo what I had done.

Luana was screaming, running her hands around the dagger in Dad's chest looking for a way to pull it out without causing more damage. But she didn't look at his face, like I did. She didn't see that it was already too late.

More shouting, and the music stopped, people running from all corners of the camps toward where I stood frozen. "Davazanto!" "It's Fastello!" were all I heard spoken. Until I heard that shrill shriek. "He's dead! He killed him!"

The camp broke into chaos and I watched helplessly as Mina joined Luana to throw herself over Dad's body, and I wondered numbly where Gilia had gone, if she'd been too old for Dad, tossed out like Mom was before she'd died.

"I'm going to a better place, my darling." Mom's clammy hand caressed my face. "I wanted to go. It's all right. You'll be okay." Creaking. Creaking. The creaking of Grandmother's chair beside Mom's bed.

I didn't know I had any memories of my mother. Not such clear memories anyway. I shook my head, suddenly aware of the daggers extended my way. "Get him! That traitorous bastard—"

"Stop!" The voice was shrill and arresting. The crowd stepped aside to reveal the woman plaguing my thoughts. The woman I could see now, rocking beside Mom's death bed, handing her a cup and urging her to drink, saying it was a gift from Ytoile and it would all soon be over. She extended an arm toward me, the silver shimmer of her dress wild with the echo of flames from the bonfire behind her. "This is your king. Your future duke."

"Rento's our king now!" shouted someone.

Grandmother looked coldly over her shoulder at the man who'd shouted. "Rento is dead. I sent him back to the wicked flames from which he'd spawned."

I clutched my bloody hand at my throat, unsure I was really awake, that I was really standing here right now, living a nightmare. I'd hated them, but I'd loved them... What had possessed me? Had I meant to kill him? Deep down? But why? Was there no other way?

"Quiet! All of you!" Grandmother raised a hand and calmed the murmurs that had broken out at her casual admission of the murder of my only brother. She clutched her hand on her silver skirt, jutting her chin out. "I'm not at all concerned that our future duke got rid of my son, and nor should you be. The man called himself our king, but he did nothing for you. It was all me. I arranged everything, so you could do Ytoile's work. So you wouldn't starve." She stepped forward and reached both arms out as if to embrace me. "All so that one day, this child would lead us. Would lead the entire duchy, and make it a kingdom of Ytoile on land." She took my face in both hands and smiled, but her smile was like a knife piercing through jagged leathery flesh.

I spun back, out of her grip. "I don't care about being king or duke." I clenched my fists. "I just want this to end." I threw my hands wildly in Dad's direction, my eyes briefly meeting Luana's. "I wanted this kind of thing to end." My voice was hoarse, my throat constricted.

Grandmother put an arm around me and guided me back to the bonfire. The crowd of people parted to let us through. "It *will* end, child. The duke is sure to bring his army to us, and we'll use the blessing of Ytoile, the cover of darkness, to confuse them, draw them into the forest, and be done with them all."

I shoved the old woman away, not caring that she stumbled. "How do you propose that exactly, *Grandmother*? Burn down the forest, like you burned down the tower? How could you? Those children. My aunts. My grandmother." I bit my lip. I didn't remember the other grandmother, to be sure, but Mom had told me she was a mother at the tower, like all of the duke's former consorts.

"I am all the grandmother you need. All the family you need." Jehanne slipped an arm around me, patting my chest gently.

"On the contrary. As his last remaining aunt, I'd like to extend my hand in greeting."

I turned. There stood the lady Rohesia, unbound, her right hand extended and scuffs of dirt and blood peppering her face and outfit.

Behind her trailed Cateline, foolishly out in the open. Where was Jiro? Why wasn't he protecting her? There he was. Far behind her. Almost out of sight. Too far to stop her approach.

"No!" I said limply, my heart hammering. *I want Cateline out of here. She can't see this. She can't know—*

"There you go!" Jehanne patted my chest again, misunderstanding. "He has no need for you."

Lady Rohesia lifted her left hand, which clutched her sword. "Then I'll have to extend my blade instead." She lunged toward us.

23

CATELINE

I couldn't scream. I clutched my hand around my neck, choking it, willing Ytoile to step in and stop this, to tell me that what I saw wasn't real. It couldn't be. Mother Jehanne. Fastello—

"Stop, Cateline!" A hand clutched at my arm, yanking it away from my throat. Jiro gripped my hand in his and he tugged. "Come! We go! Now!"

I yanked back, fighting his strength and freeing my hand from his. "No!" I searched his face. He was afraid. Well, so was I. But there was no way I was leaving. Not now. I spun around. "Rohesia, please!" I ran after her.

Rohesia was already in front of Mother Jehanne and Fastello, her sword swinging. I found my voice to scream at last, the tears blurred my vision, and it was all over. Fastello crumpled to the ground—

And so did Mother Jehanne, toward the bonfire. Rohesia stood between the two, her back to Fastello and her sword pointed at Mother Jehanne. She caught my eye as I neared. "Get him up!" she barked.

I scrambled to Fastello's side and examined him. He didn't appear hurt, although he sat collapsed on the ground, numb and not really seeing me. "Fastello!" The name choked me, the tears I'd been holding back spilled forth. I shook him lightly with my hand. "I thought you were hurt, or... Thank Ytoile!"

He snapped back to life at the name of the goddess, his eyes meeting mine, searching my face wildly. He wrapped his arms around me and embraced me, and I felt what could only be called a fire dancing across my face and through my chest and through every inch of my body. I burned for him. I *burned* like the sun spirit. *Spirit.* I laughed, exhausted, astonished. It was a sun spirit, not a demon, that had produced this sun-kissed man in my arms.

He pulled back just a bit and cupped my chin in his. We gazed at each other, and I saw how close he was, every little pockmark and light bristle of beard in the dancing glow of the bonfire. He leaned forward, pressing his lips against mine. And I felt, in that moment, as if I'd never before known Ytoile's blessing, not until I felt his kiss.

"Sinner! Harlot! You should have never trained to be a mother! You're a heathen!" It was a shrieking voice I hadn't heard in years, a crazed timbre in the shriek I associated with a demon and fire. My right hand throbbed.

"Get him up!" hissed Rohesia. I was brought back to where I was, my gaze following hers at the crowd of nomads gathering around the crumpled woman on the ground.

Fastello squeezed me, and we both stood beside but slightly behind Rohesia. Some men amongst the nomads assisted Mother Jehanne up, and she clutched at her arm tightly. I saw the red soaked in with the silver all down her arm. I felt Fastello's arm around my waist, and I rested my hands, fingerless and fingers, around his back and chest.

Rohesia studied Fastello and me briefly, but she didn't comment on the extra time we'd taken to stand. "You don't agree with her?" She nodded toward Mother Jehanne.

"No!" Fastello and I spoke both at once.

Rohesia nodded and faced forward. "Then help me put an end to her."

And end to her. She was talking about murder... "*Ytoile shall guide you, little one.*" *She rocked me back and forth in her rocking chair.* "*You are special. You have been chosen. Suffer now, and you will be repaid later.*"

I clutched at Fastello's tunic. "How did she survive?" I whispered, hoping for some sort of answer. She'd tried to stop the fire. She'd never ordered it in the first place. She'd had to be dragged, kicking and screaming from those she left to burn—

Fastello tightened his grip at my waist. "She asked some others to carry her here. Before they went back to the tower to burn."

I felt the restriction of my throat and raised my hand to clutch at my neck—my hand with the phantom fingers—but Fastello grabbed it gently and squeezed it, smiling faintly as he pulled my hand away.

Rohesia intruded. "If you were the third mother, the one who got away from the nomad raid the day of the tower fire, she meant for you to be murdered that day. Before she even decided to burn the rest of her cult alive."

My knees buckled. Fastello had to fight to keep me standing, snapping, "Lady Rohesia!" all the while.

"You knew?" I asked him, leaning heavily into his body.

My eyes searched his face. I saw the lump at his throat bounce. He pinched his lips together and nodded.

I shoved limply at him, trying in vain to get away. "Why didn't you tell me?!" If I'd only known her true nature, I'd have been able to swallow what Malle had said much sooner. She wouldn't have gone off to marry that slimy lord, I wouldn't have so stupidly defended the Stargazers—

"Now's not the time." Rohesia let go of her blade with one hand and flicked her wrist. I jumped as a dagger appeared out of her sleeve and into her hand. "Either of you got a weapon?"

I shook my head lamely. *A weapon?*

She handed the dagger to Fastello, who tucked it into an empty scabbard at his belt. Then Rohesia switched her blade to her left hand and flicked her right wrist to reveal another hidden dagger. "That one's poison-tipped," she said, hushed. "Want the one without the poison?" She held the remaining out to me, but I shook my head. She shrugged and slid it back into her arm. Fastello let go of my waist and drew out his second dagger, handing it to me.

"No—"

He smiled. It was the bladeless hilt. I took it from him, trembling. As soon as I clutched it, I felt stronger.

Rohesia nodded toward Mother Jehanne and the confused assembly of nomads standing behind her. "Any chance you can talk sense into them, nephew? Now's the time. It would go easier than taking them all on without reinforcements."

Fastello swallowed before nodding. We studied each other's eyes briefly, and he stepped forward, leaving me to stand behind Rohesia.

"I am not your king!" shouted Fastello, and I wasn't at all sure what he meant by it. He raised both hands out, to show that they were empty. "And I am not your future duke. I am your *friend*. I only want what's best for us. For all of us."

"Ha!" laughed a man supporting the bleeding Mother Jehanne. "Is that why you up and left us?"

Fastello clenched his fist and pointed behind him, at me. "I *saved* this girl. Grandmother wanted her dead, for no reason. You killed her companions, for no reason!"

Grandmother? My eyes darted wildly from Fastello's back to the leering Mother Jehanne. They'd talked about family, something about a grandmother. I'd only come near enough to hear the end of it before Rohesia had lunged and I'd felt my heart stop beating.

"They sent those women to Ytoile because I asked them to!" Mother Jehanne pointed an accusing hand at me. "Because it was their time! And it was her time, too!"

"How dare you!" The words escaped my lips before I could even tell I was thinking them. "Who are you to say who should live and who should die? You're a murderer! *You're* a demon!"

Mother Jehanne cackled and Fastello stuck a hand out to stop me from approaching. I hadn't realized I'd passed by Rohesia, my hand gripping the empty dagger hilt tightly. The crowd behind Mother Jehanne had begun stepping back from the laughing woman, those carrying blades lowering their weapons falteringly.

"Look at her!" Fastello pointed at Mother Jehanne, who had begun to sing her praises to Ytoile. *It's a dance for a festivity. But she's dancing in front of a bonfire, like the wicked creature she is.* "Is this who you want to trust with your future? You believe this murdering madwoman will bring us all to glory?"

"You killed Davazanto!" snapped one of the men still lingering near Mother Jehanne. I looked for Fastello's reaction to the accusation and was relieved that, whomever he had killed, he at least looked very pained by it. "You killed your own father!" His father. Fastello reached back and grabbed my hand.

"It was an accident. I saw it." A young woman stepped forward from the crowd. She had no weapon in her hand and kept her hands clasped before her bare midriff. Those hands were covered in blood.

The man shook his head, waving the knife he held in his hand. "Luana, how can a dagger in the chest be an *accident*? He fooled you, same as he tries to fool us."

"To Ytoile, I pray. Bless those worthy of Her love." Mother Jehanne's voice demanded to be heard, rising in volume, increasing in tempo as her silver skirt spun in circles around the flames.

The woman called Luana clenched her fists. "Fastello would never do something like that on purpose!" She started to cry, although she bit her lip to keep the quiver from overtaking her voice. "He wouldn't..." Her voice sounded less sure as she fingered a sapphire necklace around her neck.

I squeezed Fastello's hand and drew myself beside him. "No, he wouldn't," I said confidently.

The complaining man waved a hand. "Glad to see you've got the women doing all your defending for you. An appetite for the ladies, just like your father. I would never follow you—" Mother Jehanne put both hands on the man's chest and shoved him into the bonfire before he even noticed she danced before him.

She cackled and spun again. "To Ytoile, I pray," she sang, and the crowd screamed, running toward us, away from the flaming man. He shrieked and waved his arms before collapsing onto the ground.

"Enough of this," hissed a voice from behind us. Rohesia appeared, her sword extended. "She's a problem, and we need to deal with her."

Fastello's hand felt cold and clammy between my fingers. "I can't. Not like *that*—"

Rohesia nodded and stepped forward. "Well, someone needs to."

She'd only taken two steps when Mother Jehanne emerged from behind the bonfire, flaming logs of wood in each hand. "Ytoile, I beseech you! Guide my hand, and keep those who are true away from the flames! Let the sun demon devour the wicked!" She dashed forward and tossed the flaming logs onto two different tents, causing them to burst into flames.

People started running for the forest behind us. Fastello dropped my hand and shouted after them, but no one stopped, and those whose arms he grabbed for twisted away to keep running. Fastello ran to a nearby tent and grabbed a bucket, overturning it and emptying its contents. "Cateline, follow me!" He gestured, running back toward the river with his empty bucket, as if that would be enough water to stop the raging tendrils of the demon. Not the sun demon. The demon I saw dancing before me, summoning the flames.

I almost followed. I could see Fastello's back vanish into the forest, and I took a step toward him. Rohesia brushed past me, dashing forward toward the shrieking woman, and I turned to watch as she jumped back mere feet from reaching the madwoman. The bonfire grew wildly, and Mother Jehanne added a barrel she'd emptied into it to help grow the fire. I saw a man kick aside some mugs and plates to grab a bow and arrow leaning against a tent. He slid the arrow into his bow with trembling fingers and let it loose, but it died only a few feet from him, turned to ashes by a flaming tent.

He took another arrow and fit it into his bow. He was going to try again, he was going to try to shoot through the fire to reach the wicked Jehanne, and then I realized—

His arrow was aimed at Rohesia's back, as the duke's daughter waved her blade, keeping the madwoman from bursting through the flames.

"No!" I shouted. I ran toward the man, determined to knock his hand aside. I'd no love for the duke or his family, I'd even been told to shame them, never addressing them with their proper titles, keeping my thoughts about them private from the worshippers. But Rohesia wasn't the problem just then. She was trying to keep the dancing, dashing woman from spreading the flames. She was a guardian, her sword glinting in the firelight. She was who we'd come to save. The one who could save Malle and her pathetic husband.

I tucked Fastello's gift into my sash and ran, both arms swinging to get me forward faster. I'd almost reached the man, my right hand extended, when he turned to face me, his face stricken as if he'd seen a spirit. His eyes fell to my hand, my tortured hand, but the hand I'd used to dance, to live, to love. His bow was empty. And I finally felt the sharp bite in my chest, the warmth seeping across my chest. My left hand shook as it felt for the arrow sticking out of me numbly.

The man turned away, jumping back as flames spread. He tossed his bow into the fire and ran into the forest without a word, his face drained of color, his hands covered in soot.

My vision weakened. The flames were so hot. It felt like it was a hot, humid summer day.

Dancing in the meadow, the warmth of the sun caressing me. Reaching my hand out to Malle, my dearest friend, as she ran toward the bright blue of the waterfall. She jumped into the water and shrieked. I screamed playfully and ran toward her.

"Out playing! In the sunlight! You're supposed to be indoors when the sun demon reigns!" The voice was shrill and scary, the hand on my wrist causing me great pain. "Sinners! Sinners!"

"No, just me!" I saw the shaded figure hidden behind the waterfall, the water bending and keeping her from sight. "I'm alone!"

The cackling laughter.

"You shall burn for your sins! Unworthy!" The line from my past, repeated in the present. Sweat poured down my face. They were so hot, the flames. So bright. My chest hurt twice over. I just wanted to sleep and find the darkness.

"Watch out!" Was that Malle running toward me? A figure dashing amongst the flames, her sword glistening and reflecting the firelight? *No. Rohesia.*

A hand seized me from behind, knocking against the arrow and pushing it in deeper, like a monster's claw tearing through my heart. I cried out in pain, but though I had been weak, I felt a strength I didn't know I could possess, a strength flowing through my body, from my toes to my fingers, even to the phantom fingers the demon had taken from me long ago.

"*My child. You are not alone. You are never alone.*" I heard Her voice in that moment, welcoming me home.

"Sinner! Heathen! Unworthy!"

I groaned loudly and wrestled free of the frail hands, elbowing Jehanne in the stomach as I turned. I clutched her shoulder hard with my left hand, and wrapped my right arm around her other shoulder and the back of her neck. I clenched my teeth. "Let the flames burn the wicked. Ytoile, I beseech you!"

I let go of Jehanne's shoulder, my right hand strong enough to keep the squirming woman tight within my grip. I grabbed Fastello's bladeless hilt out of my sash and pretended to stab the demon through the heart. She couldn't have felt a thing, but she shrieked, her snarling face frozen as she gazed into my eyes.

"Young mother! Wait!" Rohesia. She never got to know my name.

"Cateline!" Fastello. *My* Fastello. My eyes began to glaze over. So much orange. So much flicker. So hot. But so comforting.

I leaned forward, dragging the demon with me into the flames.

24

KOJIRO

The fire lit up the night sky, tricking me into thinking it was dawn when I broke through the forest and stepped onto the dirt road. My fingers stroked the weapon at my belt. I'd fled. I'd fled like a coward, too afraid to kill my cousin, too afraid not to.

I'd promised Fastello I'd keep Cateline away from the crowd. But she'd torn away from me and run into the danger, and I'd put myself first. I'd turned and run away from it without her. I took a deep breath, clutching at my chest, willing the nausea and dizziness to go away. But it would never go away. I'd never escape who I was, what I could and couldn't do. I was hopeless. There would be nowhere for me to go. My eyes darted over the horizon and the rising sun. The farm. Maybe I could make a life there. Forget asking for their help against the duke. I could thresh wheat and grow crops and live every honest day.

And then I realized it was far too soon for dawn. In the distance, the fields in one direction—the farm I'd left just hours earlier—were smoking. *The farm is in flames. The farm is in flames!* What could I do? How could I help them? How useless I was. *No, maybe the nomads. Fastello, Cateline. Even the duke's daughter. I must tell them. Beg them for help!*

I turned back, plunging into the forest, letting the branches snap at my face and my legs. I ran and ran, stumbling, my hand resting on my weapon like it would keep me safe from the darkness, from the nausea, from the flames. I wasn't sure I was going the right direction and I almost panicked and turned around when people started running toward me.

"Run!" screamed a man gesturing the way I'd just came. "Fire!"

I froze. They knew already about the fire? They were on their way?

People continued to run past me. One would tumble and another would scoop them up. There were shrieks and screams, but the people wouldn't stop running, dripping water from their boots as they scrambled away. I reached the river and felt the heat. I saw the orange glow from behind the mottled leaves.

A solitary man stumbled through the bushes, jumping into the river and plodding as fast as he could through the coursing stream. He stared at me all the while, his face twisted as he focused on getting through the rushing water. The river was faster than I'd remembered it, treacherous if you weren't careful. The man slipped and fell. His floating body began drifting down into the forest, the trees now brimming with flames. I ran after him along the bank.

"Forget him! Help me!"

The trees on the other side of the river rustled, and my cousin emerged, a limp Fastello in her arms like an infant twice her size. She stumbled, but she plodded forward, the heat and exertion causing her face to brim with sweat. She reached the river and stepped in, clinging to the floating Fastello with all her strength.

I waded into the river and met them halfway, helping her guide the unconscious Fastello to the safer bank. I stepped backward out of the river, each step tearing at my calves, each yank on his heavy body burning through my arms, but I pulled and she pushed, and we got him to the side. My cousin panted a moment, resting her hand atop his body, and then the weakness of her exertion kicked in and she slipped, sliding down the river and away. She held a hand out, something close to panic across her steely face. I hesitated.

Let the river do the work for you.

But I didn't have time to think. I grabbed her hand and pulled before I'd even known I'd made a decision.

She climbed out of the river and collapsed on the bank, taking deep breaths as the water dripped off her tunic and scabbard and legs. I searched around, jumping back as a large tree branch on the other side of the river collapsed, shooting up a spark of wild flames.

"Where is Cateline?" I asked, seeing her nowhere.

My cousin kept panting but forced a single word out of her mouth between gasps. "Dead."

My knees buckled and I collapsed down next to her. I couldn't have understood. But it was one of the first words I'd learned in the language of the duchy: *"I want the duke and his daughter dead."* A practice sentence in barbarian, along with "I eat rice" and "I go."

"Cateline." My cousin pointed to the unconscious Fastello. "He called her that. The girl with the flame-colored hair and the wounded hand."

I nodded numbly. I couldn't feel. I wasn't feeling anything. Where was the panic, the pain, the dizziness? I clutched at my heart as if that would make it all come back, as if I could feel the pain and know I was suffering for leaving her behind.

My cousin ran a gloved hand through her hair, shaking it of some of the dampness, from the river or from her sweat. "I had to knock him unconscious to tear him from her." She exhaled. "There was nothing much left. She was shot, and then she was engulfed in flames."

At the word "shot," I fingered my weapon at my belt. As if I'd killed the red-haired beauty. The girl who'd never dance for me in the silver dress. The girl who'd called me a demon worshipper but seemed so keen to know more about me, more about how she'd misunderstood someone she thought her enemy. I pounded my fists on the forest floor and screamed, shouting curse words in my native tongue.

Rohesia stood, doubling over and leaning her hands against her thighs. "We've got to go. The water may keep the flames at bay, but they'll pass from bough to bough and engulf the whole forest soon enough." She looked at me. "Can you help me carry him?"

I stood on quivering legs, not sure exactly what she said, but seeing the meaning well enough: the fire was spreading. I grabbed Fastello under the armpits. My cousin faced the same direction and pulled his legs to either side of her waist. She led the way through the forest, away from the fire... And to the next.

"There is fire!" I said between panting breaths.

My cousin said nothing for a bit, then just, "Yes! We're running from it!"

"No!' I shook my head, even though I knew she couldn't see me. "There is fire at farms, too!" We were close now, to the edge of the forest. I wanted to prepare her for what she'd see.

My cousin stopped so suddenly, I jostled poor Fastello awkwardly against her. She let his legs slip to the ground and turned. "What did you say?"

"Fire at farms." I was collapsing under Fastello's weight, slipping to the ground gently so as not to hurt him. I noticed the large bump at the back of his head and realized my cousin really had had to knock him out before she carried him away. I felt at his neck for the throbbing of his heartbeat and relaxed a bit when I felt the movement beneath my fingers.

"Why?" My cousin put her left hand on her blade hilt, even though there were no enemies there for her to slaughter. *None but me.*

I shook my head. "I do not know. Farms hid us." I gestured to myself, to Fastello on my lap, and to the forest behind me. "We three. My people are there."

My cousin let her grip on her blade loosen, but her fingers didn't move from the hilt completely. "Who are you?"

I laughed, almost relieved that I could admit it, that she could take my life and this would be all over. "Prince Kojiro," I said loudly, proudly. "Your cousin from Hanaobi."

My cousin's hard eyes softened and her back straightened. "The heir to the throne...?" She'd heard of me.

I laughed again, wiping the sweat off of my neck with my bare hand like a barbarian. "*You* are the heir to the imperial title of Hanaobi, Princess Rohesia."

My cousin's shoulder slackened and her hand fell off her sword. "Mother was the heir?"

"Yes," I said. "She was the heir, older than my father. Before the duke stole her."

My cousin's mouth pinched. "My father didn't steal my mother. She wanted to leave your country."

"This is lie!" I shook my head, disbelieving. "He stole her and changed her heart. My father tried to take her home, and she was changed." I grit my teeth. "He killed her."

The tip of my cousin's blade was at my throat before I'd even finished speaking. I hadn't even seen her grip its hilt once more. "My father didn't kill my mother. He loved her."

I jutted my neck outward, toward the blade. "No. *My* father, he killed her. His elder sister."

I clenched my eyes and felt the rush of the wind as she moved her blade, but I felt nothing. Something clunked. I opened one eye. My cousin had stabbed her blade into the ground beside her, leaning on it for support. Her lip trembled slightly. "And *you?*" she asked. "Why are you here then?"

What could I say? *To kill you and your father. To pave the way for me to become emperor, or if Mother has her way, my sister to become empress after I'm dead. To seek justice for the treasure stolen from Hanaobi. To end the unfair trade.* "I ran," I said at last. "From my mother." I patted my stomach. "She would kill me. Not smart enough. She wants my sister for empress."

My cousin straightened her shoulders, and she looked down on me coldly. "And yet you doubt that my mother would have run, too? Of her own free will?"

The thought jolted my brain like the back of Mother's hand across my face. "The slaves," I said at last, the word so strange on my tongue. "I thought… When I listened to my father speak, I think I knew. Aunt did not like how we treated our servants."

My cousin nodded and slid the blade back into its scabbard. She crouched as if to grab Fastello's legs, but she paused before she turned. "I know…" She hesitated. "I know Father taking my mother here was a mistake. He'd gone to form relations with Hanaobi, to ensure the duchy would have enough food to last the famine, and he escaped with one of their own, making them angry." She reached into a pouch at her waist and produced a jade lion. "I know we co-exist on unfair terms, that Hanaobi allows the unfair trade in order to sneak people here." She handed me the lion and I let the smooth surface tickle my fingertips. "Father has known that for a long time and allowed it when he felt generous." She stopped, the crackling of kindle the only sound some ways behind us. "But we murder outsiders when he feels like it. We murder your people who come here." She clenched her jaw.

I thought of the little girl at the farm, of Father and Elder Brother Nobutada lying in barrels in many pieces. "My mother," I began, trying to find my voice. "She said we sneak soldiers here, but this is her lie." My stomach hurt at the thought. "She has no control over who comes. They're just farmers. They're slaves, running. They are no threat to you, to the duchy."

"I know this." My cousin sighed. "I think I've always known this. Father has let some stay, pretending he doesn't know they're there, just to help grow the crop." She bit her lip. "But he hates when they have children here, especially with his own people." Her voice grew hushed. "He kills the babies." I shuddered, and we sat still a moment. Then she reached out to take the lion back from me, securing it in her pouch. "That's not what my mother would have wanted. Father has lost his way."

I knew what she said, although the speech was long and peppered with terms beyond my comprehension. We were the children of terrible people who'd done terrible things. My eyes traveled to the unconscious Fastello. Wasn't that what he'd told us? Something about not holding yourself responsible for the actions of your parents? But to do all we could to make them right? I saw the pouch holding the weapon next to Fastello's head at my lap and shivered.

Rohesia turned and gripped Fastello's legs, beckoning me to stand and help lift him up. "I just wanted you to know. If the farm fire wasn't from natural causes, we'll probably find my father waiting." I watched her walk. Confident, large strides. Not at all like my mother or Tomiko.

The forest fire roared some distance behind us, and we stepped free of the trees. "Leave him with his people," I said, seeing the group of shivering darker people that had collapsed onto the dirt road ahead of us. "We will meet the duke alone, you and I." I thought of the weapon again, filled not with cowardice but with anger. "Your father. My uncle. Our family matter."

My cousin hesitated, but then she nodded.

25

ROHESIA

Whenever I'd felt the quivering in my chest, the shaking of my limbs before, Father had been there to pat my head gently. *"You're still a child, my dear. Those feelings are how children cope with what must be done. But you will grow. You will be stronger. And you will learn to lead —to do what must be done—without succumbing to uncertainty."*

Where was he now when those feelings returned to me? Would he tell me to push forward, to do what needed doing? But no. What needed doing was something he would never see.

Like the swirling silver skirt of the madwoman leader of that cult as she danced around the fire. That young mother, that Cateline, had seen it. The woman had to die, even if she must have been her mother figure. And Fastello had killed his swine of a father, whatever the circumstances. My hand gripped the comfort of the hilt. It was up to the child to right the wrongs of the parent.

My other hand brushed the pouch with the jade lion, my fingers trembling. It wasn't what she would have wanted. But I was raised without her. I was raised to do what needed doing.

"What do we do?" asked the prince, my outsider cousin. He jogged a few steps to catch up to me, his hand clutched at something bulky hidden in the pouch at his belt. He seemed to think I hadn't noticed how his hand would linger there, clearly contemplating drawing a weapon. "We cannot stop fire."

"No," I said, thinking of fire's finality. "But we can save the people."

We jogged over the last hill that blocked the fire from view, my eyes drawn to the smoke and the glowing embers. *If there is anyone left to save by now*, I did not add. I turned. "You stay here, beyond the hill. Stay out of sight until I need you."

The prince clenched his jaw, but he nodded, dropping to the ground. His hand was at his belt again. I continued onward.

Horses. Soldiers. Despite all I'd done to breathe deeply, to put away those childish feelings, my heart sank at the sight of the men who would follow me on a mission gathered in a circle at a safe distance from the burning barn. Of course. Who else would it be, but for an act of a higher power? *There is no higher power*, I thought confidently. *If there were, She would have intervened by now. She would have put an end to this madness.*

I was not seen approaching. "What is going on here?" I shouted, drawing the attention of the nearest soldiers. "Did you start this fire?"

"Did you start that one?" The soldiers parted slightly to reveal a black horse at the center of the circle. My father nudged Sunset and trotted casually toward me, as if there weren't a crumbling, flaming structure in the background behind him. He nodded behind me, at the smoke and embers eating up the only forest that existed on the isle of the duchy. He seemed amused. "My dear!" The firelight lit up his face, and I saw the smile that broke across his features. "You are safe! Oh, thank the skies!"

I did not point out to him that he was dangerously close to admitting he was thanking Ytoile, the goddess he'd outlawed just days prior. He dismounted and stepped toward me, his arms outstretched. "You don't know how happy I am that you are well." He embraced me, and I froze. *Flick the daggers out. Reach for the blade.* The jade lion thrummed in the pouch at my hip. I couldn't, I—

Father pulled back, placing me an arm's length away to study me. He frowned a little. "You seem a little roughed up." I looked away. "No matter," he continued. "What more could we expect from the duke's daughter? She takes on the band of nomad upstarts by herself, sets their home ablaze, and returns slightly scratched up to tell the tale! Three cheers for the future duchess!"

The soldiers lifted their swords in the air, cheering three times as ordered. It was then that I noticed, over Father's shoulder, that the men were encircling a group of outsiders who were quaking, crouched on the ground. My eyes darted over the unfamiliar faces, some pale people from the duchy included—

Sherrod and a young woman from the duchy were tied up in rope on the ground before the trembling group, their faces bruised. The ground beneath Sherrod's face was dotted with pools of red blood. "Sherrod!" I cried, surprising even myself.

Father's grip on my shoulders slackened, and I wrenched free, passing by him and the other soldiers to slide into the dirt and examine Sherrod's face. I moved his body gingerly and came face to face with the bloated features. His greasy hair was stuck against his forehead with sweat, grime and blood. One of his eyes was purple and swollen shut, but the other opened slowly as I moved him. His cracked lips twitched slightly and his mouth opened. I saw the chipped tooth dyed at the edges in red. "My lady?" he croaked. "You are safe after all." Each word wheezed through his teeth as if it were a great labor.

"What happened to you?" I asked, that feeling of childishness, of panic, flooding my body. "What happened here?"

"Sherrod left you alone outside of the castle, my dear." I did not look, but there was no mistaking Father's commanding voice behind me. "He left you alone in mortal danger. He knows his sole job is to keep you from harm."

"My lady." "My lady." Every croaking, anxious warning, every caution that I not go against something my father would wish for me, every plea for his own life and safety in those words. "Let me do my job," he was saying. "I know I'm no help to you, but I can't leave you. I can't let you be harmed." I heard the words beneath the words and felt immensely ashamed I'd ever been annoyed by him.

"Shush now, my lady." The hand caressing the back of my head, the other squeezing me tightly against him. "I know it hurts to see. But his lordship—your father—loves you. He wants you to be strong. That's all."

I buried my face deeper into Sherrod's abdomen. He smelled strange, perhaps unpleasant, but not to me. I knew that smell meant comfort. I could always run to Sherrod and bury my face against him to hide my tears.

Sherrod let me cry without saying another word, his caresses soothing me, his gentle shushing pulling the dread and nausea away. He put his hands on my shoulders and pulled me away from him tenderly, his finger sliding under my chin to get me to meet his eyes. He smiled. "You are strong, aren't you, Lady Rohesia?"

"Yes," I said. The baby. The infant's foot disappearing underneath the water... My lip trembled.

"Now, now. Dry your eyes." Sherrod tapped my nose and revealed his huge tooth as he grinned. "Don't show others those tears," he said. "Don't ever. But you're safe here, with me. You and me, we'll keep each other safe, like fami—"

"Sherrod!"

Sherrod's tongue skirted over his big tooth, and he dropped his hands to his sides. His eyes apologized silently, and he turned to go. "Coming, my lord..."

I lay a hand on Sherrod's arm and patted him gently, turning to look up at Father. "But I told him to go! I ordered it! How could you take it out on him like this?" My gaze fell over the group of outsiders, not sure I perfectly understood what had drawn Father to them at my disappearance, when he knew they were hiding there for years and let them be for the most part.

Sherrod said something faint. It sounded like "my bride." I must have heard wrong, or the damage he'd taken had addled him.

Father removed a glove and whacked it against his thigh to shake out some of the dirt and dust. "Yes, well, then he ran from me. And I found him thanks to this young lady." He gestured to a woman with golden hair who sat behind a man on a horse. Behind *Captain Tierny*. How could that be? "He'd gone and gotten himself married the instant he left you behind to track nomads. *Alone.* Then instead of telling me what had happened to my daughter, he ran off to an *underground* safe house, a tavern no longer standing, and this young woman who worked there was kind enough to tell me she'd seen him there and also here, at this farmer harboring outsiders." He held a hand out to assist the woman in demounting.

"*You!*" I hissed as the woman stepped closer. "I've seen you before!" She'd been attacked by nomads on the way back from the tower.

"Father, she's a Stargazer!" I don't know what prompted the admission. Considering all the things I was learning, hoping Father would end this woman who'd led to Sherrod's torture was a rather dark turn for my mind to take. But someone needed to pay.

"Not anymore," snapped Father, his hand escorting the woman nearer. "She's a lady. My men raided her home mistakenly."

Her too-small face pinched, and she jutted her chin out. "I never really *was* one of those filthy Stargazers," she added, as if I'd asked her to speak. She gazed at my father and batted her eyelashes, and I felt sick. Father hadn't taken another consort since Mother, but it had been so many years since she died, and this woman was clearly thinking he'd mourned long enough.

I turned away, disgusted. Sherrod groaned beneath my touch, and he said those words again: "My bride…"

My eyes darted to the woman tied up beside him. She wasn't moving. I hadn't seen her before, although it was hard to be sure with the lines of blood that ran down her head from a wound at her hairline. *When had Sherrod managed to find her?* My hand clutched at Sherrod's shoulder. I knew nothing about him, even though I'd spent more time with him than my father. Nothing outside of his groveling. His 'connections.' His *underground* connections, his history as an orphan in the tower. He had a whole life behind my back when I was safe in the castle—a *good* life, a *noble* life—and I'd never bothered to ask about any of it. Although to hear tell, any portion of his other life would have put him at risk; I'm sure he wouldn't have told me.

But he trusted you enough to let you know about his childhood in the tower. About the people he knew who broke the duke's laws.

I let go of Sherrod and crawled over to the woman, pressing my hand on her throat, searching for the beat of her heart. I saw her chest move just slightly beneath the ropes. "She's unconscious," I shouted to Sherrod. "But I think she'll be all right." I flicked my wrist to slide the poison-less dagger into my hand and began sawing at the rope around her.

"Thank you," croaked Sherrod beside me. I saw his less swollen eye squint and flicker. "My lady, you are a good person. Such a good… Almost… like a daugh—"

Just as my dagger broke the last twine holding Sherrod's bloodied bride captive, a sword plunged through Sherrod's throat.

A deafening crack, like thunder, and my chest exploded with a pain I'd never felt before.

26

FASTELLO

My head rested on her lap, the softest, warmest pillow. I felt the delicate touch of her hand on my face. Her thumbs circled my cheek like a silk scarf draped across my skin playfully. Her *thumbs*.

I sat up, the back of my head throbbing. "Cateline!"

I blinked. The clan was gathered around me. Sitting, standing, looking off into the distance. I turned to face my gentle beauty. I had to squeeze my eyes to bring her into focus. "Luana," I said, not hiding the disappointment in my voice.

The corner of her lips twitched, a poor attempt at capturing some of that feeling that had once existed between us. That smile didn't seem so shy anymore. "You were unconscious," she said, explaining the obvious.

I put my hand to the back of my head carefully, pulling it away to find no blood despite the sizeable welt that had grown there. I turned my head. "Cateline?" I stood up and almost doubled back over. Luana rushed to stand and slid her hand around my back and abdomen to support me. "Cateline!" I called, brushing Luana away.

"Fastello—"

I would not stop. I stumbled, leaning my hand on one person, shoving aside the next, looking around to find her. Elisabetta. Abella.

Mina. Gilia. So many women, so many men. Not a single trace of red hair.

Where were we? The dirt road, the charred stone. The river. The waterfall. "Cateline!"

Luana hitched her skirt up and ran to stand in front of me. "The red-haired girl? The one without the fingers? She's dead, Fastello. She's gone."

I clutched at Luana's too-small top with trembling fingers. "She can't be..." The words tasted like fire on my tongue. Fire. Cateline grappling with the old bitch...

Luana laid a tender hand atop mine at her chest. "She is. The duke's daughter and that outsider brought you to us. She said she had to knock you out to stop you from jumping into the flames."

I let go of Luana's tunic and slapped her hand away. My eyes rested not on her chest, but at the sapphire necklace hanging around her neck. I stared, unmoving.

"Fastello, we—"

I snatched the necklace. "Take it off!" I barked, yanking at it. "Now!"

Luana let out a small cry and then scrambled to release the hook at the back of her neck. The chain fell like rainwater, dangling freely as I clutched the jewel in my hand.

"Fastello, you're upset, I know, but—"

I shouted. The sound scratched my throat, echoing even over the roar of the waterfall. I felt the tears spilling from my eyelids, but still I screamed until I ran out of breath, until my head went even fainter, until I saw the stars twinkling in the black gathering in my eyes. I pulled my arm back and tossed the necklace into the waterfall basin, pitching it as far as it would go, feeling the fire roar in my arm.

I felt Luana's hand on my shoulder. "*Fastello!*"

I spun around, making Luana jump backward. I spent but a moment making note of the surprise on her face before my eyes fell on the rest of the nomads, now silent and staring in the same direction. At me. I pushed past Luana and glared at every one of them, drawing them to gather closer, causing some to look away. I threw my hands in the air angrily. "What are we doing here?! Why are you all gathered here in the ruins of that bitch's tower?!"

Mina dropped her hands from around the sobbing Gilia's shoulders and took a tentative step forward. "The forest is burning," she said, clearing her throat. "We had to get away—"

I snarled. "I mean, what are we doing here doing nothing?!" Mina clamped her mouth shut and ran a hand over her arm, her eyes on the ground. I looked over the heads of the crowd toward the forest, toward home, glowing orange in the darkness, pouring smoke into the night skies, keeping the stars from me. No one answered, so I mourned for a moment. I mourned and then—

"Turn your head. Look the other way."

I spun to see who'd spoken, and I found no one behind me but Luana. But then my gaze drifted over her head, and I saw smoke and orange. I saw fire. I turned back to the crowd. "What's going on?! Why has the fire reached that far?"

Nico crossed his arms and stepped forward. "It wasn't the forest fire that spread. Some of the farms are on fire. We saw it as soon as we exited the forest."

"So I will repeat myself." I marched up to him and faced him off. Even though he was almost a head taller than me, the man backed down. "Why are we here when there's a fire where people are living?"

Luana appeared beside me, her voice shaky. "The duke's daughter thinks it was set by the duke. She warned us to stay away—"

"Well, we won't," I said, addressing the crowd as I stepped backward. My hand rested on the dagger at my belt, the one Lady Rohesia had loaned me. My other hand searched in vain for the bladeless hilt at my empty second scabbard, like somehow miraculously feeling it there would prove the whole thing just a nightmare. I stopped, raising my voice. "Come on, men, women of the nomads! Use those bows and daggers for something other than murdering small groups of helpless travelers." I watched as the group exchanged glances, either coming to my side or formulating how they should get rid of me and stop me from continuing to berate them. I let go of the empty scabbard and pounded my chest with my fist. "I am your king now!" The anger intertwined with my voice, making the words seem all the more commanding. The looks stopped, their eyes drawn to me. "And I say, if we pretend we're noble by saying we share what we take with the farmers... If what we do is *for the farmers*—then we're going to actually save the farmers!"

I drew out Lady Rohesia's dagger and raised it into the air. It was no sword, but for the nomad people, it was as good a blade as any. "We go! Now!"

The look of confusion and fear passed between a few of the crowd's faces. Luana clenched her fists and then walked up to Nico, yanking a dagger out of his belt. She raised it in the air. "We follow our king!" she screamed.

More of the crowd fumbled at their belts or picked up the few rescued bows and quivers.

"We fight!" I shouted, shaking the dagger. "We fight like men and women! We fight with honor!"

"Honor!" repeated Luana, and the crowd joined in. Hesitantly, but passionately. We had nothing left. Why shouldn't we risk it all?

"Nomads, after me!" I turned and followed the river, the one that led to the fields and to the farms, putting the river branching out into the burning forest behind me.

A boy shouting and laughing ran by, a small meat knife in his hand.

"No!" I shouted, making the boy stop in his tracks. I turned to face the crowd behind me, my chest swelling at the sight of so large a crowd. "The children stay!" I caught Gilia's eyes, swollen red. Her hand, shaking, clutched a dagger, and she smiled.

"For the king!" she shouted. "For the duke's true heir!"

The rest of the crowd joined in. *I'll worry about the duke part later.*

This isn't just a farm that's burning. It's the farm.

Twice this same night I'd traveled away and back to this farm. But the first time I'd returned, my heart was full of the red-haired beauty, the way she'd looked in her dirt-stained farmer's dress just as stunning as she had in her sparkling silver. My heart was full of her still, but the vision of her falling into the fire, of the flames consuming her slim figure, kept jumping across my eyes. I felt some more tears escape, but I grit my teeth. The night was almost over. I couldn't tell because of the glow of the flames, but I felt the sun making its way over the horizon in my bones.

There was someone flat against the ground at the top of the hill. I turned and put a finger to my mouth. "Stay back," I hissed at the crowd.

I crept toward the figure, Lady Rohesia's dagger in front of me. The figure rolled, a flash of metal gleaming in the flickering firelight in the near distance.

"Jiro!" I shouted, recognizing the face—

A crack of thunder. The metal began to smoke in his hand. The dagger fell from my grip, and I slumped to the ground.

27
KOJIRO

Fastello fell. Fastello with the crowd of dancing tanned people behind him. I'd used Elder Brother Nobutada's weapon, Tomiko's gift, to show Mother I was worthy, at last, and I'd used it on Fastello.

"The king!" screamed a woman wearing only a skirt and a piece of cloth around her bosoms.

"Get him!" shouted a large man. I'd never seen a man so big.

I dropped the smoking weapon, which burned hotly in my hand. I clutched at my chest, but there was no way to undo what I'd done. There was nowhere for me to run. I scrambled for another pellet in my pouch, a dash of powder. I grabbed the burning weapon, dropped it, and picked it up again. I let my flesh sear a little and loaded them in, my hands shaking.

"Stop! It's all right!" Fastello sat up weakly, clutching his right hand to his chest. It was bleeding, the red ooze seeping out of his hand. It squirted up, like the Hanaobi volcano spurting lava. "He's a friend!" Fastello said meekly. He smiled falteringly.

The barely-clothed woman slammed her knees into the grass beside him, tossing the dagger she held on the ground and grabbing Fastello's arm. "He's lost two fingers!" Her eyes burned hotly into mine. "You filthy outsider!"

Fastello cleared his throat. "Enough!"

The woman chewed her lip and then ripped a piece of fabric off of her skirt, wrapping it tightly around Fastello's bleeding hand.

"What have we here? I figured the farmers might know where you scum have been hiding, but I never imagined that setting the fire would draw you to us." A sword sank into the ground a short distance from where I sat in the grass. Its tip dripped red, the color like a flame against the silver starlight of the blade. "I didn't think the nomads were actually truly in the business of helping others, you see." I got a good look at the man leaning on the sword with both hands like it was a walking stick. Pale skin, dark hair, a dark beard. The man my cousin had called "Father" surely. *The duke.*

Fastello brushed his bleeding hand against the woman who'd tended to him to send her back, and he stood on quivering legs. "Where are the farmers? The people who worked here?"

The duke nodded sideways. "Have a look."

Fastello stood beside me atop of the hill.

"I'm sorry—" I whispered, gazing up at him and noticing how pale his face had become. I watched the duke warily, but he hadn't seemed to notice the Hanaobian among the darker-skinned people.

Fastello shook his head and stared at what I'd been watching since I first arrived. The circle of soldiers on horses around the huddling farmers. Around my people. My cousin still sat on the ground, her arms around that friend of Cateline's, the one who'd left, the one with the brown hair—Malle—staring at the man the duke had been about to stab through the throat before I'd turned and fired the wrong way, startled by Fastello's sudden appearance. The dirt around the man's neck was wet and dark—the duke had stabbed him, then. My cousin didn't look to see Fastello staring down at her. She didn't seem to know where she was anymore. She clenched her chest like she'd been wounded, but she'd suffered no blow that I could see.

"What is the point of all of this?" Fastello asked. He clenched his teeth and nursed his bandaged hand against his chest. *He has no weapon now. You've taken that from him. You failure.*

"The point?" The duke lifted his sword and slung the hilt over his shoulder like it was a sack of rice. He trotted down the hill, the few soldiers who'd followed him up it falling into place behind him. The duke stopped near the outside of his circle of soldiers, sliding the tip of his sword into the ground again and beckoning us with his other hand. "Why don't you come down and join us?"

I stood, reaching my free hand out to touch Fastello's shoulder. "You cannot—"

Fastello gripped my hand with his uninjured one, letting my hand fall. "But *you* can."

"Me? No, I—"

Fastello's eyes dropped to the weapon I still clutched tightly. "Obviously you can. You must." He swallowed, visibly in pain. "You owe it to me now. You owe it to Cateline."

The pain in my chest roared to life with the sound of her name. He'd asked me to stay with her. I would have, I just... I clenched my jaw and nodded.

"Fastello—" began the woman who'd tended to him.

Fastello stopped her from approaching with a look. He gestured at the dagger she'd dropped. "Stay here. All of you. Join at the right moment."

She bent to pick up her dagger and spread her legs apart, the tension in the muscles of her arm obvious even some distance away. Fastello and I turned and began the descent down the hill to join the duke and his soldiers. And my people.

"*You!*" Fastello's voice sounded puzzled as he took in that blonde woman standing behind the duke. It was the woman we'd been with at the tavern and the farm, the one always whining. However, it was the man behind her on horseback, the one from which she'd dismounted, that drew my eye. Tierny refused to look at me.

She said nothing, sliding a delicate hand around the duke's shoulders. "Hello, Fastello." She bent in and whispered something to the duke, something that caused him to smile. The golden-haired woman —*Agnes*, I remembered—clearly looked pleased with herself. And then her expression changed completely as the duke smacked her face with the back of his hand, the metal gauntlet he wore causing a trickle of blood to escape from her nose. She cried out.

"Yes, I *know* he's a nomad, *my lady*," the duke snarled at her. "Now might I suggest you do something actually useful and jump into the burning barn?"

Agnes squeaked and gathered her skirts in one hand, the other dyeing red with the blood of her nose, a nose that looked out of place on her aristocratic face. She tried to run through the horses, but a look passed between the duke and Tierny, and Tierny drew out his sword, blocking the woman's retreat. "That way," he said, curtly, tipping his blade toward the terrified cluster of my people and the duchy farmers. Agnes quickly ran toward them, her face a mixture of blood and tears. I watched her and caught sight of my cousin, who had seemed to come back to life now, her emotionless face studying the woman as she plopped on the ground a short distance from the nearest Hanaobi farmer.

A crack of thunder echoed across the sky, and for a moment, I thought I'd fired the weapon again. There was lightning slashing through the ember glow of the sky.

The duke hadn't noticed. He gestured around him, at the fire that had spread from the barn to the cottage to the nearest crops of fields. "Welcome, nomads!" He studied my face, noticing me for the first time. "Welcome, outsider!"

Thunder roared again. Some of my people jumped and twittered at the noise. I saw the little girl who'd taught me how to harvest clutched tightly against the woman I assumed to be her mother.

"So you shelter outsiders, too? I wouldn't have thought you people generous enough to share. Not really." The duke stuck out his chest, resting both hands atop his sword hilt again.

My attention was caught by the movement at the front of the clustered group. My cousin had set the woman down and had approached the dead man. She used her dagger to slice through the ropes, even though there was no point in freeing him.

"I can add it to your list of crimes." The duke stared at Fastello, clearly considering him the more important threat, even with his bandaged hand. "Thievery. Murder. Sheltering an outsider."

My cousin did something strange. She pulled away the dead man's hair from his face delicately, as if weaving silk that might break. Then she lowered her face to his and laid her lips atop his forehead. When she pulled back, her lips were slightly redder, the man's blood smeared on her mouth and nose.

Tierny noticed. His eyes met mine for the first time since I'd descended the hilltop, if only for the briefest moment.

Fastello hugged his wounded hand against his chest, like I'd often seen Cateline do in the few days I'd known her. "Those are exactly the same crimes I find you guilty of, your lordship. And as the king of the nomads, I'll be glad to carry out your sentence."

Thunder cracked. The duke laughed, closing his eyes and tossing his head as the first drips of rain began falling. "*You?* Sentence *me?*" He pretended to wipe a tear from his eye delicately with a steel-covered finger. "I'm afraid you won't get very far with that hand of yours."

Fastello's face hardened. "I knew someone with fewer fingers than me," he said, slowly. "And she was fully capable of ridding the duchy of some of the wicked that had befallen it."

"How... poetic." The duke raised an eyebrow and shrugged his shoulders. "Maybe between the two of you, you'll muster enough fingers to grab a dagger and stab me." My cousin stood slowly behind him. Some of the soldiers watched as she rolled her wrist on the right hand, but if they found it odd, they did nothing. Tierny waved his sword, still extended, slightly to the side. His eyes met mine and they darted sideways. I took a step back, further away from the duke.

The duke lifted his sword and pointed it at Fastello. The tip dangled precariously before his heart, but Fastello didn't take a step backward. He jutted his chin out. "My mother hated you until her dying day." He swallowed. "She took poison, cursing the man who'd cast her and her mother and sisters out."

The duke's sword lowered slightly, the curiosity evident on his face. Rain started building, gushing down and hitting the fire, the hiss of the steam drowning out the crack of thunder. "I thought they all joined that tower? Became mothers serving Ytoile?"

"All except my mother." Fastello clutched his hand tighter. "She was kidnapped by nomads along the way. Held against her will. Raped." I saw the muscles in Fastello's jaw twitch.

The duke shrugged and raised the sword higher. "Then whichever one she was, I'm sure she won't mind if I do away with the trash tainting my bloodline. I have an heir, and no need for others." He lunged, and Fastello jumped back, out of the way, like he was dancing. He raised a hand. "Now!" Fastello screamed, and the rain began pouring, the cries of his people ringing out against the sky, louder than the near and distant thunder.

"Jiro, now!" It was Tierny. His sword plunged into the neck of the soldier beside him.

He was right. All this water. It could damage it. If I didn't take my last shot now, it'd be useless. I trembled, cupping a hand over the weapon in my hand to keep it from the rain. I aimed with a shaking hand and shot, the sound deafening in my ears.

And then I went flying back, the hot and drenched weapon falling from my fingers. Horses neighed and pounded past me, their metal-covered hooves just barely missing my arms, my legs. There was fire a few feet in front of me, fire roaring even in the torrent of rain, and then it quieted, leaving nothing but ash and soot and black where it had been. I scrambled up and padded over toward where the duke had been, missing the swing of a sword from a soldier on horseback just out of sheer luck when I stumbled.

The duke was smoking. His metal armor was black, blacker than if it had rusted, only a spot or two of silver left to gleam. His head was charred beyond recognition. I didn't know if my weapon hit him, but there was a dagger sticking out of the back of his neck.

I looked up to see my cousin, her arm still extended from the throw she'd made. She straightened her shoulders and drew the blade she kept around her waist. "The duke is dead!" she shouted through the gush of rain. She raised her sword. "Lay down your swords in fealty to me *now*, or accept your death!" Blood and spit escaped her mouth as she spoke.

The fall of swords from the backs of horses to the ground was like the fall of apples from a tree, if the wind rushed through the boughs and snapped the twigs holding the fruit, causing them all to fall at once.

Tierny let his sword fall with them and was the first to get off his horse. He knelt before my cousin. "My duchess. My princess." He turned and bowed to me, his face against the ground. "My future emperor."

I almost looked over my shoulder to see whom he could mean, despite what I knew, that it was I alone who had birth claim to that throne. But even that wasn't true. *I'll never be emperor*, I thought, even as all eyes in the crowd turned on me. All eyes but Rohesia's. *Not so long as my cousin is left standing.*

28

ROHESIA

The fire had destroyed everything. The water had washed it all out.

At Fastello's request, we held a memorial for Cateline at the ruins of the Stargazers tower. We'd gone back to the empty nomad camp after the rain had cleansed the land of fire, and the smoke had settled and the ground no longer burnt with fiery ash. There was no charred flesh left. We'd found bones. Fastello had laid his three fingers atop the skeleton missing the fingers on the right hand and gathered the bones in shimmering silk, spending several hours gathering each piece of her, refusing any offers of help.

"Cateline spoke often of Ytoile, and who She would bless, and who She tried to save from a demon in the sun." Fastello's lips quivered and he wiped his eyes with the corner of his sleeve. "Cateline would have us believe she's in the stars now." His eyes traveled over the group gathered, nomads, farmers—Hanaobi and duchy-born—Sherrod's bride Malle, Prince Kojiro, Captain Tierny and myself. "Others would tell us she's standing beside us now, unseen, but always watching."

Fastello gestured both hands to the twilight sky, that perfect moment between day and night, when the fires of the sun still burned bright but more calmly, soothing the land before the darkness of the night. "Maybe it doesn't matter, so long as we believe she's in a better place." He sighed. "Cateline was blind in some ways, but so right in others." He tucked his wounded hand beneath his armpit. "Flames did burn the evil. But they burned the good, too."

I squeezed the jade lion I held tightly in my lap. *"When I saw that tower burning, I thought I'd lost you forever."* There had been no funeral for him. Not for the evil duke, not for my doting father. *Could evil love, and could evil in one's eyes be good in another's?* I needed to know. For all the things I'd done.

"I ask you all now," spoke Fastello, his eyes closed, both his intact hand and his wounded hand extended. "To join hands. Whatever you believe in, to be thankful for this new night. And the new day thereafter."

Nomads grabbed onto each other's hands, and those sitting nearest the Hanaobi farmers held out their hands to them, leading the way. Captain Tierny reached out for my hand. I looked from his hand to Prince Kojiro's. Kojiro's patted his belt pouch, at the thunder-like weapon he kept hidden there. I stood without a word and traveled past the people seated on the ground, out past the ruins and back onto the dirt path. Their eyes closed, their lips murmuring a cacophony of individually cherished prayers, no one noticed my departure.

Or so I thought. I'd gotten a few steps down the dirt path when I heard my title called out from behind me. "Your ladyship! Lady Rohesia!"

I halted and turned. Captain Tierny trotted after me, a hand on the blade hilt at his hip. Prince Kojiro sauntered some distance behind him. "Is something the matter?" asked Captain Tierny. The deep grooves on his face flexed as he tightened his mouth.

Captain Tierny, who'd died at sea. Captain Tierny, who'd told me he smuggled this prince from Hanaobi, who'd claimed he'd always worked against my father, as if this would be news I'd rejoice to hear. I clenched my jaw. "I needed time to think." I slipped the jade lion into its pouch.

"My duchess." Captain Tierny saluted me with an arm at his chest, a slight nod of his head. He gestured behind him. "Prince Kojiro would like to speak with you."

I raised an eyebrow, an uneasy hand traveling to the hilt of my sword. He'd hardly spoken two words to me since Father's death. He'd lived in my castle for days, slept in the room belonging to Mother as if it were nothing. As if he were my honored guest. And his hand always twitched nervously over his explosive weapon whenever I saw him.

"Tierny says to me," started Prince Kojiro, licking his lips. The way he said the captain's name was odd, strained. "Tierny says my mother, the empress, knew I would come to the duchy. She planned for my escape."

I waited, but he'd stopped speaking. "And?" I asked at last. "You were unaware?" He'd told me in the forest he had run from her, but it hardly mattered. I didn't trust him enough to believe him then. I still didn't.

Prince Kojiro exchanged a look with Captain Tierny, who said something in Hanaobian to the prince. Prince Kojiro nodded. "She meant to kill me. She thought I would fail."

"Fail to kill my father?" I asked. "Or fail to kill me?"

Prince Kojiro took a step back, his face contorted as if I'd struck him.

"Did you think I didn't know?" I asked him.

"You are the true heir to the imperial throne of Hanaobi," replied Prince Kojiro, his eyes unsure. "You are a princess… No, you *are* the empress. Not heir. Mother is empress by marriage. Father was the younger one. Your mother the elder."

I swallowed. "If we care about birthright, Fastello is the duke of this isle."

Prince Kojiro stood straighter, pulling his shoulders back. The cape someone had given him to wear to the memorial fluttered back, and for the briefest of moments, I felt like I was looking at my own reflection. "The duchy is good now. There is hope. Fastello could be the good duke."

I clenched the hilt of my sword but then felt my fingers falter. "Are you asking me to give up my rule of the duchy?"

Prince Kojiro took a careful step closer. He dropped his grip on the pouch containing his bulky weapon and gestured toward my hand. I let him take it, clasping it in both of his own. "I ask you to accept the rule of Hanaobi." His eyes were steadfast, no sign of the fear that plagued them every time I looked at him before. I saw his cheek twitch as he swallowed. "There is evil in my home. You will help me face it."

I said nothing for a moment, reading what I could from the prince's face, his eyes, his hold on my hand. At last I pulled the hand away and looked over his shoulder at Captain Tierny. "Captain," I said, fingering the pouch holding my mother's spirit. "How soon can your ship be ready?"

"At a moment's notice!" Captain Tierny grinned. He slapped Prince Kojiro's back, making him jump, and then slipped his other arm around my shoulders, making me shift uncomfortably as well. I wasn't used to the contact, but I accepted it and walked down the dirt path beside an exuberant captain and one of the last remnants of my family.

"Save the fire. Burn everything, and there will be nothing left to rule."

I wouldn't lose sight of that. I wouldn't follow in Father's footsteps. *Hanaobi can be saved without the flame.*

I'd make sure of it.

READ THE REST OF THE STORY IN TURN TO DUST AND ASHES (FALL FAR FROM THE TREE BOOK TWO)

Impassive. Devious. Besieged. Naive. In the ashes of their parents' cruel sovereignty, four teenagers are left holding the reins with no idea how to lead their peoples to peace and prosperity.

Rohesia, told she is the true heir to Hanaobi, must choose between ruling the duchy in her father's place and returning with her cousin to seek the throne that is more rightfully hers. Without her father figure, she has little interest in either, but there is no escape from the infamous legacy of her parents on both sides of the sea.

Fastello, left to lead both his father's people and to seek the rule of the entire duchy, has never had so much responsibility in his life. Grappling with heartbreak the likes of which he's never experienced, he doesn't know if he has it in him to try to fill the hole so many people so desperately want him to fill.

Kojiro, adrift in a strange land and emboldened by the actions of the people he met there, is determined to find his courage and free his people from the tyranny of his mother's reign. However, with her number one foe defeated, the empress of Hanaobi is more unstoppable than ever.

Tomiko, the perfect daughter to the strict and controlling empress, is sheltered from the reality of the world but eager to discover the truth. Before the war is over, she must decide between fealty to her mother and loyalty to her brother, knowing full well that either way, her family will never be whole again.

The goals of each of these four young adults are bound to clash —but there's no escaping their destinies, no matter the destruction left in their paths.

TURN TO DUST AND ASHES (FALL FAR FROM THE TREE BOOK TWO) CHAPTER ONE PREVIEW
TOMIKO

I missed my brother.

I missed both my brothers. Elder Brother Nobutada might not have shown me as much kindness, but he hadn't always been the ruthless reflection of our parents that he had been in the days—months, years—leading to his and Father's deaths.

But I could not let this grief—this hesitation, this regret—show in Mother's presence. Not for one single solitary moment.

"You act as if I should care, Yeoman," she said. "Enough with the excuses. I will not stand for anything that is simply an excuse for why I should not have my men lop your head off from your shoulders where you kneel."

"No!" The man—one of the land-holding lesser yeoman farmers who oversaw the cultivation of crops somewhere outside the capital—prostrated himself once more on the ground, grinding his nose into the *tatami* mat, as if he thought that with just a little more effort, he might eventually sink into the surface beneath him.

"Rise!" snapped Mother, losing some of her composure. She stood, her handmaidens scrambling from beside the dais to step in so she wouldn't trip over any of the long, flowing layers of her imperial *kimono*. "I told you to rise already. I will not stand for endless groveling when it does nothing but waste my time and delay the inevitable."

I had to stop my mask from cracking. If Elder Brother Kojiro were here, we'd have discussed this later, huddled beneath the safety of lantern light in one of our chambers. Mother insisted on shows of fealty, on prostrations of obedience, even if they irked her. It was hard enough for her own family to find the right balance, let alone the poor layperson whose one chance to have an audience with her might also be their final one.

I had little hope for this thin, shirking farmer yeoman.

"The rains," he spat, reluctantly sitting up on his legs again, the threadbare hat in his hands surely ripping even more as he twisted it between both fists. "They flooded our crops. You can ask Lord Nakamura; his crops fared no better—"

"I am not speaking to Yeoman Nakamura right now, am I?" Mother's smile was sweet. Welcoming. But let your eyes wander a short distance above those fire-red lips, and those black eyes—so dark amidst the painted snow of her face—could never let anyone mistake something as simple as a smile for kindness.

"No, Your Majesty." The man went to prostrate himself again but flinched halfway, squeezing his hat tighter and rising back into a sitting position.

Mother raised an eyebrow. "And is that how you apologize to your empress?"

"No, Your Majesty!" The man flung himself forward, his nose back on the mat. "I apologize profusely for my offense. I spoke out of turn."

Mother's smile was genuine this time. She paced back and forth, ignoring the handmaidens struggling to keep her train straight despite her sharp movements, stepping between them as if they were mere spirits she could not see. Her eyes brightened as she looked down at the farmer. There was no mistaking that she genuinely enjoyed this—her conflicting moods, her confusing message, her refusal to let anyone do anything but displease her.

Few would dare to look her in the face to fully understand that she knew precisely what she was doing, that it was no mere accident that her moods shifted with the direction of the wind.

But I did. I could.

"I believe I just told you, Yeoman, that such prostrations are a waste of my time." She stopped moving suddenly. "And wasting your empress' time must be one of the highest forms of insults."

"No!" The man scrambled to sit up again. There was no missing the pallid tone his skin had taken, the moisture that clung to his forehead and dripped down his cheeks. "I apologize, Your Majesty," he said, inclining his head slightly. If he twisted his hat any harder, I was certain he would tear it in two.

Mother turned her back on him, her gaze settling on me seated on the dais behind her—beside where her own cushion lay in the center. There were empty cushions on either side of the imperial seat. One for Mother—for she sat in Father's seat now, just until the heir was ready, she claimed—one for Imperial Prince and Heir Nobutada and one for Imperial Prince Kojiro. I refused to sit anywhere but the seat for Imperial Princess Tomiko, at the farthest reaches from the center. I would not move into the heir's seat.

"What do you think, Princess?" She never gave Kojiro a title when she spoke to him. She never gave him an ounce of respect. "Has the yeoman wasted enough of my time?"

I took in the scene of the man on his knees, the guards standing silently flanking him on either side. The handmaidens stood with Mother's train between their delicate fingers. Other servants stood by, in the shadows, perhaps grateful to retreat from sight. They needn't have bothered. In this room, only Mother existed, only Mother mattered, and for a brief moment, she'd allowed this man to pretend he did. Now she asked me to step up. To speak. To be.

"Honorable Mother," I began, fighting every urge I had to swallow, to appear anything but the perfect heir and princess, "I am not sure there is someone who can take his place. If we are ever to get the crops back to the numbers we need, we will need experts to guide the process."

Mother's face fell as she waved a hand—slightly, almost imperceptibly—in my direction, turning back to face the man. "There is always another man. Always another farmer. And this one is clearly no expert."

"Your Majesty, please. I have a wife. Children. Grandchildren. We serve Your Majesty and the Great Empire of Hanaobi with all of our hearts, with all of our spirits, with all of our beings—"

Mother stepped forward, gracefully with small steps, although she was at his side before he could speak another word. For the briefest of seconds, his eyes raked over her face and whatever he saw there caused him to grow paler still before he remembered to stare instead at the floor in front of him.

"Do you know how many men and women have told me the exact same story?"

The man shook his head.

"How many have told me they have wives and husbands and children and grandchildren..." She sneered and began to pace back and forth in front of him, her billowing *kimono* making it seem as if she were gliding without the assistance of feet.

The man shook his head again. His hands were trembling as they clung to his hat for dear life.

"If I only executed those without families for insolence and failure, I would have to exempt all but the barren and widowed and those poor wretched souls have suffered enough, wouldn't you say?"

The man nodded, his throat bobbing.

Mother stopped in front of him again. "I am a widow, Yeoman."

The man struggled to speak. "Of-Of course, Your Majesty. I apologize. I never meant to imply—"

Mother turned again. "I have lost two sons."

She had no proof of Elder Brother Kojiro's death. No reason to assume he'd done anything but run away. She couldn't have possibly imagined where to. She never would have thought him brave enough, bold enough. But she could never have understood the well of courage she buried and suffocated and stifled in him with just a nod of her head.

"I am so sorry, Your Majesty."

She walked closer to me, pointing toward me as she turned back again to face the man, her eyes never once traveling to acknowledge the women bending and scrambling to get her train out of her way. "Were it not for my dear daughter, the final heir, my joy in this world"—she smiled toward me as she said this, but the kindness never reached her eyes—"my last remaining family, I should just die, is that what you are saying, Yeoman?"

"No!" The man straightened his back. "No, never, Your Majesty!

Never! I never meant such an offense. I only asked that you give me another chance so that I may be sent home to my family one last time."

"Yes, to your wife and children and grandchildren and all the rest." Mother fluffed her hand toward him as she sat back down on her cushion, the handmaidens crossing in front of and behind her to arrange her train like a bright red river of blood cascading through the pale brown of the *tatami* mats. "It sounds to me as if there are plenty of hands at your farm. I will give your family another chance." She nodded toward one of her guards. "But I will not give you the chance to see them once more." The guards grabbed the man by the armpits, his legs kicking as he floated above the floor and he was dragged out of the room. "From the sounds of it, your goodbyes alone would take half a day, and you do know how I hate wasted time."

"Your Majesty! I—" But the man's words were cut short as one of the guards hit him atop the head with the hilt of his sword. The actual execution would take place outside, where the mess would simply return to the soil, where the sun spirit could reclaim what she had once given.

He'd lived a long life at least. A good life from the sound of it. I knew he must be grateful. If his farm did not produce more within the year, his son would live a far shorter one.

"Sougo," snapped Mother. From where I sat, I could see the slight color of her own skin at the back of her neck, the flush of perspiration that dotted it from her trek around the room.

"Yes, Your Majesty?" Sougo, one of her trusted attendants, stepped forward from the shadows. He turned to one of the servant girls. "Fetch Her Majesty her tea."

"Thank you, Sougo." Mother looked satisfied. Despite everything, she was not above rewarding behavior that pleased her with common courtesy should the mood strike her. She did not say anything more until the servant girl returned with a tray on which sat a tea pot and two cups. With a slight tremble to her hands, she put the tray down between Mother and me and went to grab the teapot.

"Let Princess Tomiko do it," said Mother, sweetness and iciness coating her words all at once. She was in a good mood after sentencing the farmer and she would not strike at the girl for her momentary relapse.

The girl nodded and I stood, my own handmaidens rushing to take hold of my train. It was shorter than Mother's but still plenty longer than anyone else's in the room. The pale pink of the material stood out against the brown *tatami* as I took my small, measured steps forward to the tray. I set to task scooping the matcha into each cup before taking careful hold of the pot and pouring the water over the powder.

Mother turned to Sougo. "Who is this Nakamura he mentioned?"

Sougo's stiff lips grew thinner as I picked up the whisk and set to the task of making the froth appear from the tea. "His neighboring farmer, I suppose."

"You suppose?"

I stopped mid-whisk of my mother's tea.

"I will check with the records at once," said Sougo. "I apologize most profusely for my rudeness."

I let the whisk move again.

"Do not bother." Mother smiled at me—graciously, genuinely—as I cradled her tea with both hands and handed it to her. I did not complete the proper tea ceremony, but Mother was in need of refreshment, and she could only stand such a halfhearted attempt from her own family. The insult otherwise would have been too great.

Thus her desire for me to make the tea.

"Thank you, Princess," she said, sipping the tea. I returned to the tray to make my own cup, although I had no need to quench my thirst. "I am sure he has failed to produce as well. Find him and bring him to me for a chance to explain himself." Her eyes danced almost gleefully as she brought the cup back to her lips.

"At once, Your Majesty." Sougo bowed and went to exit, never once showing his back to his empress. Guards could when called to, the handmaidens had to at times to keep the train from tripping my mother, but Sougo would not dare.

"Come sit with me," said Mother after a moment, motioning to the cushion beside her. Elder Brother Kojiro's cushion.

I tapped the whisk against the side of my cup and left it on its stand, cradling the cup as I shuffled to sit beside her, my handmaidens trailing behind and then in front of me as they arranged my *kimono*.

"How go your studies, my dear?"

"Well, thank you," I said. Mother's kindness in these moments was not lost on me, but I had long since noticed the difference in how she treated me—compared to my poor oaf of an older brother, who ought to have been my equal, my superior even, and to those around us. Those invisible, visible people around us.

"Master Kondo speaks most highly of your progress." She laughed before taking another sip. "I can see how grateful he is to teach you instead of the heir before you."

I cradled my cup of tea in both hands. The tutors to the "heir before me" all wound up dead. Other than the barbarian foreigner with the golden hair. The one I hoped had safely stolen my brother away.

Mother did not notice my solemn mood. "He tells me you are quite skilled in the tongue of the barbarians."

"I am," I said, in that very tongue. It sounded coarse and sharp.

Mother laughed again. "You are lovely," she said, holding her cup out in the air until a servant scrambled to take it from her. She tucked her hands back into the billows of her sleeves. "You understand that being the ruler of Hanaobi involves intelligence and discipline. That there is reason to take pride in your accomplishments, so long as you defer to those who deserve your deference and loyalty." She reached toward me, running a soft finger across my cheek. The intimate gesture seemed so out of place in this room. "You were meant to be heir. I am sure of it. All we have been through... The spirits ordained it to see you on the throne."

I said nothing, not sure the spirits would rejoice in the deaths of my father and eldest brother, nor in the banishment of my elder brother and closest friend. But then again, it was they who'd put my family on the throne in the first place. They who'd allowed my disgraced aunt to abandon her people and lie with a barbarian beyond the sea.

"As much as it pained me to lose Prince Nobutada, I am so glad the spirits saw fit to put you next in line."

She did not say *his* name, did not mention how it might be that I'd be next in line.

She did not mention the weapon Father had had crafted for Elder Brother Nobutada, the one I'd given to Elder Brother Kojiro before I'd bade him to run far, far away. I wondered if she even imagined it unaccounted for. Doubtful.

When had Mother decided that Elder Brother Kojiro disappointed her? When had she looked at me and decided I was the one who ought to follow Father on the throne?

If Mother ever gave up her grip on it.

"Honorable Mother," I began, almost ready to defend my brother for the insult by omission, almost ready to speak up, "you flatter me."

I ran my thumbs over the warm clay cup, the unevenness digging into my skin. I could not stand up for him. I knew how hard life had been for him here—knew Mother would have killed him and thought nothing of it—and yet, the most I could do was support him from the shadows and tell him to run away. I hoped he was happier in the duchy. Part of me wanted him to have shown our mother how wrong she was about him. The rest hoped he didn't stop there and had ridden boat after boat until he was far, far away—away from Hanaobi, away from the duchy, away from any place our mother's grasp might reach.

"I do not flatter," replied Mother after a moment's thought. "I only reward fealty and talent."

"Your Majesty." Sogo returned, a strange look of triumph on his usually-taciturn features.

It didn't go unnoticed. Mother raised her eyebrows. "You have news of this other farmer so quickly?" She waved a hand at him. "You need not bother me with the details. Just summon him to me."

"Yes, of course, Your Majesty, but that isn't it." He held a parchment up that he'd kept tucked beneath his arm as he'd entered. "The trade ship arrived from the duchy just now. The captain sent a messenger from the docks with the letter he received at sea. He's on his way himself as soon as he's finished unloading."

My heart thudded wildly against my breastbone. Had Elder Brother Kojiro been found? What kind of news might make Sogo—who lived to please his empress—so uncharacteristically happy?

He's dead. He has to be dead.

The cup slipped from my fingers, but no one else noticed as the liquid soaked into my *kimono*. Even the handmaidens were mesmerized by the sight of Sogo unhinged.

"Sogo," said Mother, "if you do not start sharing the reasons for your mirth with me immediately, I shall be quite disappointed with you."

"Of course!" Sougo prostrated himself on the floor, bowing—but quickly—in apology. He shook the letter above him. "He is dead," he said, confirming my every fear. "The barbarian duke who kidnapped your sister-in-law, our empress, is dead at long last!"

A wash of relief flooded over me. He did not speak of Elder Brother Kojiro. He had run, he'd hidden, the secret weapon I'd gifted him always there to protect him.

Mother did not seem as joyful as the news ought to have made her. She looked... wounded. "Sougo," she said, recovering and intertwining her fingers. "My husband was emperor before me."

The smile slipped from Sougo's lips like a cascading waterfall had wiped all hope from his face. "Of course, Your Majesty," he said, bowing slightly, likely unable to imagine his offense.

But I knew it now. Depending on Mother's mood, she might not get over it and we might not get the rest of the story until the captain made it to the palace. And there was poor Sougo to consider. His loyalty ought to be rewarded. Mother herself had said she'd valued fealty.

"What Master Sougo surely meant to say," I said, almost surprised at my own boldness, "is the duke who has been our country's sworn enemy for nearly two decades, the one who took the disgraced princess away from our lands and turned her into a traitor to all the spirits hold dear, is dead." I widened my eyes at Sougo, letting him take the reins. Mother could be assuaged if you knew how.

"Yes, of course!" Sougo swallowed, his misstep in his exuberance now clear to him. "Leave it to the elegant Princess Tomiko to voice my thoughts more eloquently than I could ever hope to."

Mother let one eyebrow raise, but her curiosity seemed to have won over the slight. "How?" she asked simply, and I prayed Sougo would be savvy enough to know what she meant.

"Slain in battle," said Sougo, poring over the letter once more. His eyes darted madly up and down over the page. "During a confrontation with"—he gulped, and I knew he was about to say something Mother would not like to hear—"our own Hanaobi people, those runaways, those traitors," he spat, adding the latter part for Mother's appeasement, no doubt.

My heart fluttered hopefully. The expats had risen against the duke? After sneaking into the land and managing to escape their barbaric guards? Who but... Who but their prince, their heir, could motivate them so?

"Farmers," said Mother. "A band of farmers killed a ruler with the might of an army." She did not sound pleased at all that her sworn enemy had fallen. Then again, the war between them was a silent one, hidden beneath treaties and platitudes, even as we traded crops and goods with one another, Hanaobi always getting the raw end of the deal—but it did not matter, as Mother allowed some of her people to escape to the duchy for just this reason. She should not have been surprised that they'd risen up.

She had put the idea into Father's head that he and Elder Brother Nobutada should head to the duchy in secret, should command the runaways to step up and do their duty by fighting the duke in his own territory.

It was the result she had wanted. So why was she disappointed? Surely, even she could see that the invasion she'd planned to arrange one day soon was not preferable to the problem taking care of itself. There was no loss of life or resources on our side this way.

"Well, yes, the expats were the target of a raid the duke and his men made," said Sougo, consulting the parchment again. "But they were led by..." He drifted off, his eyes darting wildly, his lips turning into a sneer. "The duke's heir, Rohesia," he said, puzzling me to no end. He left it unsaid that she was Empress Momoko's heir as well. That, by all rights of succession, she was the true heir to Hanaobi.

He was not finished. "And a young man from a band of thieves," he continued, "a man claiming to be the duke's true heir."

Mother was surprised at that one. Her features barely moved, but I noticed the slight twitch of her lips.

But he was still not finished yet. "And," he said, swallowing as he looked up toward us on the dais, "Prince Kojiro and the Captain Tierny who was his tutor at his side. Your Majesty, this letter..." His face suddenly more sullen, he would not say more.

Mother's hands wrung together and her lip twitch grew more

pronounced. Sougo opened his mouth but shut it again as Mother stood and the handmaidens shuffled in quickly to remove her train from her path.

"Who sent this letter the tradesmen carried?" asked Mother stiffly.

Sougo's eyes pored over the words. "I don't know whether or not to trust what it says." He stepped forward and handed the letter to Mother with both hands. Sweat glistened on his brow.

She snatched it from him and he stepped back, bowing as she began to read. Mother's eyes widened. "Get me this messenger who handed it to you," said Mother, gliding past Sougo as fast as her measured steps would allow, "immediately." She stopped and turned to stare at Sougo, who shirked back from her glare. "And prepare for the execution of the ship's captain after I am done with him. I will not suffer the insult that he would send such an important message ahead on nothing but a piece of parchment instead of coming to my side to tell me in person the moment his ship landed." Her voice grew louder as she spoke and a pinch of red appeared at her temples, where the white makeup ended as it met up with her hairline. "It is time," she said, looking more composed. "We have been preparing for this moment. Our assault can begin."

She strode forward, gliding from the room, her handmaidens trailing after her, the guards in line behind them.

I understood at last. She could not let this go. She had to have her invasion. The duke's death was but a small part of her objective.

Perhaps it was Elder Brother Kojiro's fate that mostly concerned her.

Sougo turned toward me, his face ashen, and he bowed his head. "Thank you, Your Highness." He left the rest unsaid.

ACKNOWLEDGMENTS

Thank you to everyone who read this dark YA fantasy, especially everyone who came back to check out my next book following The Never Veil Series or who picked up an official copy after reading the book on Wattpad. You don't know how much every review, email and message means to me, and how much I appreciate your enthusiasm for my work. (Please don't hesitate to contact the authors of books you love online!)

Thanks as always to Melissa Giorgio, YA author, best friend, and beta reader/editor extraordinaire. Thank you to Kellie Sheridan and everyone else at Patchwork Press for your support and enthusiasm and for the opportunity to publish with you. Thank you, intern Amy H., for your additional edits and insight.

Cameron, Mom, Sara and everyone else: Much love and kudos to my friends and family for always supporting my dreams.

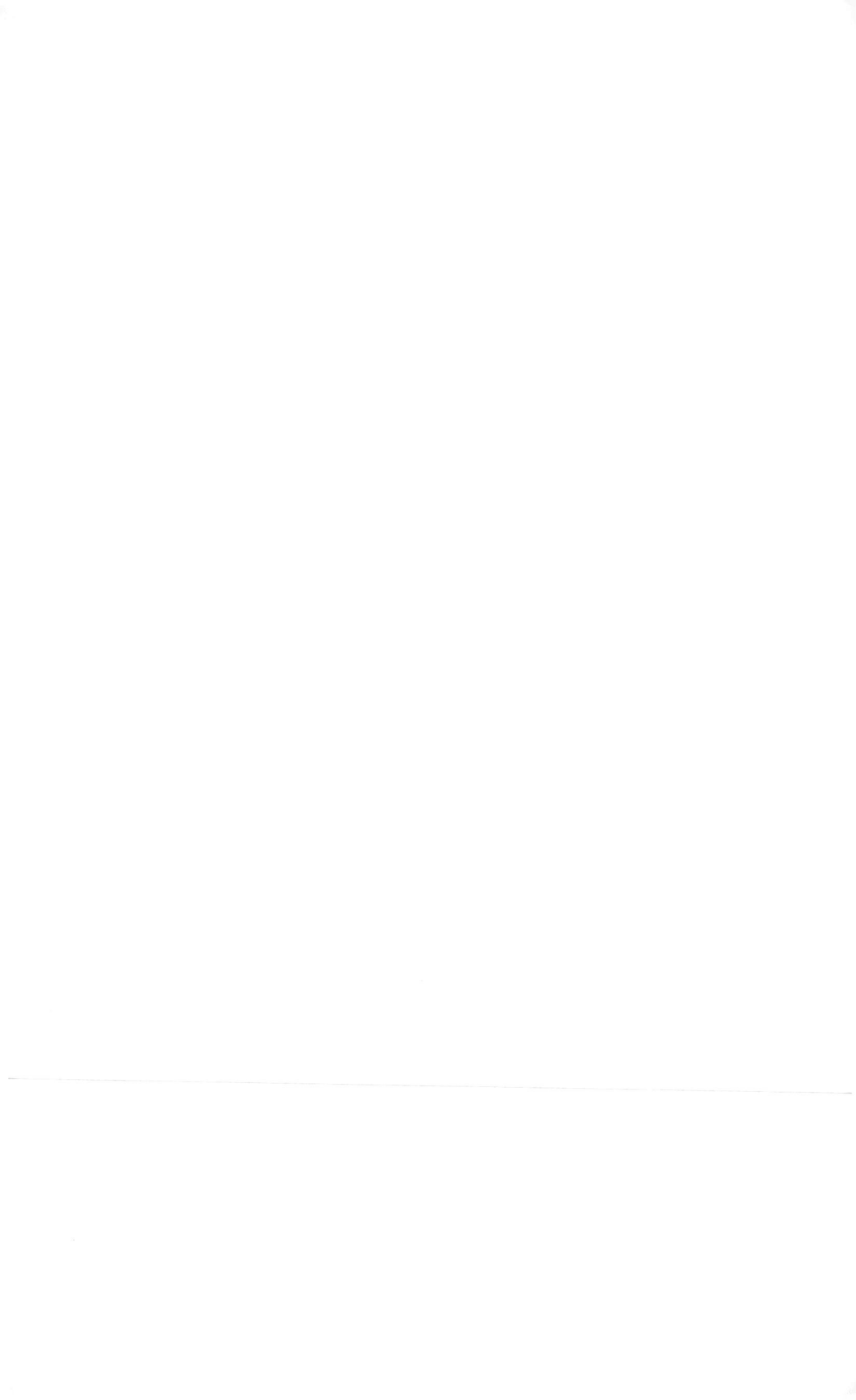

ABOUT THE AUTHOR

Amy McNulty is an editor and author of books that run the gamut from YA speculative fiction to contemporary romance. A lifelong fiction fanatic, she fangirls over books, anime, manga, comics, movies, games, and TV shows from her home state of Wisconsin. When not editing her clients' novels, she's busy fulfilling her dream by crafting fantastical worlds of her own.

Sign up for Amy's newsletter to receive news and exclusive information about her current and upcoming projects. Get a free YA romantic sci-fi novelette when you do!

Find her at amymcnulty.com and follow her on social media:

- amazon.com/author/amymcnulty
- bookbub.com/authors/amy-mcnulty
- facebook.com/AmyMcNultyAuthor
- twitter.com/mcnultyamy
- instagram.com/mcnulty.amy
- pinterest.com/authoramymc

LOOK FOR MORE YA SPECULATIVE
FICTION READS FROM SNOWY
WINGS PUBLISHING

DRIFTERS
CARMEN WEBSTER BUXTON

In the far future, sixteen-year-old Jehan Amato lives on Menkar VII, a colony world only recently rediscovered by the rest of the galaxy. After a run-in with a dangerous gang that wants to exploit his secret psy talent for opening locks with his mind, Jehan is sent to live in a Drifter caravan with his estranged father. But though Jehan, who has lived in New Hope City all his life, is initially wary of the nomadic people and their unfamiliar customs, in the caravan he comes to learn things about his family and himself that will change his life forever.

POISONED GARDEN
TRACY KORN

You Reap What You Sow...

It started with a fight at school.

The girl who attacked me burst into flames on the way to the hospital, and now, I'm starting to...change.

In less than a week, my biggest problem has gone from trying to decide what to do if I don't get into The Citadel to navigating the front lines of a looming, supernatural war.

And you know what? I signed up for all the honors classes these past four years. None of them prepared me for Eden's Bluff Academy, a school in the Bermuda Triangle with human-elemental hybrids, angels, snakes with wings, and an inter-dimensional veil that someone is trying to destroy.

Unless I stop them.

READ MORE FROM AMY MCNULTY

THE NEVER VEIL SERIES

"The story is fun and engaging, featuring a female protagonist who will resonate with young teens." -School Library Journal

"...A whirlwind of time-bending adventures that immerse readers in a maelstrom of plot twists and allusions to "Beauty and the Beast" and other fairy tale love stories, while Noll's understanding of gender-based social and cultural dynamics develops." -Publishers Weekly

Nobody's Goddess (Book One in The Never Veil Series), <u>winner of The Romance Reviews Summer 2016 Readers' Choice Award for Young Adult Romance</u>:

> In a village of masked men, each man is compelled to love only one woman and to follow the commands of his "goddess" without question. A woman may reject the only man who will love her if she pleases, but she will be alone forever. A man must stay masked until his goddess returns his love—and if she can't or won't, he remains masked forever.
>
> Seventeen-year-old Noll's childhood friends have paired off and her closest companion, Jurij, found his goddess in Noll's own sister. Desperate to find a way to break this ancient spell, Noll instead discovers why no man has ever chosen her. She is in fact the goddess of the mysterious lord of the village, a man who refuses to let Noll have her right as a woman to spurn him.
>
> Thus begins a dangerous game between the choice of woman and the magic of man. The stakes are no less than freedom and happiness, life and death—and neither Noll nor the veiled lord is willing to lose.

FANGS & FINS (BLOOD, BLOOM, & WATER SERIES)

A dapper vampire. A sullen merman. Two heirs to a great conflict—and each needs to claim a beloved to become his kindred's champion.

High school senior Ember Goodwin never had a sister, but after her mom's remarriage, she now has two. The eldest is no stranger to her—Ivy is a witty girl in her grade who's almost never spoken to the shy bookworm before—but she's surprised to find the popular girl quite amiable. Their burgeoning friendship is tested, however, when Dean Horne, a pale, besuited charmer, shows interest in them both and plans to reveal his appetite for blood to the one who'll stand by his side.

Seventeen-year-old Ivy Sheppard is tired of splitting her time between her dad's and her mom's, particularly when her dad uproots their lives to move them in with his new wife and stepdaughter. Used to rolling with her parents' whims, she tries to make the best of it and befriend her nerdy new step-sister. Her hectic life grows more unwieldy when she catches the eye of junior Calder Poole, whom she swears she sees swap well-toned legs for a pair of fins during a dip in a lake. Now she's fending off suitors left and right, all while trying to get to the bottom of the strange happenings in her town.

The first book in the Blood, Bloom, & Water series sets family against family and friend against friend as an epic, ancient war comes to a head in a supposedly sleepy suburb.

BALLAD OF THE BEANSTALK

A Library Journal Self-e Selection.

As her fingers move across the strings of her family's heirloom harp, sixteen-year-old Clarion can forget. She doesn't dwell on the recent passing of her beloved father or the fact that her mother has just sold everything they owned, including that very same instrument that gives Clarion life. She doesn't think about how her friends treat her like a feeble, brittle thing to be protected. She doesn't worry about how to tell the elegant Elena, her best friend and first love, that she doesn't want to be her sweetheart anymore. She becomes the melody and loses herself in the song.

When Mack, a lord's dashing young son, rides into town so his father and Elena's can arrange a marriage between the two youth, Clarion finds herself falling in love with a boy for the first time. Drawn to Clarion's music, Mack puts Clarion and Elena's relationship to the test, but he soon vanishes by climbing up a giant beanstalk that only Clarion has seen. When even the town witch won't help, Clarion is determined to rescue Mack herself and prove once and for all that she doesn't need protecting. But while she fancied herself a savior, she couldn't have imagined the enormous world of danger that awaits her in the kingdom of the clouds.

A prequel to the fairy tale *Jack and the Beanstalk* that reveals the true story behind the magical singing harp.